The Gold of Tolosa

Philip Matyszak

Monashee Mountain Publishing

Philip Matyszak has a doctorate in Roman history from St John's College, Oxford University and is the author of many books on Ancient History including the best-selling *Ancient Rome on Five Denarii a Day* and *Legionary: The Roman Soldier's (Unofficial) Manual.* He teaches e-learning courses in ancient History for the Institute of Continuing Education at Cambridge University. *The Gold of Tolosa* is the first novel in his series of historical novels. For more information visit: www.matyszakbooks.com

First published in 2013 by Monashee Mountain Publishing (Canada)

Second edition 2015

ISBN 978-0-9881066-1-1

Cover design by: **Ravastra Design Studio**

Monashee Mountain Publishing:
www.monasheemountainpublishing.com

The Gold of Tolosa

Foreword

Notes by the editor and translator

The sensational discovery of a lost Latin text at what the press have taken (inaccurately) to calling the 'Villa of Panderius' at Herculaneum was all the more startling for being completely unexpected. The reason for the burial of the documents in the Villa, and the veracity of the astounding claims in the text have both yet to be determined. If the claims of the Panderius texts are established, it will finally explain one of the great mysteries of antiquity and the identities of those who perpetrated the greatest robbery of all time.

It was known since the re-discovery of the villa in Bourbon times that the building had been abandoned well before the eruption of Pompeii in AD 79. Consequently, until the texts were discovered, excavation of this site was seen as secondary to the more intriguing 'Villa of the Papyri' which lies alongside. In fact this excavation was undertaken somewhat as a training exercise in archaeological techniques for post-graduate students of Prof. Joanne Baca, the researcher who oversaw the entire dig.

We are fortunate that both villas lie beneath an undeveloped area of the modern town of Ercolaneo, and were relatively well preserved under both the debris from the original eruption and the lava flow of 1672. Indeed, most of the work involved simply clearing from the site the mud and pyroclastic flow which poured from Vesuvius on that fatal August afternoon.

The site lies beside the modern Vico del Mare, just outside the ancient town of Herculaneum. In antiquity the location gave both villas magnificent views and exposure to sea breezes. There can be no doubt that both buildings were occupied by persons of considerable wealth and prestige.

Nevertheless, 18th century maps of the site dismiss the 'Villa

Panderia' with the single word 'derelict' before going into more detail about the adjoining Villa of the Papyri, a villa which has yielded a number of interesting artefacts over the years. Indeed, it is likely that had the Villa of the Papyri not been next door, the 'Villa Panderia' would have remained peacefully secluded beneath the soil of Italy, its unexpected treasure a secret for generations to come.

It is now disputed whether graduate student Christian Viggen or an Italian workman first found the section of flooring in room F laid out in the *opus vittatum* (oblong tufa block) style. It was certainly Prof Baca who decided to act upon the cryptic inscription '_cavete qua' inscribed on the flooring. Sonar mapping revealed that below the floor was a small earth-filled chamber about a cubic metre in volume. Physical excavation followed and this revealed a number of clay jars sealed with wax. The jars were carefully opened by researchers at the Museo Nazionale in Naples who discovered that they were tightly packed with papyri containing Latin script.

The language of the texts is both highly colloquial and contains a number of eccentric or even downright bizarre usages. Because of my proficiency with this form of Latin, transcripts of these papyri were passed to me for translation by Dr Mary Barba of the University Faculty of Ancient History and Classics.

I can now confirm speculation in the academic community that the documents are in a form of a memoir. Oxidation of the papyri prior to burial confirms an intrinsic date of circa 60 BC, or some 150 years before the eruption of Pompeii. This makes the Latin text near-contemporary with the lost memoirs of Rutilius Rufus (written c. 90 BC) and those of Cornelius Sulla (written c.76 BC). Indeed, content of this unique document suggests that it was written as something of a response to those two earlier texts. If so, Lucius Panderius seems to have written mainly for the benefit of his immediate family and heirs, and for a few close friends.

Those interested in the technical details of the excavation are referred to the 'Report of the partial excavation of the Villa Panderia at Herculaneum' by Baca et al. published in the

Chronache Ercolanesei of 2011. My personal contribution has been limited to rendering the idiosyncratic style of Lucius Panderius into the English equivalent. It would have been preferable to wait until a complete app. crit. and glossary could be presented for academic study, but revelation of the nature of the documents on a popular Roman history web site has increased pressure for immediate publication.

P. Matyszak. D.Phil, MA, (Oxon)
Rossland, Canada 2013

Glossary

Aedile A magistrate charged with the proper running of the city of Rome

Censor A magistrate who checks eligibility for the senate, oversees public contracts and conducts the census of the Roman people

Cohort At this time a mainly administrative unit of 400-500 men

contubernium A squad of eight soldiers who share a tent

Consul The chief legislator and war leader of Rome

Forum Romanum The main forum in the city of Rome

hastati The front line of soldiers in a Roman maniple

HS (sesterces) A coin worth about two hours wages for a skilled workman

institor A clerk - often a slave - who runs a business while the boss is away

lictor Attendants who enforce respect for a Roman magistrate

Lupara At that time it meant a brothel (today this refers to a sawn-off shotgun)

maniple A fighting unit of 120 men in three lines

Optimates The so-called 'best men' - aristocratic and conservative Roman senators

padrone Someone with power and authority

pallium A military cloak

patera A flat dish, often used to hold sacrificial herbs and other material

Pax Romana The Roman peace - later defined by Tacitus as 'They create desolation and call it peace'

peplon Body-length Greek dress (origin of the modern peplum-style dress)

Praefectus Castrorum The senior centurion charged with the proper running of a Roman army camp

Primus Pilus The top centurion in a legion, and liaison between the general and the soldiers

Praetor Roman magistrate with legal, administrative and military responsibilities

Praetorian tent Command post of a Roman general

Proconsul An ex-consul who commands when a consul is not available

tetradrachms Greek coin equivalent to a week's wages for a skilled workman

tetrarch Here one of the rulers of the Galatian tribes in Anatolia

triclinium The formal dining room of a wealthy Roman

veteres The second line of a Roman maniple which did the serious fighting

Via Decumana Road of a Roman camp from the Praetorian tent to the back gate

Via Praetoria The road to the commander's tent in a Roman army camp

Via Principalis The main thoroughfare in a Roman army camp

Vica Puellarum The woman in charge of the administration of a brothel

vigiles The night watch in Rome, responsible for suppressing fires and hooliganism

Villa Rustica Country houses of the wealthy, or simply farmhouses.

Vineae Protective trenches or sheltered ramps leading to siege engines

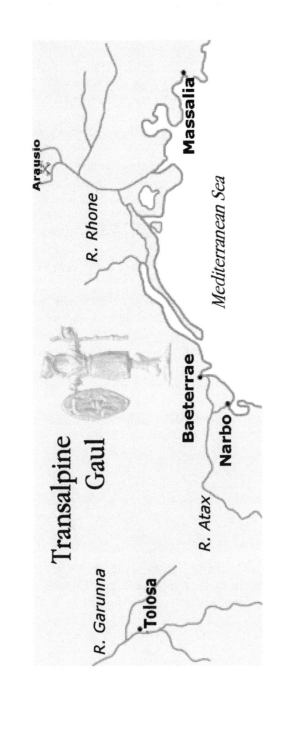

Transalpine Gaul

Massalia

Mediterranean Sea

Arausio

R. Rhone

Baeterrae

Narbo

R. Atax

Tolosa

R. Garunna

Liber I

On the morning of the worst day of my life, I awakened to the touch of Beauty and Wonder. After a while, Beauty sat back in the bed, pushed her tangled blonde hair away from her face, and looked at me critically.

'You are getting out of shape, Lucius,' she observed. 'Once you could keep going until virtually mid-morning. Now it's barely sun-up, and look at you. Nowhere near the man you used to be.'

'Before my time,' remarked Wonder from behind my shoulder. She reached past me and grabbed a handful of bed-sheet which she used to dab at the sweat between her breasts. 'He's been something of a sprinter as long as I've known him. You say he used to have more stamina?'

She swung her magnificent long legs off the side of the bed, and I lecherously savoured the sight of her bending to check the bed ropes. 'Indeed, he's hardly loosened them at all. Now Cornelius - that centurion I had the other night - he hammered the bed-frame so hard that he stretched the ropes by a handspan.'

'Well, perhaps if he had been more sober, he would have noticed that you weren't between him and the mattress,' I observed lazily.

Wonder took herself over to the silver urn of scented water that stood on an occasional table by the bed. Stretching lazily, she poured some over herself. The mosaic floor in that part of the room was slightly concave for just that reason, and the water splashed gently toward the drains.

'Tut - such jealousy is unbecoming. Failure in your own performance cannot be compensated by comparison with the deficiencies of another. 'Tis a poor innkeeper who cannot handle his own wine.'

'Failure? That's a bit harsh. Anyway, don't I keep telling you that the client is always the greatest, the best-endowed, most

1

thrilling lover you've ever had? Show a bit of professionalism here, Beaut. Talk me up a bit.'

Beauty gave me an appraising look. 'I'd say it would take Medea's best spells to get you even halfway up again. You're done for the morning laddie. Do we qualify for the usual bonus?'

'Indeed you do - enter it on the books, and I'll add it to your commission tonight. Actually -' recollection struck me, and I sat upright. 'Actually, today is the last day you'll have to do it. I'm off to Ostia today to get another girl. She'll be managing the books and appointments from now on.'

Wonder frowned. 'Another girl? A *vica puellarum*? We've been managing to sort things out between us so far. It's all been going smoothly. Why do we need someone to organize us? And while she's sitting doing the accounts, I'll be pointing my toes at the ceiling to pay her wages.'

'No wages required.' I hesitated before passing over the next bit of information. 'I'm buying her from this year's profits. She's a slave.'

I didn't think the girls would like that, and they didn't. 'A slave? But the Temple only has free girls. Is she German?'

At this point I should mention that Beauty and Wonder called each other Hedda and Thigrid when not meeting in a professional capacity. It was a conceit of mine that since the Temple of Freya's Day was named after the Germanic goddess of love, it should be staffed by members of that nation*. There was something about a statuesque Teuton, I assured customers. Once you get used to their wild, tempestuous characters, a stolid Roman matron never seems the same again. Not that you would want to marry one of

---

*The name of the temple is given by Panderius in the text as 'Eostra', the earlier Germanic form of the goddess, as 'Freya' is actually from Norse mythology. However, in the modern context 'Freya' more neatly conveys the idea of an exotic barbarian love-goddess, so I have forsaken accuracy in translation to better convey the original intent of Panderius' marketing technique.

my lasses, but every now and then a brush with the wild does a man's heart good, no? That's five denarii, magistrate, pay at the door.

Wonder pulled wide the shutters, causing Beauty and me to yelp in protest at the bright morning light. 'Amazonia's chucking Titus Didius off the premises,' she observed. 'The randy bugger overstayed again.'

'Randy bugger? Do you mean that literally?' Beauty's enquiry held professional interest. 'He's going to be tribune soon. We might as well screw a bit extra out of him by offering that as a specialist service. After all, he can screw it right back out of the Roman plebs.'

My word, I reflected, weren't my little girls getting all sophisticated and cynical? Business had been good recently. A month back, we'd had enough aristocrats through the premises for the senate to have been quorate if they'd all arrived at once. Political pillow-talk had made the girls into interested observers and commentators on the political scene - to the point where some novice senators dropped in as much for the gossip as the sex. We had come a long way in the years since I took over from my poor deceased dad. His down-market cat-house from the slums near the Esquiline Hill had now become the best *Lupara* establishment on the snobby via Patricus.

We counted some of the top politicians of Rome amongst our clientèle, which is saying something, because most would never sully themselves by visiting any old brothel. Interestingly, now that Rome was threatened with destruction by Germanic hordes from the north, the demand for the girls of the Temple had never been higher. I'd had several offers from satisfied customers wanting to buy into the business, and had finally given a share to Cornelius Sulla, not so much for the financial gain as for the political protection it brought.

It was Sulla, with his factors who handled shipping at the

3

docks on the Aventine, who had tipped me off as to my planned acquisition.

'She's a priestess, girls. A lady fallen on hard times, but a genuine priestess of Aphrodite. Can you imagine a classier deal? Fell foul of pirates somewhere near Corcyra* and her temple wouldn't pay the ransom. So we've got her. A genuine priestess of Aphrodite Porne handling the appointment books. I'm off to Ostia with a purse of silver to pick her up before some smutty competitor gets his hands on her. Pass me that tunic.'

It was going to be a wonderful morning. Leaving Thigrid's room, I glanced down the colonnade at the closed curtains marking the bedrooms where another fifteen lasses were catching up with Morpheus after a hard night's work with Freya. In the centre of the little atrium the fountain from a lustily endowed Priapus was spurting its bounty into the carp pool. The water was clean and fresh, and elegant wooden hurdles kept it that way by preventing drunken sons of the equestrian class from polluting the water by following Priapus' example. One of the slave boys who kept the vases in the girls' rooms stocked with clean water was sleeping by a pillar, curled up in his cloak like a puppy. I nudged him with my foot, and sent him scampering off to tell the stables that I needed a carriage for the morning.

We had a kitchen at the bottom of the atrium where overnight customers could grab a quick meal before facing the day. Titus Didius having been and gone, I was currently the sole patron. I helped myself to a fresh baked roll, some ham and a handful of olives. Even at the part of the house furthest from the street I could hear the rising cacophony of Rome greeting the dawn. Carts rumbled over the cobbles as they brought the day's vegetable produce to the forum Holitorum, with the usual vociferous stream

---

*Corcyra is modern Corfu. At this time, because the Romans refused to allow any Mediterranean state to become a naval power, and refused to become a naval power themselves, piracy was a major and worsening problem.

of curses when the drivers had to struggle past the crumbling block of flats opposite where builders always managed to block half the street with their material.*

There were the piping voices of a pavement class of children going through their lessons, the mind-numbing banging from the blacksmith's down the street, and over all the background hubbub of hundreds of thousands of Romans crammed into a city built for a quarter of the population; shouting, jostling, joking and relieving themselves in the gutter. This was my city, and I loved every smoke-stained brick of it.

At the vestibule I pulled on a travelling cloak and a pair of boots and stepped into the street to await my coach. 'Gaius!'

The doorman was a hulking ex-legionary who was like myself a veteran of the Jugurthan war. He came looming out from his little cubicle near the great double doors.

'Get ... ,' I winced as my instructions were cut off by a raucous shout from our sausage seller as he hawked his wares. 'Remind we why we rented that man a booth just outside our gate? He was screaming like a demented hawk after midnight last night. Does he never sleep?'

'Some blokes like to grab a late snack on the way out of the Temple, boss. I guess exercise makes them peckish. Your night-owl customers keep him going. Business has dropped since the legions left.'

'H'm yes, for us too. All those young officers getting laid one last time before they go off to fight the Cimbric menace. At least they can say that they've met at least one German face-to-face. If that's the way they like it.'

'Anyway, get a bucket and sponge, and sort that out.'

Across the doors someone had written in charcoal 'Hic futtata benne'.

---

*At this time carts with market produce were allowed into Rome in the mornings. The laws were later tightened further to forbid all wheeled traffic.

'It's not the endorsement I mind, but the spelling. Lose the last 'n' of 'bene' would you? I'd hate people to think that our patrons are illiterate *caput censi,* even if they did have a good screw on the premises.'

If you don't have class in this business, you're just running a whorehouse. So I told myself as the coach jounced along the Ostia road. As ever, the middle of the road was packed with pedestrians heading for the big city. Burly Gauls a head taller than everyone else jostled with neat Greeks in their fringed cloaks while a Numidian horse trader forced his string of rangy African ponies through the throng. All the world came to Rome, and I thought again of the children in the pavement class. My schoolmaster of a decade ago had been Greek, and hopefully his heavy-handed instruction in the language had equipped me to communicate with my intended acquisition. If not, one of the waterboys was from Greek-speaking Capua, and he could be pressed into service as a translator.

It is a morning's ride to Ostia, and you know when you are getting there because they've built the tombs so close to the edge of the road that the carriage has to go on to the stone paving. The mules don't like that since they're not shod, and they start acting up when the road gets hard on their hooves. Also, there's the salty smell of the sea, which makes me want to puke. If you've made a rough crossing to Carthage in the bowels of one of the multiple-occupancy coffins they call a troopship, you'll never look at the ocean wave in the same way again. Even Hannibal never killed as many Roman soldiers as father Neptune has done over the years. After I last made haven in Puetoli I swore a solemn oath at the temple of Apollo that I would never again trust my life to the sea.

Oddly enough, Verus Lentulus Baebius feels the same way, and the sea is his livelihood. Cornelius Sulla's factor has the censorial commission for handling the Sicilian fleet. His ships had probably brought to Rome the grain which went into my breakfast roll. (No, the other kind of breakfast roll. The one with the cereal in it.) Rome is too big to support itself from local farmlands, so we import tons of grain every year from vast estates in Sicily. It's a pretty miserable business, so we get slave revolts there as regularly as the changing of the seasons. The sooner the new colony at Carthage starts producing regular surpluses of corn, the better for everyone it will be.

Or so says Lentulus. Not a lot happens in Ostia that Lentulus does not know. He is a priest at the temple of Hercules which dominates the forum, and chairman of the crossroads guild that organizes the dockers. Though there is a fair bit of disorder and crime in Ostia, there's not a lot that Lentulus hasn't organized or taken a cut from. Anyone who does not like this arrangement can always go to the trader's guild behind the theatre and arrange for a fast ship out of town.

You'd need a quick getaway because shifting sacks of grain for weeks on end makes a solid slab of muscle out of a man, and a squad of brawny dockers wearing legionary boots with hobnails will cheerfully tenderize any political reformer once he's down. Appealing to the magistrates won't help either. Cornelius Sulla helpfully advises the Ostian electorate whom to choose, and Lentulus and the boys are on hand to supervise democracy in action. Lentulus is a friend of mine, and I had brought a half-amphora of fine Minturnian wine to keep things that way.

Once the normal courtesies were over we sprawled on couches looking westward out to sea as we sampled the wine, which Lentulus, a fellow connoisseur, correctly identified as Massic*. We had gossiped about personal affairs - Lentulus had lost a wife in

---

*Mintunae is just north of Naples, and the home of what the poet Horace (Odes 1.1.19) called *Obliviosum Massicum* - 'the Massian which brings oblivion'. Evidently Panderius stayed longer with Baebius than he suggests, for no Roman wine buff would drink Massic until it had been decanted and allowed to rest in an open urn for a while.

childbirth a few years ago, and being as lavishly sentimental in his personal life as he was predatorily purposeful in business, he had sworn never to re-marry. Now however, a widow lady had taken his fancy.

'I just don't know if the times are right, that's all. I mean getting hitched is a big thing for me, and if civilization as we know it is about to get washed away in the German tide, what's the point? I mean by this time next year it could be every man for himself. Last thing you need on the run is a wife and a new-born baby in tow.'

'It won't come to that. The legions will stop them dead.' I gestured extravagantly with my wine-cup, and hastily steadied myself at Lentulus' frown. He is generally a convivial host, but spilled wine doesn't wash out of silk coverlets. 'Marius might be a little snot-bag with the morals of a weasel, but he's a capable enough general. I loathe him and all his works, especially how he stole the credit from better men like Metellus (now there was a commander who knew his stuff!), but the troops like him, and he's energetic and cunning. Hades, I'd even vote for him.'

'Vote for him?' Lentulus screwed up his forehead in a mock-effort at recollection. 'A demagogue who could no more govern the city than could a Barbary ape? I thought you would happily see him dead.'

'Oh. I would. And even more the thieves and opportunists who hang around with him. But that's politics, you see. He was a popular tribune, so the great unwashed masses like him. He needs a chance to screw up; to screw up good and proper. It will take the shine off his image. And he can hardly manage Rome properly while he's off getting killed in battle can he now? Best of all worlds, I tell you, is Caepio keeps the Germans off our throats this year, and Marius finishes the job next year, and dies with a spear jammed through his neck while he's at it. Meanwhile the Marians have made such a mess of governing Rome that everyone hates them, and in the next elections they give their support to the best men – the aristos.'

'Talking of which, how's the new Urban Praetor? Pavonius, isn't it?'

'A Marian, and therefore a bastard. I don't know much about him, since he thinks he's a second Cato, and won't set foot on my premises. Honest, they tell me. Hard to bribe. Give me an Aemelius Scaurus if I must have an honest politician - he was a man who did what he was bribed to do. He took a fortune to go easy on Jugurtha in the African wars, and did it, even though they called a commission of enquiry into the whole bribery thing.'

'And Scaurus got himself made head of the commission ... I know, you've told me a few thousand times before. Do you want to see this girl before you buy her?'

'Of course. Momina, isn't it? Is she pretty? Or at least not scarily ugly?'

'Not ugly, no .... ,' Lentulus was struggling to express himself. 'But yeah, you'd be right to say scary. To be frank, she gives me the creeps. I mean, she's a pretty enough little thing, so how do you think she spent half a month on a pirate boat and stayed a virgin?'

I shook my head. 'Pirates know virgins get a higher price, but they're not known for self-restraint. She's having you on.'

'No, it's true. I had her checked. *Virgo intacta*. You'll believe it when you've met her. She does something to your head. It's like .... . She's God-touched, I mean it. You get the feeling that if you injure her, you'll be offending a God, or Goddess or something. On my oath. It's spooky. I'd not want her under my roof, I'll tell you that for free. You're welcome to her. And I'll be interested to see what you make of her.'

At a wave of his hand the girl was brought in.

No, at a wave of his hand, the girl came in. Those with her seemed more like retainers than guards. From Lentulus' build-up I was expecting a wild-haired Sybil, or at best some chisel-faced

Greek harridan. What I got was a tiny creature barely the height of a thirteen-year-old girl, and with a skinny body to match. She was wearing a Greek peplon of nondescript brown wool, and managed to carry off the crude clothing with a certain degree of style. Someone had done up her mousy brown hair with a filigree of vine leaves, and her feet were bare on the marble floor.

I took her chin in my hand, and looked into a pair of wide grey eyes that were startlingly large and clear - easily her best feature. She looked solemnly back with her face empty of expression.

'Momina. I am ... .'

'Lucius Panderius, brothel-keeper.' She finished for me, and dipped her head in regal acknowledgement.

Slightly nettled, I spoke more roughly than intended in an attempt to shake her composure. 'You'll be working in my brothel alongside my whores, you know that?'

A sudden smile lighted her entire face. She looked suddenly and startlingly young, carefree and full of an infectious enthusiasm.

'It would have been fun, I think. A lady fallen on hard times, but a genuine priestess of Aphrodite. A genuine priestess of Aphrodite Porne handling the appointment books. Can you imagine a classier deal? She's a priestess, girls.'

A short, shocked silence followed. I remembered not just the words I had said that morning but the tone in which I had said them. Eventually Lentulus reached over, and gently levered my jaw shut with the back of his hand. He looked at me sympathetically.

'You are right,' I told him. 'She *is* creepy.'

She was quiet on the way back, sitting docile in the carriage beside me, huddled in an oversized woollen cloak. Her head protruded from its folds as though grafted onto a statue of a tortoise. Though she said nothing, she was far from still, turning now to see a party of pilgrims setting off for some distant shrine, or intently studying a group of Gauls clad in their colourful plaid cloaks. She leaned forward to see a pack of hunting dogs trotting toward one of the *villae rusticae* where the estates of the wealthy lined the Ostia road, gasped with child-like delight as we passed an ox-waggon with cages of gaily feathered parrots, and was silent and solemn as we passed a long coffle of barbarian slaves being sent south.

I bit back the occasional urge to comment on what she was seeing, reminding myself I was a slave-owner, not a tour guide. Eventually though, I could hold myself back no longer. As the River Gate of Rome came into sight through the gathering dusk, I aggressively demanded, 'How ...?'

'Did I know what you said this morning when I wasn't there?'

'Yes, and how ...?'

'Did I know what you were going to ask just now?'

'Yes ... and ... STOP doing that!'

She fell silent, and studied me passively with those huge, grey eyes. And waited.

'Just explain,' I said rather tightly.

'It seemed the sort of thing you would say,' she told me. 'I heard a lot about you whilst I was at Lentulus' house. The other girls were happy for me that I was going to you. They like you and talk a lot about you, so I just guessed what you might say from what they said about how you talk. Laeta has a bit of a thing for you, and she can imitate you perfectly. So I did too.'

I regarded my new acquisition sceptically. What she said made sense ... sort of. It was still creepy, but maybe just a lucky guess? I respect the gods as much as the next man, but I am happier if things have a solidly mundane explanation. I had just been given one, and would have to make do with it. It was good that Momina had got on well with the women at Lentulus' house. She may be unsettling, but maybe my Priestess of Aphrodite would nevertheless get on with the girls of the brothel.

Later, much later, I realized that I had asked the wrong

question. I had been so astonished by Momina repeating my own words back to me that I had completely forgotten the words she had said for herself. The question I should have asked whilst we were there in the carriage is, 'What do you mean, it *would have been* fun?'

By the time I thought of that, it was too late.

Private carriages are allowed in Rome after sunset, but the traffic jostling about the River Gate made it easier to park the thing at its hostelry just outside the walls and make our way through the crowded streets on foot. Consequently it was dark by the time we arrived at the Temple, and the torches were flaring on either side of the doors. Doors which, at what should have been the busiest time of the evening, were unaccountably shut.

'Uh-oh,' I murmured, trying to suppress a sinking feeling in my stomach.

'Shouldn't you be open right now?' asked Momina studying the doors curiously. 'Isn't this the busy time of day for your line of work? How do customers get in?'

Agitation made me talkative. 'See those bundles of rods against the walls? And that bunch of thugs over there? They aren't the usual street riff-raff. They're the carriers of those bundles of rods. Lictors. The official attendants of a senior Roman magistrate.'

The fact that lictors had accompanied a magistrate to the Temple meant he was on official business, and counting the bundles told me that my visitor was a Praetor*. The Urban Praetor, as it turned out**. Naturally a brothel needs to be licensed, and that license is protection money paid to the biggest gang in Rome,

---

*Praetors ranked just below consuls in the Roman hierarchy. The bundles of rods were called *fasces*, and both symbolized the magistrate's power to punish and if necessary provided the means. Outside Rome the magistrates' *fasces* had an axe stuck in the bundle for the same reason, but more so.

**This supplies a small fragment of extra information for historians. The name of the Urban Praetor for 105 BC is known only from a single damaged inscription as 'Pavo[n] ...'. Panderius allows us to fill in the missing letters.

a gang that likes to keep businesses profitable so as to get maximum profit from their extortion. That biggest gang is the Conscript Fathers, also known as the Roman Senate, and an official visit from one of its *padrones* led me to expect a major shake-down. I was wrong.

'You're what?' I goggled at the hatchet-faced individual sitting at my desk, who stared flintily back. I didn't do more than goggle, because once I had muscled past the lictors at the gate two of them had followed me in. Carrying clubs. Once inside the Temple, I had seen my doorman Gaius being tended to by a gaggle of the girls. A pool of blood near his head had not so much been cleaned up as smeared around the flagstones. It was a very big smear and Gaius was still and evidently unconscious. So I respected the clubs, even if that respect did not extend to the Urban Praetor.

'I'm confiscating your filthy business,' Pavonius repeated. 'Until you pay the fine.'

Ah. Shake-down.

'That fine is one million sesterces.'

Nope. Confiscation.

In a way, Pavonius had me bang to rights, and the problem was the pool in my atrium. Rome is served by seven aqueducts, and the water in that pool had risen in the Alban hills twenty miles outside town. It had been conducted at huge expense through tunnels, pipes and canals atop mile after mile of arches all the way to Rome. In Rome that water was made available in street fountains to whoever wanted to drink there or carry off an urnful.

Naturally, some citizens had more availability to the aqueducts than others, and many a senator benefits from water piped directly to his home. The previous commissioner of aqueducts had himself suggested that we come to such an arrangement (in return for what might be discreetly described as certain services of an exotic nature). The pool had been a hit with the clientèle, and while we might have been abstracting a certain amount of water, the Temple was, after all, itself a valuable public service, was it not?

Apparently not any more. Pavonius now explained - with considerable relish - what I already knew; that filching public water was an offence punishable with a swingeing fine, and confiscation of the property of anyone who could not pay.

'But come on,' I protested. 'It's an obsolete law. Everyone does it, and just settles up with the new water commissioner when he takes over. No-one has enforced it for decades. What are you going to do when I can't pay? Cut your pound of flesh from my body, as you are allowed by the Twelve Tables of early Roman law?'

'And that was a rhetorical question,' I added, as a thoughtful expression crossed the Praetor's face.

He shook his head at me with mock sadness. 'Look at you. Lucius. You were a war hero, winner of the oak crown, and what do they call you now? Ah yes, Panderius, the brothel keeper. Is this the best you can do for yourself, for Rome?'

'There's no shame in owning a brothel. I can tell you a dozen senators who have a least a part share in one. And I've done, as you say, more than my bit in the legions. I was military tribune at age fifteen, and did almost a decade. I'm done.'

'The Germans are coming, Lucius. I'm sure Caepio will be glad to take an officer of your ability. Nothing for you in Rome. I can't imagine how you missed the last levy.'

'Rheumatism. I'm a victim at its altar.'

'You look pretty spry to me.'

'It comes and goes.'

We glared at each other for a minute, and then Pavonius returned to my books, which he had scattered over my desk. 'According to this, you were turning over a pretty profit. Yet you had little more than a day's cash in your strong box. Where's the rest?'

'You opened my cash box? Ah. That's what happened to Gaius.'

'That oaf of a doorman? Resisting a magistrate of Rome is a

serious business. I may decide to charge him. If he lives. This money, and the rest, is the property of the Roman state. And if you don't tell us where to find it, we might indeed consider reinstating some of the old punishments from the Twelve Tables.'

'Costs more than you think to keep this place running. Free girls need wages. There's upkeep and entertaining. Laundry bill is a bitch. This month, the little I had left I sacrificed to Freya.' I waved my hand at a life-sized statue of the Goddess who stood in a corner of the office, painted as a Teutonic Amazon.

Pavonius hardly glanced at it. 'We'll find the money. It's here on the premises somewhere. Oh, and we'll be summonsing you to appear before me in three days to face charges for expropriating the property of the Roman people - namely their water. Let us know where you will be staying.' He read my expression. 'Here? Dear me, no. It's not yours. You don't even own that tunic I'm so kindly letting you keep on your back. One million sesterces. Up front. Pay up and we might reconsider.'

'Where do I get one million HS?'

Pavonius smiled thinly. 'Why not ask your patron?'

Ah. So that was it.

My patron and business partner, Cornelius Sulla, was currently in Rome, raising troops for the African war. And as was generally the case while in the city, he was having a party. Cornelius Sulla enjoyed parties. These were not refined affairs in the triclinium where guests supped watered wine and discussed Greek philosophy. Cornelius Sulla's parties were rip-roaring affairs with two whores to a guest, wine by the bucketful, and bawdy comedies played by actors who happily mingled offstage with the guests. Sulla himself was sprawled on his couch like a blonde Bacchus, roaring the words to a legionary marching song with his hands busy under the gowns of two giggling girls on his lap.

Later that same year, this apparent buffoon would ride alone into the camp of the Moorish king and demand that the king hand over the renegade Jugurtha. With that act of cold-blooded courage Sulla got his man, and brought the ten-year African war to an end. Jugurtha was later executed in the dungeons beside the forum, getting Sulla wild popularity in Rome, the hatred of Marius, his jealous commander, and a whole set of future complications for me.

Now, on hearing my news, Sulla shrugged off the girls and led me to a small private room on the other side of the vestibule. Party or no party, Cornelius Sulla was stone-cold sober, and it occurred to me that I had never seen him drunk. 'Sunshine on ice' someone in my *contubernium* in Africa had called him, and my tent-mate had been right. For all his bluff hearty manner Cornelius Sulla was as cold and merciless as a snake. He had also, to the best of my knowledge, never let down a friend or failed to avenge an insult. It was one of the reasons I had chosen him as my patron.

All Rome runs on patronage. The beggar on the street has a patron, who takes a cut of his gleanings. That patron has his own patron, who is probably a gang leader. That gang leader has his own patron, probably a minor senator, and that minor senator has his own patron, one of the big wheels in the senate. The system usually works well. A client takes his problem to his patron, that patron will either deal with it, or if the matter is too much for him, pass it up to his patron. In a dispute, the respective patrons get together and work something out.

You measure a patron by his *auctoritas*, which means roughly how much he can get done and whom he can do it to. In return for helping his clients, the patron expects their support and loyalty. You can tell a man with lots of *auctoritas* because he appears in the forum with a crowd of clients at his back. No-one votes for a man with no *auctoritas*, because he can't get anything done. Unless, of course, the candidate is the 'friend' of a man with *auctoritas*. This is often the case, for those with the most *auctoritas* in Rome like to wield their executive power through others.

And that, Cornelius Sulla and I both knew, was the problem. This was not a dispute between myself and Pavonius. It was a dispute between Marius, our consul-elect, and the aristocratic party in the senate, here represented by Sulla. Marius was using Pavonius to show that Sulla, and therefore the aristocrats, could not protect their own. And since the entire point of having a patron was protection, if Sulla could not protect me he would start haemorrhaging clients and lose his precious *auctoritas*.

'You're a good choice of victim,' Sulla told me thoughtfully. 'My backers in the senate are *optimates*, men like myself, with lineages going back centuries. None of them will be particularly bothered by the breaking of a brothel-keeper, however upmarket his premises. And, much as I hate to admit it, I've not the official clout to help you on my own.'

Sulla was just starting on his political career and in any case he was about to go to Africa and place himself under Marius' orders. He could not risk a public break with his commander, especially over a brothel (Sulla's reputation already being what it was) and a fine which, though unfair, was damnably legitimate.

The cold blue eyes narrowed in thought, and Sulla muttered 'Don't worry about the personal charges. I'll get a tribune to protect you from them. Nonnius owes me a few favours. It's your business that's the problem - I'll need to go to Caepio for that, and you know what Caepio is like.' We both contemplated a mental image of the pudgy, priggish Caepio. 'He's open to persuasion,' I murmured.

'He's as thick as pig-shit and the wool is easily pulled over his eyes,' agreed Sulla. 'And he hates the Marians. Trouble is he's already in Gaul, so we'd need a fast messenger, and in any case Caepio is not too keen on me either. I'd go for Metellus, but ... .' But Metellus was under attack by the Marians who were manoeuvring to get him exiled, and Metellus had problems enough.

Sulla sighed. 'Leave it with me. What I'd recommend for now is that you get your girls - they are free agents, so once they are off the premises, Pavonius has no hold on them - and I'll set you up in one of my properties. It won't be your Temple, and I'll miss visiting the place, but you'll be back in business, which will be one in the eye for Pavonius and friends. Better do it through a front man though - I'll supply a face.'

That was Cornelius Sulla all over. The public would see that Sulla could support his clients and flout even the Urban Praetor, Pavonius would get an empty building, and Sulla, through his agent, would have taken over my business. For the moment, that was all I was going to get. We spent half an hour over a light but luxurious dinner making the necessary arrangements and then, turning down Sulla's offer to join him at the party, I left the premises in no cheerful frame of mind.

Liber II

By the time I left Sulla's house, the Pleiades in all their starry glory were rising over the rooftops to advertise that it was now the fourth hour of the night. My unhelpful patron had not moved far from his old lodgings on the Viminal hill where he had once rented an apartment in his penurious youth. (The racket of his parties had driven the freedman living in the apartment above to ecstasies of fury and frustration). Consequently my route from Sulla's mansion took me downhill towards the Forum Romanum and the looming, tottering, tenant-blocks which the average Roman pleb calls home.

Respectable citizens were by now abed, and the flickering lamplight in the occasional window failed even to drown out the starlight which was all that lit my way. The earthy smell of excrement distracted my thoughts, reminding me to move to the middle of the street. A timely manoeuvre, as soon afterwards a splashy sound from the shadows marked where the contents of yet another chamber pot hit the pavement*.

Flying faeces aside, by and large the Viminal is pretty safe. Its respectable denizens are seldom abroad at night, so thieves drift either to the richer pickings of the Caelian Hill or the easier pickings of the Esquiline. The solid citizens of the Viminal have little tolerance for violence by night, and due to local community policing policy it is a lucky mugger who survives to be brought before the Praetor in the morning.

Even after bed-time, Rome is never completely silent. A couple bickering at full volume in a tenement block were loudly advised to try an obscene alternative occupation by an exasperated

---

*As Juvenal complains in *Satire* 3 '*As there are open windows watching you, when you go by, at night. So as you go make a wretched wish and a prayer that they'll Rest content with simply emptying their brimming pots over you.*' Which tells us that chamber pots were still a nocturnal hazard two hundred years later.

neighbour. A sudden fracas in a nearby street fell as suddenly silent, possibly because the participants had seen a patrol of club-wielding vigiles passing by, and an inebriated youth was somewhere serenading his love to the accompaniment of faint catcalls and applause. I might have just lost my livelihood, but it was just another night in the big city for everyone else.

Making my way toward the Via Sandalarius, I stood politely aside for some party-goer weaving his way homeward escorted by three burly torch-bearers. Sulla, the conscientious host that he always was, had offered torch-bearers to me as well, but at present darkness suited both my mood and my purposes. So now, I faced the wall so as not to lose my night vision and thought gloomy thoughts as the little group went by. The dancing shadows from the torchlight faded from the street, and I turned once more, and in doing so caught a flicker of movement from the side of my eye. Memory linked this with the scuff of a sandal heard once or twice on my way downhill, and the occasional soft squelch which is the unhygienic side-effect of walking through Rome by night.

This was more irritating than alarming. My first thought was that some drunk was following me to pick a fight, and I rather looked forward to extracting the martial vigour from a would-be Achilles. But a drunk would be louder, and bellicose. Had Pavonius set a spy to see what happened after I fled to my patron for succour? Since I certainly did not want Pavonius to have that information, I abruptly took the next leftward turning. This would quickly bring me to the narrow streets of the lower Esquiline, where it was easy to lose a spy in the maze of alleyways and *ad hoc* vendor's stalls which crowd the kerbs. The Aediles keep clearing these stalls away, but the Roman plebs insouciantly ignore magisterial edicts and the stalls are back the next day to clog the streets again. This annoyance would tonight work to my advantage.

Plans changed as I turned the corner. Not one, but two

shadows flitted across the street in my wake. One person meant surveillance. Two suggested that someone meant me harm, and for the first time I began to consider my safety. But my original plan was sound, and the streets of the Esquiline still offered their shadowy sanctuary. I cast about for a likely alleyway to lose myself in. Then, just as I was considering making a dash into the best candidate, an even better opportunity for escape presented itself.

Three burly figures talking animatedly emerged together from a side-street and turned confidently towards the Via Patricus. Two attackers would be unlikely to engage a group of four, so I hurried to catch up. As I approached I noted the that the new arrivals were talking in some tongue other than Latin. No matter - Rome these days contained all sorts, Samnites, Greeks, Oscans and of course the Etruscans who have been here for centuries. Most would welcome company this late at night, or would at least tolerate me tagging along close by until I could find a late-opening tavern or (ironically) a brothel I could duck into for shelter.

The group were deep in conversation and apparently unaware of my approach until I was almost on top of them. As they saw me and started to turn, I caught a glimpse of a Gallic torque and huge drooping moustaches. I opened my mouth to give a cordial greeting, twisted sideways to avoid the club, and struck wildly backward to block a strike at my kidneys. Something hit me wickedly between the shoulder blades, and I dropped to the flagstones, rolling wildly for the shelter of a wall. I took a kick in the ribs and grabbed the ankle on the return strike. In fury and panic I wrenched the foot violently in a direction nature had never intended it to go, and was rewarded by a yell of pain.

Stupid me. They had let their prey see he was being followed, and like an innocent lamb I had run voluntarily into the arms of my attackers. Now they had me down in the street, and the blows were coming hard and furious. A kick in the stomach left me retching and unable even to call for help. Rough hands hauled me up, and I smashed the heel of my palm into a moustachioed face just as there was a soundless explosion within my skull, and everything. Stopped.

Some uncountable time later I came to my senses while vomiting. The human body often responds to sudden insult by unloading whatever is in its stomach, so I came to with my lungs urgently pointing out that the rest of me was suffocating on regurgitated dormouse pastries. Retching and choking I struggled towards full consciousness. In the process I discovered that my hands were secured somehow above my head, whereupon my shoulders promptly filed a complaint about how long they had been bearing my weight. The hairy shape in my bleary vision turned out to be a Gallic type watching my struggles with satisfaction. Seeing me revive, he helpfully back-handed me viciously across the face. This sent a streamer of mixed phlegm and vomit flying across the room, and suddenly I could breathe again.

This fellow was favouring one leg, and had a blossoming pair of black eyes either side of a red, swollen and very broken nose. I suspected that when I got to feel my hands again, there would be a corresponding nose-shaped bruise on the heel of my palm. I spat the remaining vomit from my mouth - getting a lot of it over the brute in front of me - and looked around sourly. Through waves of nausea I recognized that I was in some sort of gloomy cellar, with my wrists tied to a joist supporting the floor above. A few amphorae were scattered on the dirt floor, and two more men, dim shapes in the firelight, were perched side by side on a barrel quietly quaffing the contents from mugs held in their hands. A large charcoal brazier lit the room with a dull and appropriately Hades-like light.

As I struggled to get my feet underneath me, I smiled ingratiatingly at the pugnacious figure before me.

'You have the face of a leprous donkey,' I informed him pleasantly, 'the stomach of a pig with trapped wind, and the suppurating genitals of a Barbary Ape.' The guttural string of abuse I received in return caused me to add with considerable sincerity, 'And your breath would strip the skin off an elephant. Gods, man! Haven't you heard of mouthwash?'

In reply my co-loquator grabbed the neck of my tunic and tried to rip it off my body. The solid seams of good Roman needlework resisted, and the dramatic gesture turned into a somewhat comic wrestling match between barbarian and fabric. When my expensively-tailored tunic was finally hanging in shreds from my belt, the Gaul stooped to pick up a rag from one of the barrels. This rag he carefully wrapped several times around his hand. Then he turned towards the brazier and slowly pulled a bar of metal from the base of the slow-burning charcoal.

The bar had evidently been there for some time. It glowed a sullen red against the infernal shadows about the room. I eyed the thing with unease that turned to alarm as the man turned toward me with an evil leer. In the good old days of the ancient Republic, Mucius Scaevola had once voluntarily thrust his hand into a charcoal brazier, just to show an enemy his contempt for torture. But standards are just not what they once were. I'd happily confess to anything to avoid this barbaric ape doing poker work on my skin, but: primus - I had no idea what the man wanted; and secundus - even if I told him he wouldn't understand me. So it was going to be general torture for kicks and repayment for the nose modelling job. Or because the Gods had evidently designated this as 'Get Lucius Panderius Day'.

One of the spectators shouted something puzzling, in either encouragement or admonition. But I had no time to work it out. With the grin of a pantomime villain my tormentor started making mock jabs at various parts of my anatomy. These brought the metal bar so close that I could see hairs on my body shrivel from the heat. I shrank back, gibbering entertainingly with undisguised fear until my feet were firmly beneath me. Then lifting myself slightly with the support of the rope about my wrists, I kicked one foot into the man's groin with a thump so solid that it jarred me from hip to jaw. My attacker folded up slowly and squeezed a quiet and rather sad-sounding 'wheee' from his pain-locked larynx as he toppled.

In his agonized distraction, the man forgot about the red-hot metal bar in his hand until it came to rest against his thigh and started to sizzle. Then, with a yell that probably rattled windows on the Palatine hill, he flung the thing from him with great force. Despite my best efforts to dodge, the spinning bar caught me a glancing blow on the shoulder. That would probably mean a nasty burn later - something which concerned me little as I was highly unlikely to have a 'later'. Probably the Fates would cut the thread binding me to the mortal world within the next few seconds.

At least my final moments would not be without interest. The bar ricocheted off the wall into a pile of straw-filled bedding. This smoked for a second and then burst lustily into flame. This new development brought the others in the room off their barrel at speed. They flung the contents of their leather mugs at the flames, which only made the smoke thicker and more acrid. Once the pair had unavailingly searched the room for fire-fighting materials, one of them tried to pull the other's cloak off his shoulders. Gallic cloaks are thick and superbly made. They would be excellent for smothering flames, except that his cloak is every Gaul's pride and joy. Fire-fighting efforts broke down into a furious argument as to whose cloak was to be sacrificed. Meanwhile the uncured timbers of the foundation supports had started to smoulder.

A quick consensus was reached and the fire-fighters turned on the third barbarian as he writhed in pain at my feet. This was somewhat more pain than heretofore, as I had used the confusion to put in several hard kicks to his kidneys and head. Now, with concussion to add to his problems, my victim was dragged out of range. One man struggled to forcibly remove his cloak while the other desperately and totally unsuccessfully tried to slow the flames by urinating on them. From above, those wakened by the smell of smoke shouted urgent demands to know what was going on. It was unclear whether I would be stabbed or burned to death, but at least my passing would not go unremarked.

'All well, just old clothes burning!' yelled a new voice, and moments later the door crashed open to reveal the largest man I have ever seen. The newcomer took in the situation with a swift glance and barked orders that had both barbarians ripping off their own cloaks with urgency. A third figure scuttled around the bulk of the man blocking the doorway, rushed to the man still flopping on the floor like a dying fish, grabbed his cloak and joined the fire-fighters.

They can breed some big barbarians. Rome's legendary Valerius the Crow got his name from a hand-to-hand fight with some sort of Gallic human mountain and only won because a providential crow tried to peck out his opponent's eyes at a critical moment. Or so the story goes. The modern-day giant ignored me as he strode across the room and began vigorously cuffing the men suppressing the fire. Whether this constituted discipline or encouragement I could not tell. Once things were pretty much under control, the giant's companion slipped away from the action and grinned at me. With his shaggy brows and friendly smile, he resembled an amiable, and somewhat greying sheepdog. He studied my torso and the signs of wounds both past and present and grinned even more widely.

'How goes it, donkey breath?' he asked.

'You'd know a donkey's breath, since your mother spent so much time under one,' I replied amiably, and we studied each other for a second.

'Gallic auxilia?' I enquired eventually.

'Gallic auxiliary cavalry,' he corrected primly. 'Ala II Trevorum, under Scipio Aemilianus*. Were you at Numantia? Nah, too young. African legions?'

'With both Metellus and that git Marius.' Marius had cut down the size of a Roman army's baggage by making legionaries carry all their kit themselves. Jokes about 'Marius' mules' had been entertaining our auxiliary comrades-in-arms ever since. If I had heard the 'donkey-breath' epithet once, I'd heard it a hundred times.

Before I could ask what in Hades was going on, the giant returned from across the room. The two barbarians traipsed after him like chastised schoolboys. The giant tapped me firmly on the chest. I abandoned the idea of kicking him in the groin because the operation would require some form of stepladder. Piercing blue eyes studied me from atop a hawk-like nose and massive moustache. Somewhere beneath the moustache a mouth must have opened, for the giant boomed 'You Lucius Panderius!'

'I know,' I told him.

'Me Vindu!' The giant tapped his chest. 'I am Lym p'Dic.'

I glanced questioningly at the sheepdog, who was intently studying the still-smouldering cloaks in the corner. Tonelessly, the former auxiliary said, 'He thinks it means Slayer of Thousands. It's a long story. If you want to live to hear it, you had better act impressed. For both our sakes.'

I nodded. 'Ah, Limp Dick. Well yes, I mean, wow. What can a mere mortal say? A limp dick eh? Gosh.'

Satisfied with my response, the giant fired off a mini-diatribe at the sheepdog, glancing at me occasionally as he spoke. Again, I

---

*The first recorded cavalry ala with a title comes from c. 40 BC under the Second Triumvirate. The earliest ones tended to be named after a commander, but ones such as this, with ethnic titles, appear soon afterward. Obviously auxiliary cavalry were around earlier than 40 BC but this reference by Panderius is the first hint of how the early units were organized.

caught an occasional word of Greek incongruous in the 'bar-bar' sound of barbarian speech. In the background, first aid was being given to the injured man, this taking the form of attempts to slap him ungently to consciousness.

After nodding to show that he understood what he was to ask, the sheepdog turned to me. He raised his eyebrows. 'Vindu wants you to know .... '

'Vindu Lym p'Dic,' rumbled the giant from behind him.

The sheepdog sighed. 'Vindu Lym p'Dic wants you to know that we can do this the easy way or the hard way, and he's rather looking forward to the hard way. So I'll make it easy for you. Where's the statuette?'

'Eh?'

'Look, I've got a delicate stomach, and I'll have to be here to translate while Vindu does horrible things to you. The last man he questioned still comes back to haunt me on bad nights. Come on, please. Just tell. Do it for me?' He looked at me appealingly.

'Cheerfully. Just tell me what statuette you want, and I'll give you city district, crossroads and house. Ask away.'

Another sigh. 'Look. Vindu starts by breaking your little finger. Then he wiggles it around a bit. Then he breaks the little finger on the other hand, and wiggles that too. Then its your ring finger, and then all the other fingers, one by one, and then the small bones in your hand. About this point I usually lose my dinner. Then he breaks your feet ... your ankles and wrists ... .' The sheepdog shuddered. 'I once saw someone last right up to the ribs. You could see his exposed heart beating through the mess. For a while anyway.'

Vidnu made an impatient noise, and I said frantically.

'Wait, please, just tell me what statuette. I don't know what statuette you mean. In Jupiter's name, I'm trying to help you here, I just don't know what to tell you. By Pan's hairy buttocks, just tell me what in the Hecate-cursed hells is going on here!'

27

There was a nonplussed pause, and I realized that I had practically roared out the last sentence. Even Vindu seemed somewhat taken aback. Seeming much less sure of himself, the sheepdog said, 'You must have the statuette. You've got Momina haven't you?'

Momina. The discovery that my oddball slave acquisition was behind all this somehow came as absolutely no surprise.

From there things went more smoothly. The auxiliary's name was Madracaera - generally abbreviated to Madric - and he had been hired as local talent by the other Gauls, who were in fact Galatians, which explained their peculiar manners.

Galatians are Gauls, sort of. Their particular tribe forked off from a mass raid to the east and ended up bouncing around Asia Minor until they settled in an arid plateau in the middle of Anatolia that no-one else wanted. Anatolia is a snake-pit of political intrigue and warfare between Bithynians, Pontics and Cappadocians. Even we Romans join in the fun, since we hold the western chunk as a province which we call Asia. Given the amount of battle and general unpleasantness going on, the Galatians are right at home, and when not beating up their neighbours themselves, they make a comfortable living hiring themselves out to each and every side as mercenaries.

'So you are a mercenaries' mercenary, eh Madracaera?' I enquired.

He nodded. 'A thousand denarii once they get the statuette.'

By now we had established that I knew nothing about this mysterious statuette, and and this intelligence had led to my being cut down and allowed to sit while I massaged feeling back into my wrists. Madrracaera assured me, with every appearance of credibility, that the business with the poker had only been intended to terrify me into compliance. Vidnu would have appeared earlier to 'rescue' me, except while Madracaera was preoccupied with the odd sounds coming through the cellar door, Vidnu had wandered off and had to be retrieved from the arms of a passing street prostitute. Hence his vicious mood on arrival.

My report that I had only acquired Momina that morning was corroborated by the fact that the Galatians had located her at Lentulus' house at around the time I was visiting. They had seen us leave and followed the carriage back to Rome. Come to think of it, I vaguely remembered seeing a group of Gauls on the Ostia road, but they were no uncommon sight. I would not have noticed them at all if Momina had not done so. Now her intent study of the men came back to haunt me. That girl was definitely unsettling. I wondered if Lentulus would refund my money if I agreed not to return the goods.

I grasped that the Galatians wanted some sort of statuette, for reasons which neither concerned nor interested me. It was a religious thing, and nothing makes less sense than other people's religion. The Galatians thought Momina had the statuette, and I was pretty sure that did not. When I had picked her up, she came with nothing but the brown woollen tunic she was wearing. Though on reflection, I conceded that the tunic was shapeless enough to have concealed a great deal more than just the rest of Momina.

This led to the obvious question. Where was our spooky priestess at the moment? I assumed that she was still at the temple. I had left Momina on the premises with the girls making a fuss over her, and when I was escorted out by an unsympathetic lictor I had caught a glimpse of my new acquisition looking unexpectedly regal in a Greek chiton which one of the girls must have dug out of her wardrobe.

This admission was nearly the death of me. Vindu had nodded calmly when he was told that his priestess was in a temple, but once Madracaera explained that the 'temple' in question was actually a brothel, the big Galatian lost it. I noted - in the detached manner that one does once complete terror takes hold - that

Vindu's face went from tanned to startlingly red, and huge veins started to swell on his forehead and neck. Then he came to literally tear me limb from limb. If I had still been tied, it would have been over in a moment. As it was, I bounded over the barrel to safety, and then was chased around it twice before Vidnu simply picked up the barrel and threw it at me.

I ducked at the last moment, and dived between Vidnu's legs as he rushed at me. The giant turned, and smashed his fist into the face of one of the Galatians behind him before he realized it was not me. Rolling against the wall, I snatched up the poker with which I had been threatened earlier. The thing had been lying in a pool of urine which had cooled it considerably. I dropped into a sword-fighting stance, but underestimated Vidnu's reach. He plucked the poker from my hands and glared into my eyes as he slowly bent it double. Cheap iron, probably. Then Vidnu charged like an avalanche, bowling over Madracaera as he tried to get between us.

It was cat and mouse for a bit as Vidnu tried to get me into a corner and each time I managed to break free. All the while Madric scuttled around Vindu like a sheepdog trying to contain a maddened ram, urgently and soothingly explaining (I hoped) that no-one was prostituting his priestess. She was there to do the books. In the end he got the explanation down to a single sentence, which he repeated continually. This finally got to Vindu, just as he got to me; I dangled by the throat from the end of a massively muscled arm and looked along it towards a fist like a sledgehammer that was cocked to punch me into somewhere next month.

Fortunately by that time Madracaera's explanation had finally percolated into place between the giant's ears and cooled his over-heated emotions. With the Gaul talking fast and ingratiatingly, Vindu's expression slowly morphed from fury to disgust, and I was flung contemptuously across the room. I happened to land plumb on top of the Galatian I had given a kicking earlier. This broke my fall, and possibly another of his ribs. I noted the cowed expression of the prone man's two companions, and got a 'better-you-than-we' look which spoke volumes about the effect of Vindu's terrifying rages.

'So you fellows were not going to harm me, eh?' I remarked to Madracaera, though I was too shaken to make the comment as scathing as I had intended. I picked myself up and dusted myself down.

Then I said brightly, 'You want Momina, you are welcome to her. I'd make a gift of her, possibly accompanied by a small cash incentive to take her off my hands. But its not up to me. Like everything I owned when I woke up this morning, your priestess has been confiscated by the senate and people of Rome. If you want the girl, you'll have to beg, borrow or steal her off the Republic.'

'Good luck with that. But I'm out of it. Not stopping you or helping. You probably don't care, but I've got problems of my own.'

A thought occurred to me. Vidnu and his entourage had a talent for spreading chaos that might be useful. 'However, if you want to get Momina from the Temple, I was on my way there before you apes interrupted me. I've got unfinished business, and it seems that you've got things to do there too. So why don't we all go and visit my whorehouse together?'

Cornelius Sulla's factotum slid out of the shadows as we approached the Temple. 'You're late,' he told me. 'Who are these people? What happened to your tunic? Gods, what happened to you?'

'I was delayed. These people are the muscle in case the lictors weren't hungry. My tunic got torn. I refused a replacement because I prefer to be the only living thing inside my clothing. I would rather not talk about the rest of it. Are you set?'

The factotum nodded across the street to where a pair of lictors stood guard at the brothel door. 'Stood' was something of an exaggeration. 'Your girls fed them two hours ago. One has collapsed, the other should go any moment. What did your cook give them?'

'Opium. It costs the earth, but pacifies the most upset customer. Since it's not my stock any more, I told him not to hold back. Shall we see if there's anyone left standing inside?'

The lictor slumped against the door rolled a calf-like eye at me as we entered, and in a spirit of scientific inquiry I gave his shoulder a gentle shove. He pirouetted inelegantly, and collapsed almost gratefully on top of his fellow sentry. By the time we had dragged the pair into the vestibule, he was snoring gently.

Wonder, Beauty and the other girls were anxiously crowding the atrium and fussed heart-warmingly over my burns and bruises. In a low murmur I introduced them to Sulla's man, and told them that - if they so desired - new employment awaited in a new house. Sulla was a well-known and popular visitor to my establishment, so my former employees seemed happy enough with the plan once I had explained it. Technically, the girls could have walked out of the brothel at any time since Pavonius had walked in, but the law tends to be very flexible when applied to and by the Urban Praetor. While the girls were on the premises, the stark reality of Roman politics meant that they were in the Praetor's power.

Beauty whispered to me, 'They all ate the supper - it was Laevonia's best spiced lamb - even knowing what was in it, I nearly had some myself, it smelled that good. But that beastly Pavonius didn't. He's spent the evening in your study going over the books, again and again. He took one of the girls in there and whipped her. Lucius, he knows you were making lots of money.'

Another girl chimed in. 'He left the study a few minutes ago. Went to the room of that new girl. The Greek slave. Lucius?'

But I was already sprinting across the courtyard, with Madric close behind. As I came to the curtain which separated Momina's room from the rest of the world, I heard her tell someone cheerfully, 'You're not going to rape me.'

'Correct.' Pavonius replied in a careful, cold voice. 'You can't rape a thing. A slave is an *instrumentum vocale:* a tool which talks. I don't need to ask consent from a thing, and you cannot refuse it.'

'So why did you tie me to the bed?' Momina sounded genuinely interested. 'Is it a power/control sort of thing? There's girls here who are into that. I could arrange you a discount.'

Sheer surprise at Momina's effrontery startled the Praetor into a dialogue. 'Why pay for what I can simply ... take?'

'Well yes, that's what I was on about earlier. You see, you can't 'simply take' me.'

'Really? I believe I am about to do just that. Give me one reason why not.'

'Oh, okay. The reason called Vindu? He's a very *good* reason. Sorry about your head, and um ... the rest of it.'

The conversation got no further because, cat-like, Vindu had come up behind me. Hearing Momina's voice and his name, he twitched the bedroom curtain aside to reveal his priestess bent over the bed with a very priapic Pavonius approaching her from behind.

Suddenly, things happened very quickly. The almost comical expression of disbelief in Pavonius' face turned to alarm as Vindu charged him. Then it switched to stunned agony as the gigantic Galatian picked him up by throat and scrotum and hurled him with bone-crushing force against the opposite wall. Pavonius' head hit the window-frame with a sickening crack, but in the moment before the impact he saw me lurking behind Vindu's shoulder. There was a flare of recognition, and the Praetor went into unconsciousness with his eyes locked on mine. Oh dear.

If Pavonius remembered any of this when he came to, it spelled crucifixion for the Galatian and a beheading for me. It did not matter that the whole thing was over in less than five heartbeats, and stopping Vidnu was anyway impossible. Rome takes assault and battery of its senior magistrates very seriously. Perhaps the same thought occurred to Vidnu, or chucking Pavonius across the room had always been a preliminary to murdering him. He stepped across the room, drawing his dagger.

'Madric, tell your boss that killing that human cow-pat will just make things worse. Leave this to me. My town, my Temple, my rules. Seriously. Tell him to get Momina free, and they can have their heart to heart about this statuette thing. I've got things to do.'

Momina added something in a muffled voice. I glanced at her sharply to see if she was suppressing a giggle, and was amazed to see the gigantic Vidnu drop to his knees the moment she addressed him. Madric positively goggled at the sight, but only for a second. I took him by the ear and led him from the room.

'Leave those two love-birds together for a moment. I see she speaks your barbaric language. Why am I not surprised? Listen, I want you to catch up with that factotum - he can't have gone far. They will be going east down the Via Patricus. I need Amazonia, the girl who likes to dress up as a Germanic warrior queen. And, um, yes, get Circe, the one who helped me stage our 'Out of Africa' evening for the lads from my legion. I'm going to need one of the props.'

Madracaera opened his mouth to say something like 'I don't work for you' even as I added, 'You get 50 denarii as soon I see both women standing in front of me.' The auxiliary shut his mouth again. After a moment's contemplation, he ripped off a credible military salute and vanished at the trot. 'Amazonia and Circe,' I called after him, and headed for my office.

If Pavonius had not been blinded by lust he would have surely wondered where his lictors had gotten to. Or perhaps he imagined they were making use of the facilities, just as he had intended to. I imagined his remaining thugs were somewhere on the premises. If so the Temple was about to lose its charm for them. Gaius, the ex-legionary, ex-doorman and - after his beating - possibly ex-Gaius had been very close to one of the Eburoni Germans. A strapping lass. I doubted that the lictors had survived her revenge. Barbarians take things very personally.

In my office I carefully closed the door and shuttered the windows. I took a few moments to carefully bathe my wounds, wincing as the scented water from the pitcher touched the burn on my shoulder. This burn I gently salved and bandaged. (You'd be amazed how often we needed bandages in a supposedly peaceful brothel.) Then I dug around in the back of a cupboard and produced an altogether curious garment.

This resembled a vest, but it was made of stiffened linen. Some twenty narrow rectangular pockets were sewn closely together across the front and sides. It was a custom-made piece prepared especially for use should the Cimbric hordes sweep down on Rome and take the city. The Gauls had done just that over three hundred years ago and it hadn't been pretty. I wasn't staying for the next occasion, and the vest was part of my travel plans.

Now to the statue of Freya. Out of habit, I carefully checked that no-one was looking, and reverentially reached under the goddess' bronze skirt. A moment's groping, then I found and thumbed the little bump between her legs. The goddess rewarded me with a soft click. Stepping back and around, I gently pushed Freya between her shoulder blades, and the statue's cantilevered base swung up, revealing a dark cavity in the solid stone block. I reached into the cavity, and took out a slender gold bar that would keep a skilled workman in wages for a year. I slotted the bar into a vest pocket, and repeated the process again and again. Not every pocket was filled - my retirement had been rushed - but when I stood the unexpected weight of the gold made me stagger. For everyday expenses I also filled a purse with two hundred denarii, then remembered to add an extra fifty for Madric.

Returning to the cupboard, I picked out a few accessories including an elegantly embroidered long-sleeved tunic with purple dye-work on the edges. If necessary, just selling the tunic would keep me fed for two months or so. As Pavonius had promised, I was going to leave the Temple with just the clothes on my back.

Feeling altogether better about the world I stepped out into the night air. Not unexpectedly Vidnu had set a guard on my study door who stepped forward the moment I unlocked it. 'Veni,' grunted the Galatian in basic Latin. 'Come.'

Momina was sitting on her bed, looking none the worse for her recent escapade. Vidnu stood beside her, like the retainer to some ancient queen. They made a memorable pair, and I couldn't wait for the pair to become a memory. Something to recall with fascination and horror as I sipped wine on the balcony of a little apartment in Tarentum as I watched the sunset slide into the sea. It was time to say my goodbyes and make a speedy departure.

Vidnu was evidently of a like mind. He stepped forward with a broad grin and clapped his hand into mine for a hearty handshake.

Momina said, 'No!' with a voice that locked us in position like a pair of statues; I reaching for Vidnu's shoulder, and he in the act of pulling me forward on to the dagger in his other hand. I looked at the blade in quiet fascination even as part of my mind wondered at the note of irresistible command which had stopped Vidnu in mid-stab. You didn't learn that as a slave girl.

Vidnu turned to Momina and rattled out an explanation, occasionally gesturing at me for emphasis. Momina replied in the same guttural language, firmly and cheerfully rejecting the explanation. Vidnu enlarged on his topic, sweeping his arm up and down as he evidently stressed how killing my worthless self would do the world a favour. Momina was implacable. She cut into his extempore speech with a brief instruction.

Vidnu gave me a sour look. He spat on my sandals, dropped his dagger, and gave Momina a brief obeisance that stopped just short of discourtesy. The priestess watched him thoughtfully as he stalked from the room like an offended panther.

'I asked to speak to you alone,' she said, once Vidnu had stepped through the doorway.

'You are merciful,' I remarked with some bitterness.

Momina laughed. It was a bright, happy sound that chilled me to the bone. 'I am. Vidnu is perhaps not a very nice man, but I didn't want you killing him.'

'What? Excuse me. *Excuse* me!' Indignantly I pointed to where Vidnu had been standing, and mimed a handshake. 'He was going to ... going to ... ,' I pointed a trembling finger at the pit of my stomach, '... gut me like a sacrificial pig.'

Momina came over, and slid her palm over my stomach in a surprisingly sensual gesture. The small hand bumped gently over the pockets with their gold bars.

'This would not have deflected it? And let's see ... .' She gently twisted my unresisting arm and the little bronze dagger dropped from my grip. 'Bronze? Because ... ,' she lifted the blade to her face and sniffed delicately. She smiled. 'Because the poison would taint the steel. And you were half a second from dragging that blade across the big blood vessels in his neck. My poor Vidnu would not have had a chance. He'd be dead in what? A minute?'

'Three,' I muttered. 'He's a big man. What are you? A goddess? Some kind of witch? How did you know?'

She looked at me with those huge, grey eyes. 'You are not stupid. You worked out that the Galatians have me so they don't need you. Vidnu doesn't like loose ends and he's not squeamish. He's a good fighter, you know. If he did not underestimate you so, he'd have seen how differently you walked into the room. Like a man thirty pounds more top-heavy. That means serious armour.'

'And you had a cocked wrist, together with a long-sleeved tunic. Really Lucius, you could have just carried a sign in the other hand that said, 'I've got a dagger up my sleeve.' If I had any doubt, that went when you stepped into his handshake even before he pulled you. It's not black magic. Just observation. I'm glad that you two will soon be friends. Well, you'll stop trying to murder each other, and that's almost the same thing.'

'I'll step outside now. Circe and Amazonia are here, and I believe the three of you want to spend some time alone with Pavonius.'

Liber III

Eight nights after my departure from the Temple, a bedraggled and bad-tempered group slipped by night through the portals of Lentulus Baebius' house in Ostia. There were no spectators to this event. Lentulus' messenger had been very specific about this. If anyone saw us entering his premises, Lentulus himself would alert the authorities. Ill-omened as it was, this unwelcoming approach had not prevented Lentulus from laying out wine and honey-cakes for us in the kitchen, and we fell upon the food with gratitude. While the honey-cakes were superb, the wine was a studied insult - cheap stuff from the Janiculum, the kind that you drink if you can't get vinegar.

Poor stuff as the wine was, I nevertheless kept a wary eye on how much of it went into the Galatians. Fortunately there proved to be just the one well-filled urn. The kitchen itself was a secure refuge - a solid barrel-arch brick construction partly underground which ran the length of the house. Lentulus used it on occasion to entertain the guildsmen who kept his docking operation running, so the place was built to supply food in quantity. Our group had spread out comfortably before the warmth of the ovens and had elbow room to spare[*].

It was good to find refuge in the flickering firelight and friendly shadows of the room, but the shelter was only temporary. My companions had made sure of that. If Lentulus had been keeping up with our adventures, as I suspected he had (the wine was a hint) I would soon know exactly how fast and far I'd have to flee.

---

[*]Barrel-vault rooms such as that described here were not the usual Roman dining facility, but cellars and kitchens of this sort were fairly common in Greek and Roman architecture, and indeed examples can be found in ancient Egypt. A good discussion on these and other vault constructions is to be found in W. MacDonald's *Architecture of the Roman empire* (Yale 1982)

That fleeing was essential I did not doubt. My last night's sleep had been under a hedge at the side of a cabbage field, and the only news I could contribute to the current situation was that though the rabbit population was abundant this year, the miserable beasts were distressingly adept at avoiding snares. Like the rabbits, we too were evidently being hunted with enthusiasm, but also like the rabbits we had so far escaped the traps set for us. I was gloomily looking forward to hearing exactly how wide the nets had been spread.

It turned out that Lentulus was in no hurry to come downstairs. We finished our meal undisturbed. Then, once a careful check of the room had failed to turn up any further source of wine, the Galatians phlegmatically rolled themselves up in their cloaks and lay before the ovens to sleep. One man remained at the door with a drawn sword, though it was uncertain whether this was to guard against enemies entering or to prevent Momina and myself from sneaking out. Ignoring the others, the priestess and I talked quietly at the table, and tactfully tried to ignore Madracaera as he furtively rolled closer to eavesdrop.

The Gaul had wasted his effort. Momina and I had barely exchanged a few words of small talk before her head lifted like an alert hound's and she turned her attention to the door. Two minutes later Lentulus walked in. He was accompanied by a pair of burly dockers, though both were unarmed. Knowing my man, there was absolutely no doubt that a further dozen men were outside the door that Lentulus so carefully closed behind him. Nor did I doubt that those men were both armed and armoured. Bad news like Vidnu spreads fast.

'Lucius!' Ignoring the barbarians struggling upright from their impromptu sleeping positions, Lentulus strode over and gave me an affectionate hug. Afterwards he held me by both shoulders and looked anxiously into my face. 'Are you all right?' Then in reply to my traditional greeting of 'Quid agis?', which means 'What are you up to?' He asked, 'Immo vero, Lucius, quid agis?' - or roughly, 'No, Lucius the hell have *you* been up to?'[*]

'Ah,' I said ruefully. 'You heard?'

'Heard? I've been keeping track of you since before you left Rome by the chaos in your wake. The whole countryside is buzzing, man. I thought Sulla told you to get the girls, empty your strongbox and quietly - perhaps he failed to stress 'quietly'? - slip out of town'.

'We tried. We sort of attached ourselves to the back of a funeral procession. The gate guards were actually paying attention. I mean, those gates are practically rusted open, and everyone knows that the guards are basically there to shake down the carters when they arrive in the evening. Since when did Rome have security on the gates? Anyway no-one was hurt.'

Lentulus looked at Vidnu. The large Galatian and his retinue were studying Lentulus' dockers the way terriers might eye a pair of particularly obstreperous rats. The uneasy dockers glared truculently back and shuffled a bit closer together.

'He is rather hard to blend in,' Lentulus conceded. 'And by 'not hurt', you mean 'not permanently crippled.' Moving on ... there was that affair with the militia at the tavern.'

I glared bitterly at the Galatians. 'Listen, any time that these bastards tell you that they are just popping in for a drink, just one drink to wash the road dust from their throats and that they'll be in and out before anyone notices, don't believe it. I mean seriously, don't believe it. They lie.'

'It was a hell of a fight, I believe.'

'Totally unnecessary. That patrol was just stopping by. And Vidnu the meat-head here staggers over and says something like

---

[*] It would be interesting to know if one Granius (a Roman contemporary of Panderius) had sight of this text, or indeed spoke with Panderius after the events of 105, for fifteen years later he used exactly the same response when greeted by the controversial tribune Livius Drusus (Cic. Pro Planc. 14)

'You looking for me?' Fortunately this lot can fight drunk as well as sober. Perhaps I could give you something to slip the tavern owner that would cover the damage?'

'He might need a new tavern. Are you also planning to replace the little hamlet that you burned to the ground?'

'Gods no. That was their fault. We just wanted somewhere to lay low for a few days. I was hoping things would blow over. Obviously the villagers found that we had money, or perhaps there was a reward out for us after the tavern business. I don't know.'

Lentulus looked non-committal. 'I'll get to that. Go on.'

'Well, you try waking up in the dead of night surrounded by homicidal peasants. All with sharp agricultural instruments and calculating expressions. It haunts your dreams, afterwards. If Momina hadn't given us warning - I want to have a serious talk with you about Momina, by the way – I would probably be headed back to Rome with my head on top of a threshing pole.'

'Funny you should say that. So you torched the place in retaliation?'

'No, no, it wasn't like that. Some of the peasants had torches, and with all the bodies flying about in a tight space, inevitably something caught fire. By the time we got out of there, the flames had caught, and those houses were so close together … . Well? What did you expect, that we would stay and form a bucket chain?'

Lentulus smiled brightly. 'Then you vanished for a few days, until I got news of you tonight?'

'You mean the message we slipped to your dockworker?'

'No. When I was told that someone had ambushed a ten-man ... cavalry patrol. Really, you had to pick on a cavalry patrol? And steal their weapons and horses? Somehow I immediately knew it was you, and guessed I would be seeing you soon.'

'We didn't steal the horses,' I muttered. 'They are tethered near the gates. Someone will find them.'

'Would you mind telling me how you did it? Just to satisfy my morbid curiosity?'

'I'm not saying it was us. But just suppose that you had been skulking around in ditches and hedgerows for the past few days, living on rats and raw cabbage and not getting anywhere. Wouldn't you take the bull by the horns and make a sprint for it?'

'But how ...?'

'Your informants did not tell you? Maybe the cavalry saw a Gaul and our escaped slave here.' I nodded at Momina. 'Perhaps the pair were some distance away, legging it for the bushes. It maybe that the cavalry broke into a gallop without checking that someone had not accidentally left a rope strung between two trees. Hard to see a rope in the twilight, especially if someone has chosen their trees with care. And no-one got hurt. Not seriously. Lentulus, they didn't have *cavalry* looking specifically for us, did they?'

Lentulus shrugged. 'There may be a few people between Rome and Ostia not scouring the countryside for you. Sick people, geriatrics, cripples. Infants maybe.'

'Oh gods.' I rested my face in my hands. 'Pavonius?'

'Pavonius,' mimicked Lentulus. 'Of course Pavonius. That's why the military are involved. The official story is that these barbarians here tried to assassinate him on his way home. Pavonius and his men fought them off in a valiant struggle that left our noble Urban Praetor lightly wounded. Two of his lictors are still missing.'

'Ah. Gaius, my doorman. He died then?'

'I'm sorry.'

'Well, they can look for those lictors at the bottom of the Tiber. The current should be rolling them out to sea about now. My German girls tend to be rather unforgiving. Something to remember when their uncles and brothers come sweeping over the Alps next year.'

'There's an unofficial story doing the rounds as well. Rather different. This says that Pavonius was found tied to a bed in your brothel. His face was dyed blue, and a peacock-feather fan was shoved so far up his backside that it took a surgeon to remove the handle.'

Earnestly, Lentulus looked me in the eye. 'Please tell me that story is true.'

'We had a lot of the dye left. The girls used it for temporary tattoos, but they didn't like it because it takes about a week to fade.'

'And it should be about another week before Pavonius walks properly again. The story went around Rome like wildfire. The Optimates already have had little peacock feather fans made. They fan themselves in front of the Marians in the senate. Pavonius will never live this down. You've ruined that man's career.'

'Well, he ruined mine,' I muttered sullenly. 'He didn't have to take my brothel. Anyway, he saw me there, as Vidnu attacked him. There was no choice but to arrange things so that he would never, ever admit what really happened. It worked, didn't it? They are only looking for the gorilla and his hairy friends, right?'

'Someone looking like you was seen in the tavern just before the barbarians wrecked it, but obviously everyone was looking at the wreckers. No, officially I think you are clear, though you forfeited your Temple of Love when you didn't turn up to pay the fine.'

I sighed with relief, but Lentulus went on remorselessly. 'Unofficially, the Marians have put the word out that for you they are prepared to double the reward that the Optimates offered for Gaius Gracchus. Does that explain anything?'

It explained a lot. Gaius Gracchus was an aristocratic social reformer who died just before I was born. His social action plan had snowballed into an unofficial popular revolution, provoked partly by senatorial opposition to Gracchus. But just because they wear the purple stripe on their tunics, this does not mean that our Conscript Fathers play fair. They don't take kindly to their monopoly on power being challenged, and they play for keeps when it is. When it came to blows, Gaius Gracchus fled from town. He did not get far because the senate offered the weight of Gracchus' head in gold to whomever presented that head to the scales.[*]

No wonder the countryside had been so hostile to us. Try to kill an Urban Praetor, and those country folk who gave a damn would probably help you to do it. But offer your average Alban peasant a decent price for one of his grandmothers, and you'd get the other at a discount. Offer to make those same peasants millionaires for a simple beheading and you would get the kind of search we had spent the last week evading.

'Well, it explains why the gentleman in a dark cloak tried so hard to take my head off with a scythe when I bolted out of the door at that hamlet,' I admitted ruefully. A thought suddenly occurred to me, and I looked at Lentulus with alarm.

Reading my mind, he grinned back at me. 'And we are not such good friends, are we Lucius? More like business associates really.' He sighed. 'I seriously considered it; but no, I won't turn you in. Sulla, you understand?'

I did. Sulla stands by his friends no matter what. And after what we had been through together in Africa, Sulla counted me as a friend. Lentulus was tough, brutal and occasionally sadistic. Perhaps because of this side of his character, he understood Sulla better than gentler folk such as I, and what he understood scared the daylights out of him. I was safe, for now.

Vidnu had been patiently letting Lentulus and I get up to date, but now he was twitching irritably. Madric had given me to

---

[*] 'It was proclaimed that an equal weight of gold would be paid the men who brought the head of Caius Gracchus. So Septimuleius [who found and decapitated Gracchus] stuck the head on a spear and brought it to Opimius, and when it was placed in a balance it weighed seventeen pounds and two thirds. This was because Septimuleius was a fraud as well as a villain; for he had taken out the brain and poured melted lead in its place.' (Plutarch *Life of Gaius Gracchus* 17)

understand that the gigantic Galatian was something of a big wheel back in his homeland, and he was accustomed to a degree of respect.* He had certainly gained a lot more of my respect after after we had wrapped things up at the Temple. On doubling back to his quarters Vidnu had unearthed a cash reserve that put mine to shame. As a devout Roman, I respect gold next to godliness. Why else would we cloak our statues in the stuff?

My new-found respect for Vidnu had dipped sharply after the unpleasantness at the tavern, but that same incident had taught me that placating the giant barbarian was generally the path of least resistance. Through Madric I did the introductions.

'Lentulus Baebius, this is Vidnu - and I must stress the importance of keeping a straight face here, okay? - Vidnu Lym p'Dic. No, I don't know why either, but he insists on it.'

'Why haven't you ditched the guy?' asked Lentulus, never taking his eyes off Vidnu's face. 'He's more trouble than he's worth. Someone like you could have easily sneaked away, quietly joined me here and left him rampaging through the countryside.'

'I'm not sure that I could. His fieldcraft is good, and those men with him are excellent. You don't think they disarmed the gate guards, militia patrol and cavalry by good looks alone? I thought I had seen the best, but these guys are better. They got me here despite every man, woman and child along the way on the lookout for us. But yes, indeed. Now we are actually here, it's time for the sweet sorrow of parting.'

'What's your plan?'

'Vidnu wants to charter a boat. With your connections it should not be hard to get a small merchantman. He'll take it east and they'll cross to Greece and drop Momina off at her temple.

---

* From clues implicit in the text, it looks as though Vidnu was a scion of the royal family (Tetrarchs) of the Tectosages. This fact is interesting in itself, as in 105 BC the Tectosages had both a Galatian branch, with Ankara as their capital and another, the Volcae Tectosages, who inhabited the Tolosa region of Gaul.

They came to get her, and now they have her, they can go back to their gods'-forsaken highlands with their vows fulfilled.'

'Me, I'll stand at the dock and wave a handkerchief until they are out of sight, and quietly make my way to Tarentum. There is a little apartment there that I am renting out through an agent. Nice views, and convenient for the city gate for someone needing a quick getaway. I might even learn Greek.'

Lentulus grunted. 'Only if you want your Greek to have a broad Laconian accent. The Spartans founded that place, and some of the traditions have stuck. You never seemed that fond of austerity to me.'

'All in moderation, as our Momina from Delphi would say. Especially moderation. You need to be very moderate with moderation.'

'Hmmm. And how to you plan to get to Tarentum alive?'

'Gods. In Africa I got through countryside infested with wild Berbers while being hunted by Numidian cavalry. Italy, my home and native land, should be easy.'

Lentulus shook his head. 'The chances of capture are too high. Sulla and the Optimates are having a wonderful time rubbing Marian noses in the discomfiture of Pavonius. If word gets out the insult has been avenged, that spreads balm on wounds our masters would prefer to keep raw. We need to be certain you get out of Italy without trace, sonny boy.'

'Out of Italy? That's even riskier. No, make that impossible. I'd have to go north, through Tuscany, into Cisalpine Gaul, over the Alps, through the Boii - and that's a head-hunting bunch of Gallic swine. They are probably still swilling wine from the cup they made from the skull of the Roman consul they killed a few decades back.* Oh, no. Then Macedonia. They hate Romans in

---

*This would be the unfortunate Lucius Postumius Albinus, of whom Livy says 'The Boii stripped the body and cut off the head. They carried the spoils in triumph to the most sacred of their temples. According to their custom they cleaned out the

Macedonia. If I ever made it to Greece intact, and I wouldn't, I'd not be happy there anyway. So, my vote for leaving Italy is a no. No, and after mature consideration, no again.'

Lentulus sighed. 'Well, let's consider alternatives then. The Optimates can't let you be taken, so you have to disappear. There's lots of ways to vanish without trace in Italy. Rather as Pavonius' lictors have vanished - permanently. Sulla assures me that it won't come to that. The twenty armed men, who are at this moment wondering why they are sitting in my atrium, assure me that if it does come to that, it will.'

'Or ... we get you out of Italy easily, safely and painlessly. On a ship.'

My stomach gave a violent surge of nausea at the very thought, but Lentulus went on remorselessly, 'I can get you a good, steady merchantman. Hades, I could get you a small fleet of merchantmen if you really needed them. The captain will take you wherever you need to go and ask no questions. I'd recommend Africa. I'm sure you still have friends in those parts. Then the ship can sail on and drop off your friends in Greece. Simple.'

'And if we get shipwrecked and drown?'

'Well, that works too. From our perspective. But your capture would be a major embarrassment, Lucius. Remember, you've practically declared war on the Roman Republic.'

'Oh, come on, now ... .'

Lentulus ticked off the points on his fingers. 'Attacking and raping a Urban Praetor with a peacock feather fan. Assaulting the gate guard in the course of their duties. Looting and pillaging a tavern, severely dilapidating a foot patrol in the process. Burning homes and generally devastating the hamlet of Morsapulici*,

---

skull and covered the scalp with beaten gold. It was then used for libations and also as a drinking cup for the priest and temple officials'. Livy 23.24 Panderius exaggerates how recent the event was. In fact Albinus was consul in 234 BC .

*Since it is unlikely that a place with a name which translates as 'Flea-bite' ever assault and robbery of a cavalry patrol. Name any invader since Hannibal who has managed the half of that, why don't you? No? Since you can't, it's the sea for you, old boy. Better to think that you're dying than to actually die, you know.'

I lifted my head and regarded Lentulus mournfully. At sea, they say, nobody can hear you scream.

Seven hours later ... .

'The Galatians would like you to keep the groaning down,' said Madracaera. 'They are trying to sleep.'

I unhooked one arm from the stern-rail and tried in vain to puke over Madric's sandals. My aching stomach had been comprehensively emptied several hours earlier, and I managed only a greenish dribble of bile. The ship chose that moment to lurch sideways, and another wave of nausea hit me. I groaned. It had taken only minutes for seasickness to hit after our boat had slipped out of harbour into choppy waters off Ostia. In the uncountable eternity of misery which had followed I had gone from worrying that I was going to die to worrying that I wasn't. It had occurred to me that since I had met Momina I had been bankrupted, knocked unconscious, kidnapped, burned with a hot metal bar, and made a fugitive. And now this, which was worse than the others combined. It appeared that the only way was down, which gave me an idea.

'Drop me overboard,' I moaned as the world swirled about once more. 'Ask Vidnu ...,' I paused to retch again. 'He'd ... love to.'

Madric seemed seriously to consider my request. My eyes were screwed tight so that I didn't need to see the stars making crazy ellipses in the sky, but I knew the night was bright and the waves

---

existed, either Panderius or Lentulus Baebius obviously cannot remember the real name of this unknown hamlet.

pitch black. We were a few hours from morning, making our way along the Italian coast with the sail banging occasionally in a stiff breeze. By daybreak Ostia would be a dozen leagues behind. The decking under my hands was worn smooth by the busy feet of the crew of our ship, so a larger-than-usual wave sent me sliding easily against the feet of the helmsman at the steering oar. He pushed me off again with a friendly kick to the ribs. There were three of these crewmen and a captain, and their sociable exchanges with harbour guard showed that the sentries were well used to this little coaster slipping out of the harbour, probably to do a bit of fishing before dawn.

Italy has hundreds of ships like this, bringing cement up from Puteoli, shipping oil lamps to Gaul and Spain, and olive oil from Africa. No-one keeps track of them, and apart from customs checks at the harbour, no-one pays much attention to passengers or crew. It was the kind of free-wheeling, rootless lifestyle that would have appealed to me, were it not that even fake waves on a pantomime stage make me queasy.

The ship's stern performed a coquettish wiggle as it slid over a wave, and I groaned again, even louder than necessary since I had discovered it was annoying the Galatians. I became aware of cool arms lifting my head, and unless Madric's limbs had become considerably slimmer and softer in the past few minutes, he had left and been replaced by Momina.

She held a cup to my lips, and the liquid within smelled of mint, rosemary, and something slightly rotten and sickly sweet. I had smelled this combination before, as we were leaving for the harbour. A servant had passed a bag to Lentulus, who had passed it on to Momina saying, 'Here's the stuff you asked for. Not easy to get it all. We had to chase down a good few herbalists for the exotic items.'

Momina had thanked Lentulus gravely, and I had inquired, 'She asked for that? When?'

'While she was here, twelve days back. She said you would need it. I didn't ask for details.'

Now I fought weakly against whatever was being administered, but hours of violent seasickness had debilitated me to the point where even Momina had little difficulty in pushing my arms down while she forced the evil-tasting brew into my mouth. I choked and retched, but a little hand was clamped firmly against my lips, and a thumb and forefinger pinched my nostrils shut until I swallowed. It must have been like feeding an oversized baby. One that spat and dribbled. Yet though I felt violently sick, my stomach made curiously little attempt to expel the potion. Eventually I actually gulped down a mouthful of my own accord. The world stopped spinning, and somehow felt emptier and darker. Then, Momina and the sounds of the ship were abruptly gone. In the darkness I felt myself falling, and falling far further than the short drop from stern-rail to sea.

I fell – into a dream.

For days she fell from godly Olympus, a golden comet incandescent with humiliation. Bad enough, that father Zeus had married her to Hephaestus, the lame craftsman-god. Bad enough, that she could console herself with her lover only when Hephaestus was busy in his workshop. Ares, the proud lover of Aphrodite, would have been outraged at being cuckolded (he was indignant enough that Aphrodite sometimes slept with her husband). But Hephaestus hid his fury and continued labouring in his workshop.

The fruit of those labours dropped from above her high-bowered bed when next Aphrodite lay with Ares. It was a golden net so cunningly contrived that once it wrapped around them, neither lover could move a muscle. They must lie there, and listen to the reproaches and imprecations of Hephaestus as the vindictive Craftsman God flung wide the ivory doors of his home and invited the denizens of Olympus to view the hapless living tableau.

Then once the Gods had laughed their fill, Hephaestus contemptuously divorced Aphrodite who threw herself into the arms of Gaia, her mother, the Earth.

Falling to rest in Sicily*, Aphrodite was soothed and consoled by the demi-goddesses known as the Graces. Gentle Thalia, bright Aglea and joyful Euphrosyne nursed her wounded spirit with flowers from the mountain groves, and by coaxing her to join in their songs, games and dances. Yet still Aphrodite was despondent, an exile and an outcast among the Gods. She had little hope of return, for though the Gods were powerful, like the forces they embodied, they were seldom compassionate or merciful. And yet . . . .

One morning Aphrodite was roused from her misery by the song of the Graces as they returned to her cave. There, the three showed her a wonder. An effigy, wrought in gold, and as small as a man's index finger. Beyond the cave, an arc of solid, iridescent colour stretched from the island to the heavens, a manifestation of Iris, the rainbow goddess and messenger of the goddess Hera. This small effigy was a gift from Apollo, the bright one, companion to the Graces. By his gift of the statuette, Apollo revealed his understanding and sympathy, and his regret for his earlier mirth. Hera's messenger told Aphrodite that the Queen of Olympus endorsed Apollo's gift, mother of Hephaestus though she may be. There was still a place for Love among the Gods.

Yet Aphrodite dallied in Sicily, now taking her own time to return. So rejuvenated were her spirits that she took a human lover and even bore him a son. When Aphrodite felt ready to leave, she left the statuette with her lover. She placed a cross-bar behind the knees of the little golden figure, so that a hand

---

*Here Panderius is repeating a well-known legend. Note though that Homer in *Odyssey* 8.267 has Aphrodite fleeing to Paphos in Cyprus.

grasping the waist could hold it firmly. Above the statuette's head she fixed a small circular mirror, but this mirror showed not a reflection but Aphrodite herself. (This shape, the circle of the mirror and cross of the handle has since come to represent Aphrodite and all her gender, just as the shield and spear of Ares represent the male.)

The son of Aphrodite founded a shrine to the Goddess of Love in the city of Eryx which bore his name*. In my dream I saw the statuette there in the sanctuary, shimmering in the soft light of the oil lamps, as outside the walls, the slow centuries slipped by.

A sudden shift. A small rivulet of water cut through mud, and in the mud lay the statuette. The mirror was broken and the cross-bar snapped. I stood in a woodland clearing beside a riverbank flanked by stripped and leafless trees bare against a sky heavy with rain. I bent to retrieve the statuette at my feet, but a voice said, 'Don't. They will find it in due time.'

'Momina?'

She looked different. Less fragile, and dressed in a pure white chiton. Her lair was long, black, lustrously oiled and curled in the manner of the Greeks. She was smiling at me with friendship and sympathy, yet this Momina had an erotic attraction which could move planets – elegant, raw sexuality blended with grace and empathy. Looking at her, I could understand why Cupid would risk the wrath of heaven to find his Psyche, why Agamemnon would plunge two continents into war to retrieve the wayward Helen.

She raised an amused eyebrow, and I became aware that I had spent the last few seconds goggling like a love-addled adolescent.

---

*Pausanias 8. 24. 6 (trans. Jones) 'In Sikelia (Sicily) too, in the territory of Eryx, is a sanctuary of [Aphrodite] Erykine, which from the remotest times has been very holy, and quite as rich as the sanctuary in Paphos.' Today Eryx is a town called Erice. Visitors are commended to the falsomagro - stuffed meat roll - at La Pentolaccia restaurant. (Just don't ask for a translation of 'falsomagro')

Regarding me thoughtfully, she murmured, 'Momina .... no. Part of me will be her ... she will be less than me. And more. I am Lais.'

Lais. Yes, I believed it. Once an Asian king had wanted to spend a night with Lais, but he had no appeal for her. She charged that king so much for his pleasure that he had to raise taxes when he got home. Frankly, he got it cheap. Lais was that good.

'The mirror' - she gestured at the sad, broken ruin in the mud - 'That came from my predecessor.' I knew the story. What self-respecting brothel-owner would not? Captured as a slave-girl by the Athenian army in Sicily, the elder Lais had been brought to Corinth. Sold to a brothel, she swiftly earned her freedom and continued with the profession into which she had been forced. In her prime, a night of her favours cost 10,000 drachmae - about what my entire Temple earned in a year. Her extravagant fees had inspired the proverb 'not everyone can go to Corinth'; which to a Greek means that some pleasures are simply out of reach.

The most prized possession of the elder Lais had been that mirror, the sole possession she had brought from Sicily. When she retired, it was again placed in a temple of Aphrodite with this dedication:

> *I am Lais, who laughed exultant over Greece*
> *Who gave her lovers great delight*
> *Now aged, I return this mirror to Aphrodite*
> *Since what I was, now I cannot be*
> *And what I am, I do not wish to see.*

'Her tombstone,' I remarked, 'shows a lioness tearing apart a ram.'[*]

'And I,' rejoined the younger Lais, 'have no tombstone'.

---

[*]There are various sources for the elder Lais (cf Athenaeus 12.544, 13.588.). For her tomb see Pausanias 2.2,&4. The epigram of the mirror had various versions in antiquity, though the version here quoted by Panderius is perhaps the earliest. The story of Lais being brought to Corinth as a prisoner from Sicily is quoted by both Plutarch and in Pausanias 2.2&5. Several of the tales, including that of the Asian king are also told of Phryne, a contemporary.

She stepped past me, to show a bare, dirty foot protruding from beneath a small pile of stones. Looking further, I saw a bruised and bleeding back, and blood pooling beneath dark hair and a torn scalp.

Suddenly Lais looked more like my Momina, fragile and slightly scared. 'They killed me,' she said, her voice the sound of the cold wind that blew through the clearing. 'They stoned me to death a few hours ago.'

I made a gesture, somewhere between confusion and compassion.

'It was a mistake to come here,' Lais said. 'I thought ... I did not realize ... Thessaly is not central Greece. My beauty did not inspire, it threatened. They feared me, I think.'

'But why ...?'

'Because I looked men in the eye and spoke my mind. Because I laughed at their pretensions, and acted as their equal. Because I would not allow myself to be sold off in marriage to live within the walls of a house as a brood mare. Because I was free. They hated that, so they hated me. They surrounded me and stoned me while calling me filthy names. As I lay bleeding and dying, they lifted my head by my hair and each spat in my face. And they broke the mirror.'

I looked at the body with horror and shame. 'I'm so sorry. It ... just ... sometimes men can be total bastards.'

Lais was startled. 'What? Oh. No. No, you don't see. ... It was the women.'[*]

---

[*] Pausanias (ibid) tells the story that Lais followed her lover Hippolochus to Thessaly, where she was stoned to death in a temple of Aphrodite by Thessalian women. She misinforms Panderius that she would have no tombstone, for she was buried by the banks of the river Peneus where he found her, and the inscription on her monument was preserved by Athenaeus 13.589.)

This time I immediately knew where I was - the camp bed, the carefully stacked weapons, the large space enclosed by weather-stained leather - the field tent of a general on campaign. Not a Roman tent - the patterning on the tent and the weapons looked Gallic. And the figure swaddled in furs on the bed definitely resembled friend Vidnu, though his luxuriant moustache was red and Vidnu was a blond.

(I later discovered that Vidnu means 'blondy' - Gauls seldom give anyone their 'true' name, and think the Romans fools for telling theirs to anyone who will listen. So every Gaul goes by a nickname - and I knew the Gaul I saw here called himself Acichorius, but to the world he was called Brennus*.) Brennus was not dead, but he was dying.

Brennus had the familiar gold statuette, now stripped of the mirror of Aphrodite. He held the body of the statuette loosely in one hand, and rubbed the side of its head with his thumb, all the while staring into the little effigy's face as though to decipher some hidden message. The cold wind still blew, but it was a hard, dry wind now. It rippled the fabric of the tent and infiltrated the interior with a dozen insidious drafts. A charcoal brazier by the bed produced more smoke than warmth. It must have irritated the Gaul's lungs, though it was not the cause of the cough that was killing him.

The leather entrance flap was briefly lifted, and a Gaul in full battle armour stepped inside. Behind him I caught a brief glimpse of an army in turmoil.

The new arrival kept to the point. 'The Greeks are coming. We must retreat. Are you well enough to move?'

Brennus never took his eyes off the statuette. 'Do you know

---

*By some other accounts of this, the huge Gallic raid on Greece in 279 BC, Acichorus was another of the Gallic commanders. Those who want the detailed story are commended to 24.7-8 of Junianus Justinus' *Epitome of Pompeius Trogus' 'Philippic Histories'*.

where it all went wrong?' he asked.

The armoured Gaul studied the fur-swaddled Brennus for a moment before deciding to humour him. 'Delphi. It all went wrong at Delphi. We spent too long looting their thrice-accursed temples and the defenders counter-attacked. We didn't hear them coming in the thunderstorm, and couldn't shout orders over the wind and rain. They gave you that wound the next morning. So now we're running with what we've got, and hoping to get out of Greece alive. So, Delphi. Offending Gods is a bad business.' The armoured man spat.

'That's why Delphi went wrong, Commatus. Because of that temple we sacked in Thessaly.'

'We sacked many temples in Thessaly.'

'Remember the temple of Nantosuelta ... the Goddess of Love? It was built because the townswomen killed a servant of Aphrodite.* The temple appeased the Goddess, and by pillaging it, we brought the curse on ourselves.'

'How do you know this?'

'I'm dying Commatus. I know. He knows.' To my vast surprise Brennus indicated me with a gesture that sent a fur sliding from the cot to the ground. 'He knows about the statuette.'

Commatus could not see me. He turned back to Brennus, his eyes hard and calculating. 'Listen. Your chieftains want to make a stand near Thermopylae, where we beat the Greeks on our way in. It's folly. The Thessalians will be waiting. I'm taking my Tectosages and cutting west. We'll take our share of the booty and no more. But this raid is over, and we're running all the way back home to Gaul.'

---

*This would have been the temple of Aphrodite Anosia. This was built, as Brennus told us, to avert the plague which Aphrodite was said to have inflicted on the townsfolk who killed Lais. From our perspective, it is interesting that Apollo, the giver of the statuette, was also the god who inflicted plague. Nantosuelta is the Gallic version of Aphrodite.

Brennus coughed. 'That was not the plan. Comontoris is talking of taking his part of your tribe even further east. To Asia Minor. We can find a new homeland.' He coughed again. 'But not in Greece.'

'It's over, Brennus. Half our men are dead. More will die at Thermopylae. I'm taking my tribe home.'

Suddenly Brennus sat up, his eyes fever-bright. 'Then, take this back.'

He held the little statuette out with a trembling arm. With a troubled expression on his face, Commatus took the effigy from him.

'Put it back. It was never ours to take. I feel the anger of the gods, and would die knowing that anger will be appeased. This effigy must be back in place at that temple before the army reaches Thermopylae. Or we will be defeated. I know it.' The effort of talking made Brennus break into a series of hacking coughs. Blood dribbled down his chin onto the furs of the cot.

'Keep this from the other treasure. If you go west ... you must put ... back the statuette, or everything will be cursed. Everything, all your treasure. Cursed. Keep it away ... .'

There was a brief commotion outside. A warrior thrust a pigtailed head into the tent. 'Greek cavalry. A strong force, several thousand.'

Commatus turned. He tossed a dagger onto the cot beside Brennus, 'Do it. The Greeks will certainly kill you anyway. We're leaving.'

Outside the camp was bustling like an overturned ant-heap. Striding through the confusion Commatus snapped out orders. He halted briefly to sort out a debate between two of his henchmen, and while expostulating, became aware of the statuette he still held.

He glanced at it briefly, and frowned. Then he tossed the effigy to his bodyguard. 'Put this in a saddlebag with the rest of the booty. Get the baggage mules moving. We're going home.'*

Shift, shake. Shake. A temple treasury, an underground vault lit by oil lamps, a tattooed figure with long white hair laying the statuette on a shelf. Shaking. I became aware of stiff muscles and a cramping stomach, and the fading image of the treasury became the earnest face of Madracaera, his eyes as blue as the sky behind him. I squinted into the light, and heard Madric saying, '... three days now. Lucius, come on, wake up. We're landing in Gaul.'

---

*This Commatus was evidently a chief of the Volcae Tectosages, and thus a different branch of the tribe to our Galatian Tectosage Vidnu. Therefore, for Commatus 'home' would have been the area of modern Toulouse and Aquitaine. Panderius obviously believes that because the statuette was not returned the Gauls were wiped out by the curse when they made their stand at Thermopylae. The famous 'dying Gaul' statue now in the Vatican museum commemorates this battle.

Liber IV

Gaul. That had been the plan all along (though Version A of the plan, before we discovered exactly how intense the hunt for us had become, would have taken us north on the dry, and above all, very steady surface of the via Aurelia.)

So I had lied to Lentulus about going to Tarentum. Of course I had lied. Think about it. Why share plans about my immediate health and safety with a gangster who would happily betray me the moment it suited him? Anyway, I'd not want to insult Lentulus with the truth. That would mean that I did not worry about him enough to take precautions. When he's not breaking fingers or skulls, Lentulus has a sensitive nature. He likes to think that people take him seriously. So lying to him was the least I could do.

Wanting to part company with Vidnu and his merry band was also a lie. Well, not about wanting to part company. I was still pretty keen on that, but I had lied about intending to. For the moment we were all stuck with each other.

I had reluctantly come to that conclusion while we were running for Ostia shortly after the débâcle at the tavern. The occasion was firmly lodged in my memory. It was soon after one of the Galatians had found a nest of rats in a hedgerow that the others insisted on grilling and eating for dinner that evening. I'm as partial to dormouse baked in honey as the next Roman, but I generally draw the line at rats. Especially because, as the only person thinking clearly during the riot at the tavern, I had used the chaos to commandeer a couple of fine cheeses from the kitchen.

But Vidnu decreed that cheese would keep and dead rats would not. To give the Gauls credit, they managed to produce a small but intensely hot cook-fire that gave off little more than an undetectable shimmer of hot air, and that under a large oak with leaves which diffused what little revealing smoke the fire produced.

Nevertheless, chewing roast rat totally failed to produce any feeling of congeniality with my companions. So after my first mouthful of rat thigh I announced that I was going my own way. Momina and Madracaera promptly joined forces to persuade me that my way was their way. Firstly, they explained the matter of that accursed statuette, and why I should take the 'accursed' bit literally. Though she dodged the question of how the Gods had told her, Momina was clear that Apollo and Aphrodite were in agreement that the statuette would remain accursed until it was returned to Greece, and all the while it would exercise a malign influence over the other treasure it was stored with.

The statuette was now in Gaul, which was bad news for Gaul. More particularly, it was bad news for the Gallic city of Tolosa, where the statue now resided. Two years ago a high-powered delegation had gone from Delphi to Gaul to explain this in detail to the city council of Tolosa. Greek high priests and priestesses had informed the sceptical Gauls that the curse had become active. They offered to take the statuette into protective custody, and offered more than the effigy's weight in gold in exchange. The Gauls took the gold, kept the statuette, and contemptuously rejected the delegation.

'So this is this second attempt?' I asked Momina incredulously. 'You? How are you meant to get the statuette out of Gaul? It's not a job for a girl. You should be clearing away the sacrifices from the altars and dancing at your friends' weddings. This is a job for an army, or a highly-trained ... group ... of special forces operatives ... .' My gaze travelled around the camp-fire, and I finished lamely, 'Rather like the one you have here.'

Which led the conversation to Vidnu. Providentially (for a given definition of 'providence') he and his men had turned up in Delphi soon after Momina had left on her mission. The Galatians had gone directly from their ship to the Temple of Aphrodite and there had sworn themselves into the service of the Goddess.

'Isn't that sort of unusual?' I later enquired of Madric. 'I thought Vidnu was some kind of Galatian prince? The son of a ... a ... .'

'Tetrarch.'

'I was going to say 'bitch'. But go on.'

'He's going to be one of the four most important men in Galatia one day. Assuming he can keep his authority with his tribe. And there, well, he's sort of hit a hitch.'

'Ohh. Gossip. Do go on.'

'Well, the group went raiding in Phrygia. No biggie. It's what high-spirited young men do. You know, ride over the border, loot a farmhouse or two, drive off a few dozen head of cattle. Who hasn't done it?'

'Civilized people?'

'Look, if you are going to keep up the catty comments ... .'

'I am. But you're dying to tell me anyway, so keep going.'

Madric delicately nibbled a rat-rib with every sign of enjoyment. 'So while on the road in Phrygia Vidnu and his men came across this luxurious carriage, with just the two retainers escorting a fine lady. So of course ... .'

'They killed the retainers and raped the lady. Doesn't everyone? If they are uncivilized, I mean.'

'Er ... no. They shouldn't. They should first check and find out why the lady is travelling with just two retainers. She might be a priestess. Of Aphrodite. And Vidnu has found out what happens if you screw with the servants of Aphrodite .'

'What happens?'

'You don't get to screw with anyone else. Ever again.'

'Ahhh. Suddenly the Lym p'dic appellation becomes clear. You mean it's literal?'

'Keep it to yourself. The big lunk annoyed me once and I

called him that in a fit of temper. I didn't think he heard me, but
he did. He demanded a translation, and I had to think fast to save
my life.'

'So Prince Floppy has lost a bit of credibility with the tribe has
he? Ah, and then there's the question of heirs to the throne, or
whatever a Tetrarch sits on.' I smirked. 'Altogether not exactly an
ideal chieftain for a warrior race, is he? They like their leaders to
be hard men. Hard but upstanding.'

'You know, it's just that sort of joke that will get you killed if
Vidnu even *thinks* you've made it. He hates it. He tried his luck
with a prostitute back in Rome when he was meant to be
'rescuing' you from Condrusix and that hot metal bar. Total failure.
That's why he was so, um, moody, when we did finally show up.
Anyway, his tantrum stopped the men from asking questions. The
tribe don't know. All Vidnu has let on is that he's under a geas.'

'You mean a *geasum*? What's he doing under a javelin?'

Madric sighed. 'A geas. It's a kind of mixture between a curse
and an obligation. It happens a lot to Celtic heroes. It's mysterious
and romantic, and the sort of thing that bards go on about all the
time. So if Vidnu spins this one right, and does not let on the exact
circumstances of the geas, he could come out of it with a lot of
credibility.'

'Anyway, he and his dad consulted with religious experts, and
the verdict was that our hero had to report to Delphi. At the
temple of Aphrodite he had to swear himself into the service of
the Goddess until such time as she releases him. Very heroic.
Something very similar happened to your Hercules.'

'What? The Labour of the Statuette?'

'More or less. I'd imagine the head honchos at the temple had
their doubts about sending Momina off on her suicide mission.
When Vidnu and company reported for duty it must have seemed
as though the Gods had sent them.'

Madric gave a superstitious shudder. 'The creepy thing is, I'd say they did. The more you get involved with this business, the odder it seems. Trust me, if I could get out right now, I would, and to Hades with my commission. But I can't leave.'

I lowered my voice. 'Why not?'

Momina's arm snaked around my shoulders and I almost jumped out of my skin. I *always* know when someone comes near to me, yet I had absolutely no idea how long the priestess had been sitting at my elbow. She beamed happily into my startled face and informed me, 'I can be very persuasive.'

Here's the thing. I had been a very good pimp and panderer. And I had loved it. It was a party every evening that ended with willing and skilled bed partners, and we were all getting paid sacks of money for doing it. What's not to like? I had figured out what still appeared a secret to my competition; that to be good in bed a girl needs, above all, enthusiasm. So I'd asked around for German slave prostitutes who put their backs into their work, purchased the girls and freed them. After all, even when freed, what party girl - and I had very carefully picked party girls - would want to go back to German forests and bogs to live with misogynistic menfolk who'd regard her as a ruined chattel?

If sexual exploitation was going to happen, I explained to my new employees, why not exploit the over-sexed scions of the aristocracy? And party while we were at it. Before I'd met Momina, my lasses had been literally screwing money out of Rome's patricians for five years, and things had been going splendidly. After I had met Momina, I had been bankrupted, kidnapped, outlawed and fed roast rat. The Gods - especially Aphrodite - had dropped the turbulent priestess into my life so I reckoned they owed me a brothel. Even before they had put me on a boat.

While I'd been moodily contemplating my rat-on-a-stick, I had come up with a plan. Firstly, I needed to hide out somewhere until the Marians screwed up. That the Marians would screw up I had no doubt. Marius, their leader, was a good general (something that still surprised me). But he had the people skills of a dead catfish, and had only got far in politics because he had the morals of a shithouse rat. But Marius had run out of people who trusted him enough to be betrayed, and had racked up more expectations and obligations than he could possibly repay.

So Marius would make consul next year. He would disappoint his allies (he had no friends) because he'd promised everything to everyone and simply could not deliver. For example, even if he broke his promise to improve the state finances and kept his promise to upgrade the army he would still get his plebeian backside kicked by the Germans.

It seemed a safe bet that after a year of Marius, popular reaction would lead to the Optimates storming back to power in the next elections. Though the self-styled 'best men' of the senate are nothing less than a gang of amoral cut-throats, they are at least amenable to bribery. And, after all, they owed me for wiping the priggish Marian Pavonius off the political map for them. So a few choice words in the right ears, a few large bribes judiciously distributed, and this time in eighteen months, I'd be back to wine and women (song optional) in the triclinium of my beloved temple, with my crimes forgiven and forgotten. And yes, I vowed, I would even get that aqueduct filling my atrium pool once more.

Apart from the fall of Marius, which was only a matter of time, the problem was the bribe. It was going to take a large, no, a huge war chest of gold to buy redemption. You can do anything in Rome with enough gold. My old enemy Jugurtha had once looked back after leaving Rome and remarked, 'That whole city is for sale - and doomed if it ever finds a buyer.' Thanks to the antics of Vidnu and his boys, I calculated that I needed to buy a couple of senior senators, a good advocate and an entire jury. There was not only a civil offence (no aqueduct license) but also various crimes against person and property to be expunged. While Sulla and his friends could prevent actual criminal charges being brought against me, it was going to take lots more money to smooth everything over. There is no point in having an unpopular brothel.

'Tolosa has gold,' Momina had told me. 'Tons of gold, waggon-load after waggon-load of gold. Did you know that the temple treasuries are so full of gold that they've been literally throwing the surplus treasure into their sacred ponds and lakes? For hundreds of years, Gauls have been bringing their plunder to Tolosa, dedicating golden bowls, silver drinking cups, torcs, wrist-braces, ingots and yes, statuettes of precious metal. There's silver drachmas, golden staters, emeralds, rubies, lapis lazuli and pre-cious spices, but above all gold. More gold than you can spend in a lifetime. More gold than you could spend in two thousand lifetimes. Cellars literally packed with gold to the ceilings.'

'And not only do Apollo and Aphrodite permit you to take all the temple gold you can carry, they even want you to. The Gods themselves will help you to steal all the gold you can - so long as you also steal the statuette. What the Gods have taken from you up to now, they can return a thousand-fold, if only you help their servants. And after all, with your Temple of Love, what have you yourself been all these years but a servant of Aphrodite?'

'When we get to Gaul, we'll hire a waggon. When we leave Tolosa, that waggon will contain all the gold it can carry. Or - you can leave us now and take your chances at getting to Tarentum and there living the half-life of a fugitive. Always fearful of being recognized, never trusting your barber to trim your beard, and indeed, never being able to ever fully trust anyone again for the rest of your life.'

'Oh, and one more thing. Aphrodite and Apollo would be very, very disappointed in you. So I would not count on the rest of your life being very long. Or at all happy. I'm just saying, Gods do not take rejection well. And don't expect your impending horrible death to get you off the hook. These are Gods, and they can be even more creative once they get a soul into the afterlife.'

Momina held out two pale little hands as though weighing something invisible. 'So - on the one hand, long life, love, huge wealth, happiness, your brothel and the favour of Aphrodite. On the other hand, poverty, rejection, interesting diseases, pain, unending misery and divine vengeance. Just taking one little statuette is all the difference between them. Please Lucius? Come to Tolosa?'

Oh yes, Momina could be very persuasive.

Madric had awakened me from my coma as the ship rounded the Olbia headland, and over the next three days while our little vessel scudded across the southern coast of Gaul, I actually started feeling pretty good. With me in dreamland, my body had adjusted to life at sea. Apart from occasional queasiness when the sail hit a crosswind, my seasickness had totally vanished. I took actual pleasure in walking the rolling deck, staring over the rail at the passing scenery, gossiping with the sailors, and joining the occasional dice game.

Every evening we pulled the boat ashore on a suitable beach, and camped for the night in the shadow of the hull. There were general complaints about the amount I was eating, as my four-day sleep had left me with an appetite that could eat a wolf down to the toenails. The ship picked up supplies at Massalia, and the Gauls delightedly rolled a barrel of foul-tasting water aboard. I had heard of the stuff called 'beer', but only slaves drink it in Rome.

Myself, I enjoyed a small urn of Massilot wine*, as full and flavoursome as the sparkling-eyed Grecian lass who sold it and herself to me that evening. I took great pleasure in her eloquent grunts and squeals, knowing full well that a fulminating Vidnu was somewhere in earshot. The next morning I left the girl with a

---

*This would be the wine described later by Pliny the Elder as 'sappy', and particularly full in flavour. (*Natural history* 14.68) The Greek doctor Galen drew the same analogy with the feminine as Panderius. In the *Epitome of Athenaeus* 27c he calls Massilot wine 'full and fleshy'.

generous tip, had the rest of the wine with water at breakfast and was delighted to find the drink still in my stomach at lunchtime despite the very best gyrations of the ship.

So good was I feeling that by the time the fortress town of Baeterrae came over the horizon, with our destination of Colonia Narbo just on the other side of the bay, that the Galatians decided that I could decently be killed.

'I'm not fighting a damn duel,' I told Madric flatly.

'Then you lose your honour,' came the implacable reply.

'Okay. I'm good with that.'

Madric shook his shaggy head. 'No, you won't be. You've not seen how the Gauls treat a dishonoured man. You'd be the servant and errand boy for the whole group. You'd eat last and alone from whatever scraps they decide to leave you. God's teeth, if Condrusix feels like a bit of the other, you might end up as his bum-boy. You want that?'

I glared across the deck at Condrusix who glared right back. He was the Galatian whose nose I had broken when we first met in the alleyways of Rome; he who had failed so spectacularly to torture me and then had his head and ribs kicked in for his pains. All this might have been taken as the sort of rumbustious fun that Gauls so enjoyed, but my crime was worse. Condrusix's cloak was a scorched wreck that still smelled faintly of urine. That cloak once had been his pride and joy, and now the others ostentatiously held their noses whenever he wore it. After several beers in the evening the unfortunate warrior had been the butt of jokes that left his companions rolling helplessly on the sand with drunken laughter. Condrusix blamed me.

It did not help that his nose was setting slightly skewed, and remained hideously swollen. His eyes were no longer black. With added shades of green, yellow and midnight blue, they resembled an oriental sunset. He looked a mess, and held me wholly responsible. Watching me bounce cheerfully about the deck and joke with the crewmen had apparently been the last straw.

'I'm a Roman,' I said haughtily. 'We don't fight duels. If he's got a problem let him take out a lawsuit when we reach Narbo. The idiot.'

'Err, that might work in Rome. This is Gaul. It doesn't wash here. And we're not going to Narbo. Vidnu decided that someone might remember us, and connect it with the gossip from Rome. We're stopping at Baeterrae which is a good Gallic settlement, and going inland by waggon.'

'Not going to Narbo ...? I've been looking forward to getting to a decent Roman town, and having a few drinks with the boys. The colony's not settled with veterans from my old legion, but any Roman ex-soldiers would make a change from you hairy-assed ape-men.'

'Now see, that's the kind of statement that gets you into duels in these parts. I'm not taking exception to your hurtful words because I am the bigger man, and because I know you are upset about going to be dead very soon.'

'I am not fighting. Bloody primitives.'

'Well, I'll tell them then. He's a well-set up lad, is Condrusix. I'll ask him to be gentle with you when he takes you for the first time. After all, he looks well-endowed. You might have fun.'

I looked around. Vidnu was standing like a giant statue, massive arms folded and his face set like stone. Momina was no-where in sight, which was unusual in a ship so small. Condrusix was surrounded by his companions and evidently delighted by my horror at the thought of fighting.

'How do these things end?' I asked wearily.

'Death is acceptable. Or a mortal wound. Surrender means that whole loss of honour thing. So basically if you fight, only you or Condrusix is getting off the ship alive. If it's any help, the odds against you are five to one. You might as well bet on yourself. What have you got to lose? Cower a bit next time Condrusix looks at you and I might get you eight to one.'

So it was that an hour later I stepped out into the warm sunlight on the deck wearing nothing but a subcingulum wrapped around my hips and and a small, round shield in my left hand. In my right I clasped a good, solid *gladius hispaniensis**- a legionary sword given to me for the occasion by the ship's captain himself. If he needed that kind of expensive weaponry I guessed being captain of a small merchantman had its problems too.

The crew had set up an impromptu gladiatorial amphitheatre at the poop - or whatever the round part at the back is called - with the stern-rail itself making up one border of the arena. Condrusix had evidently planned this for some time. He had acquired some whitish powder to lime his hair back across his head and the hairdo had set like a dry and spiky horse's mane. Then the warrior stripped naked to reveal a body on which the tattoos writhed like living things as he went through a work-out with a huge two-handed sword around three times the length of my own. Madric was right - he was indeed a well set up lad.

I vaguely heard the Galatians cheering as I stepped into the fighting area. The deck was smooth under my bare feet, and I flexed my calves carefully, getting the feel of the ship as it rolled. When he saw me, Condrusix abandoned his shadow-sword fight and pulled himself up to his full height. Instead of beginning the fight, he began some kind of declamation, pointing at me with extravagant gestures and to where his kit - including the notorious abused cloak - was rolled up by the prow. He launched into something with a sonorous rhythm, and I wandered over to Madric to ask quietly, 'What's this?'

Madric shrugged. 'It's his ancestors, and the ancestors of the men he has fought and defeated. By the way, I got you ten-to-one

---

*This was the earliest version of the famed Roman legionary sword, in use until around 20 BC. It was longer and heavier than later versions, and capable of inflicting fearsome injuries.

odds in the end. Emptying your bowels over the ship's rail was a good move.'

I had indeed cleared my intestines. Any veteran will tell you that doing so helps prevent gut wounds from becoming infected. That is probably why animals in danger do it too, but evidently the Galatians considered such pragmatism a sign of cowardice.

Condrusix had finally run down. There was an expectant silence. I studied my opponent thoughtfully. 'Has he finished?' I asked loudly, 'How rude of him not to bid his companions good-bye.' Madric translated, and there was a smattering of laughter.

The sun was on my left shoulder, and I strolled across the deck so that my back was against the left stern-rail. That way, if the Gaul lifted his head as he made a downward swing, he would get the sun in his eyes. Then I took my stance, and waited.

Vidnu said something, and Condrusix lifted his sword in both hands. Then he charged, swinging the sword around hard with the evident intention of cutting me in two at the waist. That's the thing about long, heavy swords - you can predict with some certainty where they are going. So I stepped back, batted the sword point down with my little shield, and swung a backhand at the Gaul's neck as I stepped past him. He was evidently expecting that and spun away so that my sword cut through empty air.

The first traces of uncertainty appeared in the warrior's eyes as we squared off after that first pass. That move with the shield had required tight timing, and had been the first indication that I knew what I was doing. Nor did I appear worried. Of course I was worried, because these things are so unpredictable, but it's a beginner's mistake to let it show. In any case, worry was already overwhelmed by the rush of being in mortal combat, a hot, taut excitement that is like nothing else. It can be dangerously addictive.

Balancing on the balls of my feet, I grinned savagely and without pretence, then raised both eyebrows at my opponent, inviting him to make the next move. It would all be over in the next minute or so, because Condrusix was taking some wild chances. He lifted his sword high over his head, meaning that the next attack would be the old cleave-'em-in-two overhand strike, a blow aimed to cut straight through skull, neck, chest and ideally groin, allowing the deceased to drop to the ground in two mirror halves. Legionary armour is built for this. Our helmets slope from the crest to deflect exactly this killing stroke, and the shoulders of our armour have reinforced chain mail and padding to catch blows deflected on to them.

Not having armour or a helmet left me with three ways to deal with the attack. One was to make a mighty leap backward and hope this carried me beyond the reach of the sword. The other was to hop sideways as the sword swept down, and hope that Condrusix couldn't react in time to change the angle of his swing. In either case a feint by my opponent would leave me vulnerable, because after you have jumped it takes the last half-second of your life to get your balance back.

That left option three. As soon the sword swung down, I charged under the swing to body-check the warrior with my shoulder. He anticipated that, turned and swung sideways, but as the sword scythed overhead, I had already dropped to the deck and rolled against his knees.

Since I lost my sword in the manoeuvre, there the fight would have ended with me crouched unarmed at Condrusix's feet. But we were on a ship. As the Galatian reversed his sword to stab me through the back, I grabbed his ankles and flipped him over the stern-rail. A glimpse of an inverted bearded face, mouth comically open in surprise, and then Condrusix vanished out of sight with a splash.

Breathing hard, I pulled myself up and looked into the ship's wake to see if the warrior could swim. Decidedly not. He was just going down for the second time, thrashing his way underwater in a frenzied panic. Aquatic ability is not a required life-skill on the arid Anatolian plateau of Galatia. There was a bang as the ship's captain brought the sail down, and the helmsman set the ship dead in the water with a deft twist of the steering oar. There was a practised drill for man overboard. A crew member grabbed a coil of rope hooked near the captain's quarters. This unwound behind him as he sprinted across the deck and dove smoothly over the rail into the sea. By the time he reached where Condrusix had been, the Galatian had floundered underwater again. The sailor did not hesitate, but immediately plunged under the waves.

Both bodyguard and crew applauded as the sailor came up with Condrusix, who lay so passively in his rescuer's arms that he was clearly at least half-drowned. From there, it was a matter of attaching the rope beneath the warrior's arms and letting his brawny companions pull him to the deck while the sailor swarmed up via the cat's heads to the congratulations of the rest of the crew.

Puking up seawater, Condrusix lay flopping on the deck like a pale landed fish, his hair a mess of dissolved lime. As I strode over, Madric saw the sword in my hand and asked with alarm, 'What are you doing?'

'What does it look like? I'm going to kill him. The whole 'to the death' thing, you remember?'

'But he's totally helpless!'

'Can you think of a better time?'

Condrusix had picked himself up on to his knees. He screwed his eyes tight shut at my approach, and without stopping I drew back my elbow so that my walk would add momentum to the killing stroke. My sword point aimed for where his rib cage arched above his stomach, and where an upward thrust would split his heart with a single clean blow. But my elbow could no more move forward than if it were set in cement.

Vidnu's huge hand was almost completely wrapped around my

bicep. The giant's face was as flinty as ever, but there was a hint of entreaty in his eyes as he rapped out a single sentence to Madric. 'Oh wow,' murmured Madric. He looked at me and translated verbatim. 'Vidnu son of Brogitarus asks you as a friend and colleague to spare the life of his companion.' The words seemed to awe him. 'He's acknowledged you as a friend and colleague. That's um, a very big deal.'

When I got to learn a bit more about how Gallic society operated, it became clear that Vidnu had little option but to do as he had. A chieftain's relationship with his retinue is a complex one, but basically he has to protect them and their interests, while they in turn die for him when and as necessary. The duel had been outside that social contract. Condrusix had taken it on himself to issue a challenge, and therefore could take his own chances in the fight. However, as it happened, the fight had ended before the duel. This left me with the right to kill the hapless retainer as he lay gasping on the deck, and left Vidnu in a quandary.

Here's basically what he could do.

Option one: Stand back and let his sworn follower get gutted like a fish right before his eyes and the eyes of his men. Such pusillanimity would certainly lead to muttering in the ranks. Vidnu was supposed to protect his people.

Option two: Let his man die, but let one of his men challenge me directly afterwards, thus avenging both Vidnu's honour and that of the group. A sound plan, were it not that Condrusix was the group's best swordsman. Given my recently demonstrated ability, Vidnu might end up with his honour intact but his retainers markedly less so.

Option three: Do the job properly by doing it himself. It certainly never entered Vidnu's thick head that he might lose a duel, and to give him credit, it would not have stopped him if it had. But if he won, he would catch hell from Momina who considered me essential to her plans, and Vidnu was deeply awed by the little priestess. He might be able to distance himself from my death at the sword of an impetuous retainer, but getting personally involved put him in a lose-lose situation.

Option four: Ask me not to kill Condrusix. Vidnu knew that I was - or at least had been - a man of some property and wealth who had connections in high places. And I had just proven myself as a warrior. True, a sneaky warrior who did not fight fair, but Gauls respected that. Acknowledging me as an equal was not a great exaggeration, and had the added benefit of promoting me out of the league of the rest of Vidnu's men, who no longer had the social status to issue a challenge. Which would keep Momina happy.

As a sort of prince by appointment, I did my royal duty to ease tensions with Vidnu's men by buying the dratted Condrusix a splendid new cloak the moment we got off the ship. This was less of a sacrifice than it would appear, since the bodyguard held the swordsmanship of Condrusix in high regard and had laid substantial bets accordingly. Only Madric and myself had put money on Team Rome, and collected a handsome windfall off the chastened losers. When I remarked on Madric's somewhat surprising faith in my durability the Gaul would not meet my eye. He muttered 'Momina' in a somewhat abashed manner and handed over my winnings as though he needed to be elsewhere in a hurry. A man stuck between two worlds was our Madric, with a Goddess on his case as well. We all had our problems.

The downside of being a colleague of Vidnu's was that Lucius Panderius could have left the Galatians to their own devices for the first evening in Baeterrae and spent the time enjoying a quiet beaker of wine with the leading Roman merchantmen in the town. Most wine in Gallia Comata is made from fermented carrots and is best appreciated in the narrow margin between getting drunk and going blind. However, Baeterrae actually produces a remarkably palatable vintage which is exported cheap by merchants looking to ballast their ships after selling a cargo of Italian goods in Narbo. I had even on occasion stocked the wine in my own cellars.

There was no chance of getting re-acquainted with the drink in Roman company. Vidnu was to dine with the town's big-wigs, and any (newly-promoted) guest-friend travelling with him was doomed to go along. Since Lucius Panderius was an endangered creature, that guest-friend was currently passing himself off as a minor scion of the Oscan aristocracy.

The Oscans were a good choice. A reclusive tribe of provincial Samnites from south-central Italy, they did not get out of their beloved mountains much, so I considered that the chances of meeting a 'fellow' Oscan in Gaul were slim. The tribe had been unwillingly incorporated into the Roman state since getting thumped in the second Samnite war two centuries ago. Therefore most Oscans could speak standard Latin as well as their own tongue-twisting perversion of the language. As long as I broadened my vowels into a sort of bray, I'd pass. Finally, the Oscans hated and resented their loss of independence to Rome, so any desire to avoid the Roman authorities would be sympathized with and understood.

It turned out that an Oscan vouched for by a Galatian prince got to discover a heck of a lot more about Gallic sentiment in Transalpina than any Roman ever would. I should point out that at the time these events took place, Rome's stock in the province was pretty low and dropping fast. Rome likes to give the idea that her legions are unstoppable and invincible. With personal experience I am here - and only by the grace of Fortune - to tell you that this simply is not so. I have seen legions that were stopped dead - and that 'dead' is not a figure of speech in this case. In my time legions have also twice been passed under the yoke by their conquerors.

Being passed under the yoke is the nastiest thing you can do to a beaten army short of massacring it wholesale. It's rather like the loss of honour Condrusix had tried to force on me the previous afternoon, but on a large scale. It is when an army admits that it has been totally, utterly and abjectly defeated and opts for the most grovelling and humiliating of surrenders in order to survive. The yoke is usually a bar - often made of spears - set so low that the soldiers passing under it have to bare their buttocks to their conquerors and bear a stream of abuse and insults as they stoop. Jugurtha had done it to the army in Africa just before my legion got there.

It also happened in Gaul just last year. The Romans had been beaten yet again by the Germans, so Rome sent out another army under a rather jolly old buffer - and regular patron of my establishment - a senior consul called Cassius Longinus. His orders were to help a local tribe stubbornly loyal to Rome and in consequence getting roughed up by both the Germans and Gauls. Not unexpectedly, given our current form in the region, a convincing defeat followed, culminating with Cassius' head on the end of a Gallic spear. The last surviving officer, Popillius Laenas, had saved the remnants of the army by paying a ransom of half of everything he and his soldiers had, and then trotting under the yoke.

When I left Rome they were planning to try poor Popillius for treason, though from what I could see he was a decent fellow who had done the best he could under impossible circumstances. Popillius had committed 'treason' because his humiliating surrender had done more than anything else to turn popular opinion against Rome in Gallia Comata. Certainly no Gaul at the banquet had a good word for their Roman masters, and many went out of their way to inform me of the fact, assuming that an Oscan would approve and endorse their sentiments.

'No ladies here,' remarked the Gaul I was sitting beside at the banqueting table. 'It must be getting very boring for you between courses.' The fellows across the table guffawed at the witticism and the knuckles of the hand holding my knife whitened slightly. The Gauls had heard lurid tales of what goes on at Oscan dinner parties. As it happens, Oscan men and women dine together at social gatherings - a gross breach of morality from a Gallic perspective. The assumption that Oscans enjoyed freestyle orgies between main course and dessert was but one of the jokes of elephantine subtlety I'd endured so far.

'I see there are no Gallic women at our meal,' I remarked politely.

'Don't worry. We'll save you a serving wench to enjoy after the table is cleared.' This was somewhere between a joke and a genuine offer, and my efforts to work out which caused further amusement. Taking pity on me, a pigtailed individual down the table explained. 'Our wives keep the company of other Gallic wives. Their kingdom is the home, and their glory and honour are our children.'

'Who dine separately as well?'

'Of course. A man should not even acknowledge his own son in the street until the boy is grown old enough to be a warrior'*.

There was a general murmur of approval around the table, and talk turned to the corrupting influence of Narbo across the bay. A white-haired gent declaimed, 'They take not just our land for their colony, and our money for their taxes, they take from us even what it means to be sons and daughters of the Volcae. The other tribes too. You wait and see, one day soon our daughters will sit at table and criticise their men, like Roman sluts.'

A pause.

'Not like Oscan sluts, of course, erm ... that is, not like Oscan ladies, who ... I mean, I'm sure they are properly deferential to their men. Um.'

There were covert glances my way from around the table. Vidnu, via Madric, had informed me that swords were compulsory

---

*Confirmed by Caesar's *Gallic Wars* 6.18

at formal dinners, just in case - for example - that someone inadvertently insulted the womenfolk of my assumed nation.

'There's the occasional sword-fight at dinner,' Madric had informed me nonchalantly. 'Sometimes someone makes a playful feint with his sword at someone else, and it gets serious. Or someone takes offence, or someone keeps giving offence until it can't decently be ignored. Then the cut-and-thrust around the table becomes more than conversational. In fact, if the others don't stop it, someone ends up bleeding all over the main course.'

'Oh, and that reminds me. There will be a hind quarter of pork roast on the table. Don't touch it unless you want to fight for it. Tradition says that cut is reserved for the bravest warrior present. Assuming good manners by your hosts, that should be Vidnu. And if it's not Vidnu he will make it so, and you'll get your steak bloody.'[*]

So I had purchased the *gladius hispaniensis* off the captain for about three times its value and strapped it on. A damn nuisance on my uncomfortable and crowded dinner bench the thing was too. I really did not want to use it. The old duffer's once florid face had gone as white as his hair, and conversation waned as my reaction was awaited. Clearly my victory over the vaunted swordsmanship of Condrusix was known to the diners. Vidnu glanced my way, and casually started a conversation with the man beside him. Taking his cue to downplay the moment, I helped myself to one of the broken loaves scattered generously around the tabletop, and mopped up a bit of grease on my platter.

'Oscan ways are not Gallic ways, and every people has a duty to defend its ways - and to strive to be free.'

There was relieved agreement from those present, and the conversation got back on track. The 'liberty of our people' was a popular and repeated theme of the meal, asserted with increasingly drunken fervour as the wine cups were filled and

---

[*]Athenaeus 4.40 confirms Madric's observation here

energetically drained.

This was no surprise. Senators go banging on about 'Republican freedoms' for more or less the same reasons. The genuinely poor and oppressed worry about getting their next crust of bread rather than getting liberty and self-determination. People who insist on 'freedom and liberty' are generally rich and politically well-connected bastards. They need the 'freedom' to keep oppressing the poor and the peasantry, and the 'liberty' to grind their victims into penury without interference.

That was certainly true of the people around the table. (Gauls eat at long banqueting tables instead of reclining on couches like civilized people.) As I later discovered, the aristos treat their own common people abominably. For a Gallic aristocrat the world exists for fighting, drunken partying, pillaging and raping, with accompanied sporting activities pretty much indistinguishable from the above. The general population pay, and not just in astronomical taxes. It's usually they who end up getting pillaged and raped; perhaps because chieftain A made an insulting comment about the beauty of the bride at chieftain B's wedding - or whatever. A Gallic noble is very sensitive about his honour.

'It's good to see a prince of the Galatians here. Even in strange lands across the sea, these Galatians are true Tectosages.' My neighbour offered this diplomatic conversational titbit, possibly aware that further jokes about Oscan dining habits might be dangerously unwise.

'And your plan, well, it interests me. You need slaves that much in your mountains, eh?' The Gaul lifted a haunch of venison and bit into it, his eyes shrewd between the meat and his shaggy brows.

'The Gallic palate is becoming refined. There's a demand for more sophisticated wine, such as the Oscans are specialists in making.'

We both glanced ruefully at the wine in the huge beaker at my elbow. It was a remarkably vicious local variety; a Vocontian red, smoky and doctored with aloes to hide its bowel-numbing astringency. Although the Gauls chugged the stuff as though it was apple juice, it seemed that some were aware that the world offered better.

'If the quality of the wine is good enough I can give you one healthy slave per amphora,' offered my entrepreneurial dinner companion. He correctly read the surprise on my face and smoothly upped the price, 'plus shipping and taxes, of course.'

'It would appear slaves are abundant here.'

The man shrugged. 'The Romans are too busy to keep the peace, and everyone else is always feuding. Warriors get captured, sometimes their chief can't pay the ransom. Or won't.' This prompted him to glare at a stout individual down across the table. 'Some love their gold more than their honour. Those whom the Gods favour with victory hold more of such captives than they need.'

'No insult to our host intended, but you would be prepared to exchange these prisoners for something that actually tastes of grapes?'

'Come round to my villa tomorrow, and we can draw up the contracts. You didn't bring samples, did you? How do they taste undiluted?'

This statement was noteworthy for several reasons. For all their fear of *Romanitas* corrupting the common folk, the aristos were happy to dwell in Roman-style villas. But they still drank their wine unwatered - something that must certainly rot the brain, especially with the local varieties. With Lentulus' shipping contacts it would be easy enough to import some of those heavy Sicilian reds that hit the palate like a lead brick. Too earthy for the Roman taste, those wines would literally and metaphorically go down a treat here. So now I needed to talk my way out of an actual sure-fire money-making business opportunity. It hurt.

'It is flattering that you would want to do business with me. But it grates that Rome will get a cut from the shipping and taxes you mention. I'd prefer to cut thieving by the taxman and go on to Tolosa.'

The Gaul spat onto the rush-covered floor to mask his disappointment. 'Tolosa has allied itself with the Romans for decades. They've been kissing Roman backsides since the Hannibalic war.'

'But all that has changed after the Cassius-Popillius débâcle, no? The city is now violently anti-Roman.'

'Because the Romans never know the difference between allies and subjects. One of their governors built a fort in front of the city overlooking the plain.'

'And?'

'Oh, it protected the city, but dominated it too. Imagine if the Etruscans built a fort on one of the hills around Rome. The Romans would hate it, and the Tolosans considered that fort a symbol of Roman arrogance - and Roman imperial ambitions.'

The Gaul burped, adding bad breath to the aromas of scorched meat and unwashed warrior swirling about the sweltering banquet room. 'So when the second Roman army got massacred - or was it the third? - the Tolosans decided that they didn't have to put up with Rome. The fort's gone now. Most of the garrison are buried under the ruins. I think they still have the governor's wife and daughter hostage. That's why Tolosa is an independent city. Don't think we wouldn't be too. But across the bay, there's that accursed Roman colony.'

'Which is exactly why it's there,' I pointed out, and got black looks from several of the nearby Gauls who were none-too-subtly eavesdropping on our conversation. A surprising number of them evidently spoke Latin. As the evening went on, I had been forced to concede to myself that, despite being a bunch of oafish boors, my hosts were in no way fools. They might quaff their wine by throwing it at their faces, but most were trilingual in Gallic, Greek and Latin. They were also alarmingly well-informed of Roman political affairs.

'The Roman army here can be ignored,' one aristo told me firmly after insisting that taxes on my wine imports would not be enforced. 'The soldiers are not here to make us obey minor laws.'

'Servilius Caepio's army?' someone chimed in. 'They need a legion to keep his lardy backside from dragging on the ground as he walks. And that backside is more intelligent than the rest of him. He loses the best part of himself every time he takes a shit.'

'That's maybe true, but it's still an opinion,' retorted another, speaking Latin as a courtesy to me and to show off to the others. 'What's a fact is that the Germans broke up into independent pillaging parties while ripping through Gaul. Now they've taken anything that can be lifted, and then raped everything that can't run, they've formed back into an army again.'

'Caepio has no chance. Better Roman generals have tried and failed. This butterball will march confidently north, meet the Cimbri somewhere around the Tarnis river*, and get wiped out. Just like all the others.'

Someone leaned across the table to me. 'I've got contacts with the Cimbri. I do a good bit of business brokering prisoner exchanges for cash. In fact some aristocrats with the Roman army have put down deposits with my agent already. What does that tell you about how confident the Romans are feeling?'

'Anyway, after the last battle with the legions, the Cimbri were left with masses of second-hand armour that they couldn't shift. You Italians, if you don't mind me saying, are too small for your stuff to fit the average German or Gaul, and you can only tailor chain mail so far.'

'If you are interested in changing that wine of yours for

---

*The modern river Tarn, a tributary of the river Garonne which latter river flows north-west past Tolosa to the sea.

second-hand Roman armour, I can soon offer you all the business you can take. Would you care to invest in a futures option?'

None of this reflected well on Rome's allegedly invincible army. But I knew Caepio, and the offer was extremely tempting. Twice now this evening I had been forced to turn down opportunities that would have made me rich, but at least this one gave me a twinge of patriotic pride for doing so.

As a former intelligence officer, I could not help listening to such conversations as I could understand and automatically filleted them for information which might be of use later. Such conversations became less discreet as the evening progressed - and they were not that discreet to start with. Sadly as inebriation took hold, most guests reverted to animated and increasingly slurred Gallic, leaving me to concentrate on my meal.

Soon the serving boys switched from shovelling on to our plates the slabs of pork and venison being grilled or roasted on spits in the huge fireplace at one end of the room (not a vegetable did I see through the course of the evening) to exclusively pouring out huge beakers of wine. I pretended to quaff the stuff so as not to offend my hosts, and privately speculated how much of Gaul would be Roman by the year's end.

Despite my reservations about the Gallic aristocracy as a class, individual members were enjoyable company. Their bluff and hearty approach made an appealing contrast to the reserved and catty one-upmanship of an equivalent Roman social gathering. The sheer determination of everyone present to simply have fun was remarkably infectious. The evening culminated with drunken singing in which I joined lustily without anyone noticing or caring that I did not know the words. The singing was accompanied by freestyle eructations in which I did not participate, being easily the most sober person in the room. One drunken slip might compromise my assumed persona - assuming anyone was sober enough to notice. Nevertheless deciding it was better to be safe than dead, I drank lightly. The wine certainly encouraged abstinence.

Eventually, as the candles burned low, the party did not so much break up as pass out. I was helped up to my room by a slave while three others carried away the body of an inert Vidnu as though it were a felled oak tree.

Liber V

The rest of Vidnu's bodyguard had enjoyed their own impromptu party with sundry tavern ruffians and serving wenches. Their wine was even cruder than the stuff I had reluctantly sipped last night, and their hangovers correspondingly more devastating. This left Momina and I as the only two members of the group capable of standing upright the next morning. Since in Gaul women above a certain status never do business on their own account, it fell to me to organize a waggon to Tolosa. It had been explained at dinner the previous night that decent horses were out of the question. Vidnu might want to ride as befitted a prince, but any horseflesh of cavalry standard had been already commandeered by Caepio's army on its way north - to bitter local resentment.

It rapidly became apparent that Transalpine Gaul might be a Roman province, but it was a foreign land nevertheless. This was brought home by the Gallic businessman from whom I tried to rent our transport. He, like many of his fellow countrymen, had served in the Roman auxiliary cavalry and had started his enterprise with the lump sum of cash received on discharge. We passed part of the morning bargaining and swapping war stories over a drink (wine for me, ale for him) and agreed on the use of a cart and a set of six half-decent ponies for what I considered a reasonable sum, especially as the cart in question was the equivalent of our Roman *carruca dormitoria* - a large covered waggon. In this Vidnu and company could sleep off their alcoholic excesses and later we would be spared the bedbugs and urine-saturated mattresses which Madric had gloomily assured me were standard fare in the hostelries of the interior. The problem came when, after I had handed over the necessary payment in silver coin, the carter rather diffidently told me, 'I'll also need a name.'

'My name? It's Sepiis Mamercus of the Opici', this being my Oscan *alter ego*. The carter looked embarrassed. 'I can't recognize that name.'

My detailed explanation of Oscan nomenclature did little other than spread further confusion. The carter insisted stubbornly, 'I'm sorry. I still can't recognize this name. Do you have another you can give me?'

A Roman name invented on the spot elicited the same response, so I went to drag Madric from his wine-sodden slumbers. 'The man won't part with his cart without a name. Yet he says he does not recognize any of the names I give him. Should I write a name in charcoal on a large board and bang his head against it?'

Madric merely groaned and shambled beside me in grumpy silence down the winding streets (town planning was evidently not a Gallic forte). On arriving at the scene of my failed negotiations, Madric rattled out a long string of Gallic at the carter, and then went off to be sick in a gutter. Without another word the carter began hitching the ponies to their traces.

A 'name' I discovered that afternoon, when everyone was well enough to travel and Madric felt condescending enough to explain, was 'recognized' as a form of deposit. The carter was not going to rent his expensive - and buttock-numbingly uncushioned - vehicle to any Caius, Marcus or Aulus from the Apennines without an assurance that he would get his property back. So if we absconded with the waggon, the person whose 'name' we had given was the person to whom the carter would go for redress. Since the cart was rented 'in his name', that individual was honour-bound to make good the carter's loss - and then find and decapitate the scoundrel who had taken his name in vain. Acting in someone's name without clearing it with them first was a major breach of etiquette, but naturally Vidnu had sorted all that out last night without anyone bothering to tell me. Sepiis Mamercus could not guarantee five minute's use of a latrine, but if I had opened negotiations with the names of Vidnu and some of the local bigwigs, our transport would have cost a third less. Ah well. As we used to say in the army, one lives and learns, and he who learns, lives.

Gaul was fascinating. When one travels with the military, Rome comes along for the ride. You never really leave home when you go abroad with the legions. Everything is done Roman style. You live in a Roman camp, the language is Latin, and the local population are merely surly survivors standing amid the smouldering rubble of their homes. To the average legionary, if one cannot fornicate with, loot or obtain wine from them, native peoples are basically background colour.

It's totally different to be dunked head-first into an alien culture where no-one even knows you are Roman. I had discovered this first in Africa, and now in Gaul I discovered it all over again. One saw the occasional trousered individual in Rome, but with the advent of the German menace, such apparel was not popular. Visitors from the north quickly learned to adopt a tunic unless they liked their vegetables free, over-ripe and delivered at high velocity. Here in Baeterrae, trousers were the norm, and it was my tunic which attracted dirty looks and muttering.

Gallic women wore skirts, naturally, and were constantly having to hike them up to cross dodgy parts of the street, which was most of it. Urban roads were a well-compacted mixture of dung, mud and rubbish amongst which the occasional pig rooted in search of something relatively fresh. The houses were solid-looking affairs, mortared stone with well-fitted doorways and windows that would look out of place in a Roman apartment block only because their quality was substantially better. The thatch roofs were something of a shock, as I'd always imagined that they would be a sort of golden blond, rather like the hair of the Gauls themselves. Instead the thatch was the dark grey of forge-worked metal, and sometimes darker than the stone walls beneath.

For inhabitants of a city in danger of being wiped out by

Germans in the next few months, the Gauls seemed a remarkably cheery bunch. Madric and friends constantly exchanged good-natured jests with members of the public - many of which jests appeared to relate to the nature of my clothing. Neighbours gossiped by the simple expedient of bellowing at each other through their opened windows, and I don't think I saw anyone in the street communicate at less than a shout.

Even the gate-guards bade us a jovial farewell at top volume as we finally rolled out of town. This actually took some doing as the streets had been remarkably crowded, and (for example) the gentlemen unloading hay at a stables seemed to take it for granted that until they had finished blocking our way we would be happy to put our feet up and relax; which is exactly what we did. On clearing the gates we ended up behind a funeral. Madric exchanged a few words with one of the cortège and informed me that the deceased was a well-to-do local merchant who had died suddenly a few days ago. The body was on a richly-decorated cart, but on looking over that way my attention was drawn, not to the corpse on the bier, but to the woman with bound hands who limped alongside. 'Who's that? A slave girl?'

Madric looked a bit discomforted. 'Um, no. I'd say that's his wife.'

'Wife? Why is she dressed like that and tied? She's limping. What happened to her?'

'That's probably from the torture.' Madric would not meet my eye. 'She confessed to poisoning him.'

'You torture citizen women? And did she,' I asked caustically, 'confess before or after being tortured?'

'He died suddenly. She supervised his meals. It was a reasonable thing to do.'

'So what happens to her now?'

'She will be killed after the funeral, and her body left for the dogs. Don't you strangle poisoners in Rome?'

We did. Come to that, Roman magistrates might also torture the household slaves if a death looked suspicious. But a *widow?*[*]

'You know,' I told Madric, 'one of my girls used to have a saying, 'Better a whore in Rome than a wife back home.' (In fact, though I didn't mention it, that particular girl had gone for neither option. She had married a love-struck client and now efficiently administered his bakery just off the Forum Boarium. She still sent fresh bread rolls round to the Temple every market day.)

Madric griped, 'Well, you are not in Rome any more.' And I sat silently grappling with homesickness as our waggon bumped down the road into the countryside.

'Isn't it unusual for a Sybil to marry?'

We were two days on the road, and three hours out of the village where we had passed the previous night. We did not need to stay in the village, having our own accommodation in the cart (or under the cart in the case of Vidnu's retinue), but Vidnu had this annoying habit of stopping at every hamlet and crossroads to establish diplomatic relations with the local headman. Since 'diplomatic relations' involved drinking large quantities of some abominable local vintage, we often stayed overnight. In the morning the Galatians were seldom inclined to conversation, so Momina and I would coax their semi-animate carcasses into the back of the waggon, and then sit together on the bench at the front guiding the ponies as they plodded towards Tolosa.

That's how I learned - without any great surprise - that Momina's mother had been the voice of the oracle at Delphi. Many Romans have the wrong idea about the oracle, and can't shake off

---

[*] 'When the father of a family has died, if the circumstances of his death are suspicious, they hold an investigation upon the wives in the manner adopted toward slaves; and, if proof be obtained, put them to severe torture, and kill them.' Caesar *Gallic Wars* 6.19

the odd idea that the oracle is some demented priestess who howls drug-induced gibberish in an underground cave. In fact even I only knew better because Sulla - who was not averse to seeking the odd oracular pronouncement about his own future - had informed me that the Delphic oracle works in an altogether more civilized manner. The priestess does indeed sit underground, but on a stool in a very tidy little room. Her questioners sit on the other side of a curtain and are answered not only in coherent Greek but generally in verses of iambic pentameter. Even Marcus Brutus, the man who overthrew the Tarquins and established our noble Republic, only did so after he had popped across the Adriatic and had a quick consultation with the oracle (which gave him the go-ahead).

It was rare for a Sybil of Apollo to marry, which she might only do once she had stepped down from her duties. For the god of culture and the arts, Apollo can get pretty barbaric at times. For example, he no doubt did a very artistic job of skinning alive the satyr Marsayas as the penalty for losing a music competition, but most people prefer their critics to be milder.

So, eligible as a Sybil might be - they usually came from the very best families - they tended to remain spinsters. Prospective husbands felt that once Apollo had possessed a woman he might take exception to anyone else doing so. Being Apollo, that displeasure might be ingeniously lethal. Of course, Apollo was being very unfair and unreasonable, but then the Gods often are.

For pretty much the same reason our own Vestal Virgins have trouble finding husbands once they step down from their thirty years of service - and the record shows that those ex-Vestals who do get married proceed more or less directly from virginity to widowhood. The threshold between divine and mortal is not a comfortable place. Few men are keen to join the women who have dwelt there, and generally don't last long if they do.

'Your father had no issues about touching what the God had

touched?'

'He too was touched by the divine. At Eryx in the temple of Aphrodite in Sicily. He went there to sacrifice to the goddess. When he got to the altar, a sheep was already there, waiting. No-one saw how the sheep arrived and the priests refused to take money for it. But my father insisted on giving Aphrodite her due. So he dedicated an inscribed golden band which was fitted to the leg of one of the temple pigeons. Every year at Eryx they celebrate the departure of Aphrodite to Libya, and every year the pigeons depart as well. My father's pigeon turned up at Delphi, which brought him there to meet my mother. She was expecting him, of course.'*

'So how does prophesy work?'

'My mother always used to worry that it would not. The words of the Sybil can start or stop wars, and change the destiny of entire countries. What if the God did not speak through her, and it was not the words of Apollo, but of a mortal woman that changed the fate of nations?'

Yet when she sat in the chamber, she could feel the presence of Apollo. The air would be sweet and almost exhilarating. Her mind would become perfectly composed and clear, and when the question was asked of her, she would simply know what to say, and said it without the slightest hesitation.'**

'And what about for you?'

Momina laughed. 'Oh, I'm no Sybil.'

---

*This extraordinary story is substantiated by the ancient writer Aelian. His *De animalia 10.50* describes the occasional mysterious appearance of sacrifices at the altar in Eryx while his *Miscellania* 1.15 describes the Anagogia (departure) of the pigeons.

**This is nowadays ascribed to the effect of the natural gas Ethylene which probably built up in the underground chamber when it was not in use. Those who have sampled the gas at low concentrations have felt similar sensations to those described here by Momina. Those who have sampled the gas at high concentrations have never felt anything again, so do not try this at home.

'So what are you?' I asked, very earnestly.

The girl did not answer immediately, and I let her mull the question. After all, we had the whole morning. It was a peaceful sunny day, and apart from the scolding of a jay, even the birdsong which had accompanied us from the autumnal woodland at the side of the road had now hushed. We were at the crest of a hill and I watched a magpie swoop at some bushes at the bottom of the slope, and then swerve away as something else attracted its attention. The only sound was the gentle clopping of the ponies' hooves on hard-packed clay.

'Vidnu thinks I'm an angel. It's why he is so deferential toward me.'

'An angel? What's that?'

'It's Greek. An *angelus* is literally a message from the Gods. In the Levant and Anatolia they have this concept that the will of a God can take human form. Word made flesh, if you like.' * Aphrodite and Apollo desire something - the statuette – and according to Vidnu, I am the human incarnation of that desire.'

I considered this while contemplating the pattern made by the autumn leaves on the road ahead.

'Later I'll ask what *you* think you are. But now I'd better ... .'

'Wake Vidnu and the boys? They're already gone.'

I looked back into the body of the waggon. The sleeping pallets were empty, with hastily discarded blankets strewn on the floor. Of the Galatians and their weapons there was no sign.

'So you are no Sybil?' I asked accusingly. 'Then how did you know there's an ambush on the road ahead?'

Momina's answer was placid and composed. 'The same way that you did, I suppose. The birds went quiet which means there is a predator in the area. The alarm call from the jay confirms it. And that magpie swerved away from those bushes, which means

---

*Even today, some religions have this concept - notably Christianity where John 1:14 says explicitly 'And the Word was made flesh and dwelt amongst us.'

that the ambushers are probably hidden there. It's not a fox, because foxes don't drag in branches for extra cover. The wind did not make those leaf patterns across the road. So, um, that bush is an am-bush.'

'And you are not worried?'

'Oh no. Vidnu and his men are well on the way to ambushing the ambushers by now. They left when they spotted the archer by that tree we've just passed. He's there in case anyone breaks free and comes running back this way. The Galatians left him for you.'

The archer was an amateur and therefore would not be a problem. An experienced ambusher would know that it is all very well pressing yourself against a tree trunk as a cartload of prospective victims goes by. But the sun is quite low at this time of the year, and it's not much use being perfectly concealed if a shadow, complete with the outline of one's bow, stretches out on the ground behind.

'Pull over,' I told Momina loudly, and the waggon came to a halt, the ponies twitching their ears at us as they turned their heads in curiosity. A bucket dangled on the side of the waggon, and I unhitched it, ostentatiously taking out the sponge on a stick it contained. Then, without any attempt at concealment, I took myself into the bushes by the side of the road, hitching up the hem of my tunic as I did so.

One can be absent for some time with a bowel movement, especially in a country where they serve undercooked beef, toxic wine and little in the way of roughage. The archer had not even begun to fret about the delay before I was standing so close behind him that I could see the ripe pimples on his neck. Momina's call floated across the clearing just as I was about to guarantee that the youth would never have to fret about acne again.

'Lucius, it's very important that you don't harm him.'

Ah. Great.

Pimples stepped closer to his tree and peered around the trunk to see what was going on. Irritably, I snapped my arm out straight in front of me, and the palm of my hand brought his skull and the tree trunk into violent contact. There was a solid 'clonk' and my archer gave a sort of sigh and collapsed gracelessly to the ground, causing me to stoop at record speed to prevent him from impaling himself on his own arrow.

It is not that easy making one's way silently through under-growth while carrying an unconscious body over one shoulder, but I reckon I made a fair job of it. Of course, I was helped by the discussion at the bottom of the hill. This was being conducted at top volume between our would-be ambushers and Vidnu and his men. The shouting stopped briefly when I joined the group and dropped my cargo (tied hand and foot by his own bowstring) onto the ground between them. The strangers were unarmed, while Vidnu and his men still had their swords. In addition they had collected some rough spears and a variety of crudely-adapted agricultural instruments. Why, I wondered, did people keep trying to kill me with scythes?

Though they outnumbered us by a considerable margin, the scales were very clearly tipped against our would-be attackers by their monumental ineptitude and the wolf-like efficiency of the Galatians. From the way that Vidnu was haranguing the others it was clear that he felt indignant and insulted rather than threa-tened. Red-faced and with veins bulging in his forehead, he had his bristling moustache shoved right against the face of a obviously terrified Gaul, whom he alternately prodded in the chest and sprayed with spittle.

'Local villagers,' remarked Momina who had secured the waggon and wandered over to join the fun. 'Your army took all their grain, and they are a bit desperate. Winter is coming. And, oh you poor boy!'

She rushed to my victim, who was still lying on the ground but had progressed to moaning feebly. Momina knelt and indignantly felt the bloody bump swelling up on the side of his head. 'I thought you were not going to hurt him. Knife.'

She reached imperiously behind her, and one of the Galatians automatically put his dagger into her hand. I stopped her before she cut the bowstring. It was a nicely waxed affair, and if we were supposed to play nice - though I still could not for the life of me see why - there was no sense in ruining a good tool. I pulled on one end of the bowstring and the knot writhed briefly and undid itself. I grinned proudly and stepped back remarking, 'You can learn a lot in the company of sailors.'

Everyone ignored me. Vidnu was questioning the leader of the Gallic band with something now approaching concern, and I was startled to see that the man was actually sobbing quietly. Madric came up behind me and quietly muttered in my ear, 'Roman bastard.'

Caepio's army had passed that way ten days ago. Until that moment the villagers had believed that they were peaceful and law-abiding subjects of Rome's growing empire. However Caepio decided that the villagers were close enough to the rebel city of Tolosa to be considered hostile. Three maniples of legionaries arrived at the village unannounced, and with no warning began pillaging. They also helped themselves generously to the wives and daughters of the village, and killed not a few in the process of raping them. The headman had immediately succumbed to the demand that he show where the grain stores were kept, but despite this, for some reason the soldiers crucified him anyway. Then they left with virtually everything that could be carried. Only the fact that most villagers were away working the fields and tending their cattle had prevented them from being enslaved as well.

Now, bereft of their food reserves, the villagers were looking at a bleak winter - and they were also looking at anyone coming from the direction of Narbo with a distinctly unfriendly eye. Vidnu gave brisk orders, and one of his retinue scuttled back to the cart and returned with several substantial bags of silver denarii. I eyed these dubiously. 'How many in the village?' I asked Momina - the only member of the group still talking to me.

Even she seemed to hold me somehow responsible. 'Before or after your army came along?' she enquired tartly.

'After.'

Madric supplied the answer with a terse, 'Two hundred and eighty-two. Though some women won't survive the week.'

'Then that money won't be enough,' I observed. 'Not for that many people for the whole winter.'

'They'll have more,' Momina told me. 'And not all the harvest was yet in. With our help they'll scrape by.'

'More' turned out to be finger-sized bars of gold. I yelped as I saw Vidnu begin handing out generous fistfuls of what I had fondly believed to be my well-hidden retirement fund. At my indignant look Momina shrugged prettily.

'I didn't tell anyone. There was no need. Gauls have a natural affinity for gold. They dig it out like truffle hounds.'

'But ... but ... .'

'Relax. There's plenty more where we are going.' Momina gave me a subdued smile, but after being that abruptly bankrupted I wasn't easily cheered.

Madric suggested diffidently, 'Alternatively, I could sort of mention, loudly, that we have a genuine Roman officer right here. Afterwards, assuming there still is an 'afterwards' for you, the women of the village could demonstrate their feelings about the Roman army fraternizing with the natives?'

He smiled, but the smile came nowhere near his eyes.

'Ex-officer,' I responded promptly. 'And you were in the auxilia.'

'Want to put it to a popularity contest? If not shut up, smile, and see your money being well spent.'

I shut up, smiled and watched my gold being distributed to pathetically grateful villagers. 'There's some babies that will see next spring because of you,' Madric informed me grudgingly.

Vidnu came over once the distribution was done and clasped me firmly by the forearm as he gave thanks for my contribution. He had the good grace to look sincere about spending my money, but his smirking retinue ruined the effect.

Then we bumped onward to Tolosa. As we approached the city, it was clear that, even if the Romans were not exactly expected, precautions had been taken in case they came. Caepio had, or should have, his hands full coping with the threat of the fast-approaching Germanic tribes. However, Tolosa was a city in revolt, and uncomfortably aware of the tempting amount of treasure within its walls.

Momina had been increasingly solemn as we approached the city. Now she regarded the walls with wide eyes, turning her head this way and that to take in the details. The rest of us likewise gave the walls our professional attention. They were *muri Gallici*, 'Gallic walls'. Unlike city walls in Italy or Africa, which were either hastily raised earth ramparts or finely worked stone structures, these seemed something of a combination of the two.

Madric had evidently seen this design before. 'Stone facing,' he remarked. 'That protects the timber behind - and the timber is banked with earth. Those walls are positively elastic. The earth and timber combination will soak up the impact of anything our siege engines can throw at them. And look at the ramparts.'

We both lifted our eyes. Even though the ponies pulling the cart were now clopping almost directly under eyes of the suspicious sentries manning the walls, I could still see piles of stones and logs rising beside them.

'Logs?' I asked. Madric nodded.

'You stick spikes in them, and then when the enemy infantry

rush the walls with siege ladders you point the log down the ladder and let go. The log collects soldiers on the way down and crushes them at the bottom.'

Scaling ladders would be needed. The walls plus ramparts were about five times the height of a man, and fitted with towers and javelin platforms besides. There was also a deep red scar of a ditch running alongside the wall - and through where a number of outlying houses had once stood. The city authorities must have decided these were too close for comfort to the walls and had them demolished so that legionaries could not use them as a forward base. Here and there wet hides and 'sails' were being prepared. The 'sails' were basically gigantic nets intended to catch missiles, especially the flaming variety, that an invading army might lob over the walls to burn the houses within. The wet hides were for throwing over, or mounting on, exposed woodwork to prevent it catching fire.

At the city gates themselves we stopped while several cartloads of arrows, spears and stones were brought within the walls. We passed the time watching some warriors on a nearby stretch of wall practising 'catch the ram', a game they might be playing in earnest before the month was out. It is a simple game. One set of players attempt to thump the gates open with a battering ram. The defenders try to catch the head of the ram with lassos and pull it up. In the real game, the winners get to live. In the practice, the defenders seemed to be doing pretty well, though as Madric remarked, no amount of practice can fully prepare for reality.

No food carts were in evidence, but I guessed that the Tolosans knew that if he did come, Caepio would not be able to stay long. At most, the city would have to weather a brief storm before Caepio was compelled to move on to the Germans. The Germans were after all the reason why he was in Gaul. I wondered if the Tolosans had any idea of how intense that brief storm would be.

Within the city, the thatched roofs of the houses had new meaning for me. Madric saw and correctly interpreted my look, and nodded towards a street corner where a collection of long-handled hooks were stacked upright against a wall. 'If a roof catches fire, they'll tear the thatch off with those. And you can bet that every house has buckets of water inside so that they can soak the thatch if things get nasty.'

Even with these precautions, I would not want to be in Tolosa on a windy day if Caepio did come. Burning straw carries far on a stiff breeze, and buckets of water won't do much to soak thatch that is carefully designed to shed rain. It was a mild relief to note that the hostelry to which Madric led us was roofed with good Roman-style baked clay tiles.

Servants stashed the baggage in our rooms. Momina went after them without saying a word, and did not come out thereafter. In the courtyard of the inn Vidnu's retinue set about brushing road dust from their cloaks and helmets. As was his social duty when arriving in the tribal capital, our prince was off to meet the local civic dignitaries.

I was doomed to come along as well. This was partly because Vidnu was a man of his word, and having called me his 'colleague' he was determined I should live up to the designation. Secondly, my cover story was an 'Oscan aristocrat' dirtying his hands with trade. Such a man would be expected to do the social round with Vidnu in the hope of making new business contacts. Finally, it was plain to the Galatians that I would much prefer to slip off to spy out the land on my own, and they took a petty satisfaction in frustrating me.

Whatever the reason for taking me along, that bright idea nearly caused our enterprise to come unglued at the very first stop. This was at the mansion of some fat individual with an enormous red moustache, the edges of which drooped below his chin. Geese scurried around the yard where this Gaul sat at a bench with a large tankard in front of him. Vidnu had to shout to be heard over the clanging of the house blacksmith who was evidently beating his patron's armour into shape. Possibly to accommodate an expanded waistline.

Vidnu made a great show of introducing me, which elicited surprise and a voluble stream of Gallic from our host. Behind me, Madric quietly murmured, 'oshit'.

I turned to him. 'What?'

'How's your Oscan?'

'Eh?'

'No, seriously. How's your Oscan? Can you speak it like a native?'

'No, I can fake the accent for a joke at a dinner party, but that's about it.'

'Pity. How fast can you learn?'

'Why?'

'Because big Red here has a genuine Oscan in residence as a guest-friend. He's delighted to have the chance to bring together two countrymen so far from their native soil. Ah. Now he's calling a servant to get the guy. He will be here any moment.'

'Gods. What are the odds? We've got to get out of here. If the Gauls find I can't speak any Oscan we'll all be arrested as spies.'

'We? Hey, you fooled us as well. None of us speak Oscan, so you tricked us into believing you were the genuine article.'

Madric gave me a pleading look. 'You'll remember that when they are torturing you, right? We being your comrades in arms and all that.'

My indignant reply was interrupted by a stocky, dark-haired individual who hailed me from the porch of the mansion. Madric had been right that we hadn't much time. I suspected the guest had been watching our arrival from an upstairs window. Now he called a greeting in something which sounded like Latin but wasn't.

There was nothing for it but to fake a cry of delight and hurry across the courtyard while surreptitiously checking that the dagger under my tunic was ready for immediate use. If the worse came to the worst, I was going to knife the stranger. Possibly we could persuade our host that the stabbing was related to some old family vendetta which the Oscan's family and mine had been waging in the Italian hills.

Selling this story would be tough, and in any case, Red Moustaches would take a very dim view of the murder of someone in his protection - especially with the deed committed under his roof. Besides it was rather unfair to kill someone merely for being Oscan.

So with a welcoming smile, I wrapped the stranger to my bosom in a huge hug, and pretended to kiss him on his leathery cheek.

'I hope you understand Latin, because I'm not Oscan. That object you feel under my tunic is a small but sharp knife. Tell anyone I am a fake, and the pointy end is the last thing you'll ever feel. On the other hand, how do you feel about strangers giving you lots of money?'

Calmly the stranger kissed me back and quietly replied, 'Relax. Just talk gibberish. Go by the tone of my voice.'

With that he slapped me heartily on the shoulder and exclaimed something like, 'Gooblendum de gookunt!' to which I obediently replied, 'Rhubarbo, rhubarbas rhubarbat.'

We exchanged repartee in this way for a few seconds with our Gallic audience looking on. Benignly in the case of our host, and with barely-concealed relief on the part of Vidnu and his men.

Then my interlocutor asked something with sympathy evident in his manner, and I replied, 'Rhubarbamus, rhubarbatis rhubarbant?' with some concern. After his reply, talking to Madric in Latin was something of a relief. Speaking fluent gibberish is nowhere as easy as it might seem (though the girls at the Temple assure me that I do it effortlessly after a second flagon of wine).

'Madric, my fellow countryman has grave news from home which affects our plans. He and I must confer within. My apologies to our host for breaking up this gathering, but these tidings are most important.'

Red Moustaches gave us his gracious permission to use the vestibule, and the stranger dragged me by the arm to a low marble table. (Gallic aristos certainly did themselves decidedly well.) The Oscan plonked himself opposite on an elegant wrought-iron chair.

'So what imbecile decided on that cover story? Or is it a suicide mission? Are you meant to be the fool they capture so that no-one suspects the real spies? Do you even know who the Sidicini or Ausones are?'

I rather sullenly replied that both were Oscan tribes.

'Okay. We are from the Aurunci. Even other Oscans think their accent is barbarous, and it's closer to Latin. Just remember to finish your infinitives in 'um' and your passives with 'r'. And if you can't write Etruscan, just don't write anything. Aurunci generally use Etruscan script, rather as these barbarians do their writing in Greek. Now, who sent you?'

Pretence was useless, and there seemed no harm in letting this stranger know that his catch had powerful allies. 'Cornelius Sulla. While he is in Africa he wants someone keeping an eye on what Caepio gets up to in Gaul. Who are you, I mean, who are you really?'

The stranger gave a short bark of laughter. He remarked cryptically, 'If you want to know what Caepio is up to, you've come to the right place. I'm Quintus Sertorius; at your service. I really am an Oscan, as it happens, but currently a military tribune on detached duty from the army of Servilius Caepio. I would be obliged if you did not mention that last detail to our current hosts.'

'So not just an Oscan, but genuinely of a good family. Even I've heard of the Sertorius clan. What gets you into something as dangerous as the spy business?'

Quintus Sertorius shrugged carelessly. 'Minor branch of the family. I'm expendable. This is banking away a few exciting memories before I settle down to being a sheep-farmer in the Nursine hills.'*

We chatted lightly for a while, but the conversation was literally dead serious. I kept my dagger handy in case this 'Quintus Sertorius' did not know people and things that someone in his position should know.

From the way he favoured his left side while sitting, and kept his leg tight against the table, it appeared Sertorius was of the same mind. His right hand had not been visible since he had introduced himself, probably because he had palmed something sharp into it. My guess was a *sicarius*, the little assassin's knife specifically designed to be slipped under a tunic. This muscular little aristocrat was braced and deadly. It was just as well I had not gone with my original stab-first-and-explain-later strategy.

Now - fortunately for my ongoing health - Sertorius knew of Freya's Temple in Rome. ('Never had the pleasure of visiting, though a colleague speaks highly of it.') He had friends who had served in Africa, and we knew many of the same people. Some quick questions confirmed for him that beyond doubt I knew Sulla personally, and knew him better than Sertorius did.

'So you are that Lucius Panderius? Well, if Sulla sent you, you could have done a better cover story. There was an Oscan merchant here a ten-day ago, and you'd have been in a pretty pickle if you'd met him.'

---

*Sertorius was being economical with the truth here. In fact he had passed a brief sojourn in Rome trying to break into politics. He failed, mainly because he was an appalling public speaker (or 'ranter' as Cicero preferred to call him). Since he didn't want to go home with his tail between his legs, Sertorius joined the army, and discovered a natural aptitude for intelligence work. (Plutarch *Life of Sertorius* 1-5)

'Since when was this cursed province swarming with Oscans? Is he coming back?'

'That my dear Panderius, does not matter. I'm leaving at sundown to rejoin the army, and you'd really better come along as well. Mallius, my commander, will be happy to update you in person for Sulla's benefit, and we can always use another able officer.'

A servant came in with a message for Sertorius. While they exchanged a few sentences in Gallic, I pondered my options, and immediately resumed the conversation as the servant slipped out.

'My thanks. But I'd like to look around here for a bit before going on to the army.'

Sertorius gave a sinister smile, 'Oh, but who said you would have to go to meet the army? It is coming here to meet you. And all these lovely Tolosan rebels, of course.'

'But ... .'

'The army is around two hundred, two-fifty stades away. The artillery is closer, because it is coming ahead for the army to catch up on a forced march tonight. The legions will be around Sostomagus* by now. Come dawn tomorrow Tolosa will wake up to an army camped under its walls. With a bit of luck you won't have unpacked your waggon yet. Maybe I'll hitch a ride? I'd like to find out more about this Vidnu of yours. Is he really a Galatian prince as he claims?'

'So far as I know. He's got fighters with him who'd make any royal bodyguard proud, and he throws money around in right regal fashion - even when it's not his,' I added with residual bitterness.

'Well I assume he's with you. I saw him sweating as we were

---

*The Roman stade was around 600 feet, making Caeio's army some 30 miles from Tolosa at the time of this conversation. Sostomagus is modern Castelanudry in Aude, France; about one day's journey east of Toulouse. Its position made it the first imperial post-house from Tolosa in the later empire.

introduced. How far can he be trusted?'

'Not at all. He's a prince of the Tectosages, and this is his tribe. A single Roman snooping around he can tolerate - just. But an army? He will probably be unhappy.'

'Very unhappy?'

'Lethally so.'

'Better not tell him, then. Forget the waggon. Can you slip away?'

'Do you mind if I bring a priestess?'

'Can she ride?'

'Oh, I suspect so. You'll find her ... remarkable.'

"Remarkable' seems a good description for your entire group. I'll not even enquire why you are traipsing around Gaul with a priestess in tow. We will find out when Caepio debriefs the pair of us tomorrow morning. Does she do divination?'

'You have no idea.'

'Well, she can talk shop with Caepio. He fancies himself as something of an augur. He even sometimes sets strategy by the flight of birds.'

'Can't quibble with that. I recently changed my plans radically because of the flight of a magpie. And it worked out.'

Over the next few minutes we briskly sorted out the details. Towards sundown, as the Galatians prepared for their nightly revels, I would leave the group. (I would claim to be taking an early look at the temple holding the statuette, though I did not share that detail with Sertorius.) He would be waiting by the city gates with three fast horses, and we would be back with the Roman army before dawn.

There were a few drawbacks to this plan. Momina would probably baulk at leaving when she was so close to her precious statuette. Also apparently, Caepio would be keen to conscript me into his army. This would protect me from the authorities at home, not least because Caepio loathed the Marians as much as anyone. However my long-term future would remain in doubt. Furthermore, I remained flat broke in a hostile world, and desperately needed to loot a temple or two before leaving town. But again I could hardly share this last fact with Sertorius.

It turned out that the servant who had stopped in earlier had come to tell Sertorius (and myself - though Sertorius did not bother updating me until the end of our conversation) that Vidnu had left us to it, and moved on to his next appointment across town. Since this appointment was with a friend of Red Moustaches, the Gaul had gone along for the ride. On past form, there would probably be a house party rolling across town by nightfall. Ah well, eat, drink and be merry, for tomorrow ... .

'You die?'[*]

As I crossed the courtyard, Madric had materialized out of thin air beside me. The man could move like a ghost when he wanted to. So preoccupied had I been with the fast-developing situation that I had evidently been muttering under my breath. Such negligence can get a man killed. In fact, Madric seemed to be considering doing just that.

'I'm shocked. Yes, shocked and hurt, Lucius. Did we not break bread with you? Welcome you into the bosom of our little group? Did you not drink our wine?'

'Yes. I've not forgiven that wine.'

'The point is not the quality of the wine. Forget the wine. Let us discuss how you were planning to betray us, leave us hanging in the wind. Abandon us to our fate. Where's your honour?'

'Where's the honour in lurking by the door pillars with your ears pricked? You slipped in behind the servant I assume?'

'How I discovered your black-hearted treachery is not relevant.

---

[*]It is generally speculated that this famous quote, also used by Shakespeare and by St Paul at Ephesus, is based on the famous *Cena Libera*, at which gladiators and the condemned were traditionally treated to a splendid dinner the night before they faced death in the arena.

Are you seriously planning to leave Vidnu and his men to die horribly when the Roman army comes over those city walls? Think of all we have been through together!'

'Exactly.'

There was a brief pause as we mentally recapped the lowlights of my acquaintanceship with Vidnu. Then Madric asked, 'Can you arrange an extra horse?'

'No problem.'

'I'll be there at sundown.'

Liber VI

Having decided to cut short our stay in Tolosa, Madric and I found ourselves with an afternoon on our hands. At my suggestion we wandered over to look at the temple where, according to Momina, the statuette was being kept. My vague idea was that we might find a loophole in the temple's defences which would enable a quick raid just before we fled. More probably we'd find that security was tighter than a mouse's bum and that would be our excuse to persuade Momina that her mission was hopeless. Either way, if we gave the temple a quick survey, we could at least say that we had tried.

The building in question lay on a wide street with a tavern a few doors away. It looked like no temple I had ever seen, and that is because it wasn't. There are - were - temples in Tolosa, and a splendid one on the hilltop overlooking the city centre[*], but there were far fewer than a pilgrim would find in any Italian city. As I discovered, the Gauls are not much fond of temples, preferring to take their religion *al fresco* beside lakes or sylvan groves. Partly this is because Gallic religion is closer to nature ('druid' means something like 'truth of the oak'), and partly because druids are keen on burning, drowning and/or disembowelling human victims, and it is easier to get rid of the bits in the great outdoors.

So 'warehouse' probably described our target more accurately than 'temple'. It is my experience that - sacred bull in Egypt, holy holly bush in Gaul or whatever - there isn't a god in existence who'll say 'no' to gold or blood. In Gaul, blood could be left splattered around a sacred grove, but even the most devout nation has its atheists, so the gold was securely locked away in town.

'Do you know what the druids do to people who try to steal sacred treasure?' enquired Madric with morbid relish. 'I'd tell you

---

[*]The Tolosa which Lucius describes was in the hills now overlooking the modern city which lies on the plain some ten miles to the north.

in detail, but we'll want our midday meal soon, and I don't want to spoil your appetite. Let's just say it is not pretty, though the spectators learn a lot about basic anatomy, and the amazing amount of it a person can do without and still keep screaming.'

'Shut up.'

We wandered around to look at the back of the building, which was against an alley so congested with foetid rubbish that we only ventured into the squelching mess for a couple of paces before Madric withdrew with a disgusted 'ewww'.

Adjourning to the tavern, we braved a chilly autumn wind to sit outside in the watery sunshine. My lunch was a roll of coarse bread accompanied by a whitish cheese and a solid slab of ham. Madric preferred to drink his meal from a large leather mug, explaining, 'If things come unstuck, I don't want rotten milk and pig flesh floating around a stomach wound. My intestines will be purified with beer.'

He studied the contents of his mug thoughtfully. 'Okay, purified is a stretch. This stuff is truly appalling. I'll be glad when I've finished it.' He did so in a few heroic gulps.

'So,' I said, as Madric wiped beer suds from his moustache, or rather, smeared foam over his lower face. 'What do you think?'

Madric was not fool enough to blatantly study the treasure-house, though we had a good enough view of it from where we were sitting.

'Two guards at the door. Not a problem, though there's probably some sort of inspection system at night. A basement, because you can see those heavy grilles letting in light at toe level. One door, bronze by the look of it, and no windows up to twice the height of a man - and those are, firstly, facing the street and anyone walking by, and secondly, are slits too narrow for a cat to wiggle through. Best way in, I'd say, is to con our way past the guards. We need either a good bluff or an even better battering ram.'

'Alternatively ... .'

'The roof?'

'The roof. Put a ladder across the alley from the house at the back. Fortunately, the treasure-house is higher up the hillside so it's a shallow climb. Then lift the tiles, and slide down a rope. Of course, you would have to do it at night, and pacify the people in the house you are crossing from, but Vidnu and his lads do pacification so well.'

'And this afternoon? Do you have any clever ways of fooling the guards that would allow me to nip in and filch the statuette?'

'None that don't end with you as the star of a subtractive anatomy lesson.'

'Okay.' I wrapped the remainder of my ham in my napkin and stashed it within my tunic for later*. 'Let's go and break the bad news to Momina.'

It was evident that Momina had been crying. Her red-rimmed eyes and trembling lip caused the serving girl at our hostelry to give Madric and me a dirty look, as though we were somehow to blame. In reality the serving maid herself was responsible, though certainly not to blame.

'I can't take it,' the usually irrepressible Momina muttered. She squeezed her eyes tight. 'That's the owner's daughter. She's fourteen. She will see her father tortured then cut down before her eyes. Her own body will end up on the dung-heap there, raped then gutted. She'll die when the stables catch fire and the wall falls on her.'

'Everywhere I look, I see people, and what is going to happen to them. Him;' she nodded at a stableboy. 'Enslaved. Those two - children playing in the street - suffocate from smoke while hiding

---

*Management would see nothing wrong with a napkin being carried off the premises. Diners were expected to bring along their own napkins - and their own cutlery, if it came to that.

under the bed of a burning house. Their mother gets thrown into the flames later. By the time the soldiers finish with her she's too damaged to walk. That man ... .'

'We get the picture, Momina,' I said gently.

She sniffed, and made a visible effort to pull herself together. 'Oh, and some tunic-wearing fellow came round with a message for you. He said I was to put it into your hands personally.'

'When was this?'

'About an hour ago. I didn't want to speak to him, but he insisted. He survives, at least. He's a soldier - and not a Gallic one.' She shook her head, mousy-brown hair spilling across her face. 'I wasn't paying much attention.'

The message was on a wax tablet bound with coarse twine. Fortunately Sertorius had not trusted me to read Etruscan, because I couldn't. His message betrayed his rustic origins, for it was scratched in schoolboy-style Latin. 'Change of location. Ride from stables near River Gate. Be there at nine paces exactly.'

Madric and I turned and squinted at the sun. There's a quick way of telling time in the army, and that is by using yourself as a sundial. Make a mark on the ground and turn to face the sun. Then take nine paces (or whatever time you are looking for). If, when you turn, the shadow of the top of your head just touches the mark on the ground, then you are on time. If the shadow falls short, you're early. The system works well because shorter people take smaller steps, but you do need the sun. After a quick experiment, Madric discovered that his shadow was currently at two paces. He looked at the sky with an accusing expression. 'Nine paces is going to be cutting it fine.'

I nodded and turned to Momina. 'You are probably wondering what this is all about ... .'

'He's not coming.' Since this was about the twentieth time Madric had said this, I simply ignored him, and went on scowling at the gates. The guards there were chaffing with a couple of new arrivals, the context obviously being that the latecomers had been within a few minutes of camping overnight outside the walls.

We were lurking in riding gear near the stables, where the horses stamped and blew in expectation of their evening meal. I might have considered purchasing three horses from the stable owner, but all anyone does by trying to buy horses at very short notice is to attract unwelcome attention - and the gate guards were well within earshot. So we waited, and time passed like liquid gold running out of a water-clock.

Madric strode impatiently into a stretch of street where the dirt was lit orange by the setting sun. He paced out the length of his shadow. 'Ten and a half paces.' He reported. 'I tell you, he's -'

'Madric,' I said in a perfectly level voice, 'if you tell us he's not coming, just one more time, I swear by all the Gods of the Underworld that I'll put all ten inches of my knife into your belly.'

'It's too late anyway,' replied the Gaul with a sigh. 'They're closing the gates.'

Sure enough, the five guards had put their shoulders to one wing of the huge oak gates and were slowly pushing it closed. I peered up the road once more in the vain hope that I would yet see Quintus Sertorius hurrying towards us, but the street was empty apart from a few stray pedestrians and a bored-looking donkey.

And just an hour before I had been so pleased at having persuaded Momina to abandon her enterprise and accompany us out of the doomed city. On reflection, I had told myself, it was not so surprising. Not many people will voluntarily remain in a city that is about to be sacked if they know what a sack involves, and in some inexplicable way, Momina knew. Her demeanour as we had entered the city suggested that somehow she had always known, but it is one thing to know in the abstract, and another to walk the streets where the horror is soon to happen. I too had seen a city or two go up in flames, which is why I wasn't leaving Momina in Tolosa if I could possibly help it. Officially she might be an escaped slave and property of the city of Rome, but she was also my responsibility.

It was a good thing that we had scouted out the treasure house earlier. Madric and I had given a graphic description of its strong points (omitting the vulnerability of the roof), and explained that Tolosa just did not have enough time left for us to get the statuette from the doomed city. Momina barely argued. All the fight seemed to have been knocked out of her.

It was disturbing to see the little priestess like this, and a reminder that she was not a lot older than the serving girl at the inn whose fate she had foreseen. It's how Cassandra must have felt as she walked the streets of Troy, knowing that the bronze-clad Greek warriors would soon be unleashed on her beloved city, yet powerless to prevent it.

The only hope for Tolosa was if the Cimbri were pressing close. The more time that the legions had to spend in the city, the tougher things would be for the inhabitants. Some cities take over a week to be thoroughly pillaged - and several generations to recover afterwards. I looked up again at the ramparts, and Madric read my look and shook his head slowly. Tolosa was strongly garrisoned and well fortified, but it would not be enough. Not against Rome.

The guards were now fitting immensely thick wood planks into brackets across the gate, and a small squad were making themselves at home in the guardhouse. No-one now would be leaving Tolosa, and consequently our little group in riding gear was attracting curious looks from passers-by. It was time to go back to our inn.

Madric murmured hopefully, 'If we hurry, we can put back Vidnu's money before he gets in.'

'We?' I gave Madric a startled look. I had certainly helped

myself to travelling expenses by picking the lock of Vidnu's sturdy but unsophisticated money-chest, but had no idea that Madric had done it too.

'So much for tribal loyalty.'

'Puh-lease. He's Tectosages, I am Allobroges. For time imme-morial Tectosages have been raiding our territory, stealing our women and raping our cattle. The only loyalty I owe him is that of mercenary to employer. And this afternoon I resigned, taking my back wages and a bonus. It's not like he's going to need the money, is it?'

'Well, if the past fortnight is any guide, he will roll in about midnight drunk as a sailor on pay-day, and by tomorrow there will be other things to occupy his mind. We might as well order a slap-up dinner on credit tonight.'

Momina made a little sound of protest, and I turned on her more roughly than intended. 'Look, why on earth not? We'll get a good meal, it will make the innkeeper happy that we're spending money - and the size of our bill is going to make no difference whatsoever. Anyway, he's going to get the waggon and our belongings. No doubt Vidnu will want to fight and die on the ramparts as a prince of the Tectosages is supposed to do, and his men will be gutted along with him. But I'm Roman and Madric and I won't fight our own army. It's over the wall on a rope for us - as soon as I can arrange a rope. My invitation to come along remains open.'

The discussion continued as we reached our inn. As soon as she saw us, another of the landlord's daughters scuttled out of the building with a message. Momina murmured under her breath, 'Enslaved. Ends up as a street whore in Milan.'

I couldn't look at the girl as I took the wax tablet from her hand.

The twine around this second message of the day was of finer quality, and the handwriting was clear and sophisticated. The text read - 'What happened to you? Can't wait any longer. Good luck. Q.S.'

Madric had been reading over my shoulder. As one man we swivelled to stare at Momina who had wandered off, chatting with the innkeeper's daughter. As though feeling our stares drilling through her shoulder blades, Momina turned and called back over her shoulder, sounding slightly more cheerful than she had for a while.

'By the way, Lucius, while you are arranging the rope, why not arrange a ladder? One that goes over a ten-foot-wide alleyway ought to reach that roof. I'll see you at dinner.'

It was a frustrating evening. Vidnu arrived back at the inn as we were finishing a splendid meal of beef and beans. After being escorted to his cellars by the landlord I had managed to dig out a half amphora of Rhaetian wine – which, if the seal was genuine - dated from the consulship of Scipio and Flaccus[*]. The cost of the thirty-year-old wine was as hair-raising as the taste was superb, and I found myself wondering what was going to happen if Caepio and his army did not actually arrive after all. Then I watched Momina listlessly pushing food around her plate, and realized that there was no point in trying to fool myself. Tolosa's doom was almost upon the city.

We urgently needed a rope (and possibly a ladder), yet instead Madric and I had to sit and watch Vidnu souse himself in wine far too good for his callused palate. All the while he drunkenly regaled us with details of his visits of the afternoon, of how the Gauls and Germans were going to slaughter the Roman sons of pigs - with myself ('hic') excluded - and how all the beautiful girls in Gaul and Galatia would not be walking properly for a week once, well, once ... and here Vidnu screwed his scarlet face into a

---

[*]Rhaetian wine is regarded as good by Vergil, just not good enough to share a cellar with his prized Falernian. (*Georgics* 1.95.96)

hideous wink, and calmly helped himself to the beaker of wine directly in front of me, well aware that any Gaul would have considered that a mortal insult.

Eventually the princely oaf had staggered to his quarters, bellowing a drinking song calculated to wake everyone on the west side of the city. The moon was well overhead before Madric and I could slip from the courtyard for our nefarious business of the night. The moonlight was welcome, for the streets of Tolosa were no more well-lit than the streets of Rome, and rubbish and pig-shit on the street were even more abundant. But the height of the moon was also a warning that the midnight had passed and we were well on the way towards morning.

Of ropes (and ladders) there was very little sign, and after we had explored our fifth hayloft we were very discouraged.

'All we've found so far is how to really ruin the evening for clandestine lovers,' I complained to Madric, 'you must look exactly like someone's father'.

'And she looked rather like my daughter,' growled the Gaul. 'If I find she's been up to any of that hanky-panky while I've been gone, having a terrified boy crap himself on her will be the last of her problems.'

'You mean the least of her problems.'

'I know what I meant.'

'The lad almost fainted when you asked about rope. Did he think you were going to hang him?'

'It's what a conscientious father would have done. For the boy's own good.'

Madric paused. 'You know, we've been looking in the wrong places. All the rope and ladders will be at the walls. They don't know that the Romans are coming, but that sort of thing will have been moved there. Can't have enough rope when working on counter-siege preparations.'

'Ah, sneaking up on gangs of armed men on a wall where there is nowhere to run. I was wondering what little treats this evening was missing.'

We finally found our rope at the foot of a guard tower, and to my delight, a ladder was propped up on the wall beside it. I had abandoned my plans to go temple-raiding, but the ladder would get us up one side of a wall while the rope got us down the other.

There were, as expected, armed men lounging on the ramparts nearby, so stealth was useless. We simply walked up and helped ourselves. One of the men shouted down a query, and Madric informed me afterwards that he had answered the challenge with an invitation to take the matter up with Red Moustaches, whom we had met that morning. Satisfied that we were Gallic, knew the townspeople and were apparently on official business, the warriors let us depart unmolested with our booty.

By now I had determined that moonlight gave insufficient light to avoid the filth on the street, and I simply squelched through the noisome mess regardless. We were moving westward down the main street, but even this important thoroughfare, like other Tolosan streets, served secondary duty as a sewer. With a heavy coil of rope on one shoulder and my share of ladder on the other, I was slow to react to the urgent drumming of hooves behind me. Suddenly the rider was around a twist in the road and almost upon us. Madric's violent evasion saved me from being trampled, although at the cost of landing me face-first in something soft and putrid.

The Gaul ignored my soft but fluent cursing, and the observation that my tunic was ruined.

'You Romans wash your clothes in piss anyway,' he remarked absently*, looking in the direction of the departing horseman. 'That's not good.'

---

*Urine was indeed an essential whitening agent for clothing. So much so that fullers placed large urns on the street into which Romans could voluntarily contribute a bladder's-worth of detergent whenever the urge took them.

I picked up the rope and my end of the ladder. 'He bears urgent news.'

'And we can guess what it is.'

As we tramped westward, we heard shouts from around the area of the city square. The shouting spread, and soon the occasional shutter was thrown open and questions asked of Madric and me on the street. As the noise and confusion slowly grew, lamps came on in houses, and windows brightened as fireplaces were stirred back to life. By the time we reached our inn, Momina and the staff were up, as were Vidnu's retinue. Madric parked the ladder against the upper window to the hayloft of the stables, where it blended into the scene as though it had been there all along (and may well have been until recently). Hopping onto a waggon outside the courtyard, I looped my rope over a projection near the thatch of the eaves on the inn, and slipped down to join the throng in the courtyard.

No-one noticed apart from Momina, who was, naturally, watching me with wide-eyed interest. I responded with a narrow-eyed glare. It was almost certain that the little witch had followed us around town that day. I'm pretty good at knowing when I am being followed, especially as the eavesdropping Madric had already embarrassed me once that morning - and I had seen no-one. But how else could Momina have scuppered our escape plans? I tried to ignore a small voice in my head which kept asking, 'How else indeed?'

There was a general movement by the crowd in the direction of the city walls, and we fell in with the jostling flow - though given the state of my stinking tunic, I had more elbow room than most. There was little point in going along, because there was no surprise about what we were going to see, but a morbid compulsion to know the worst drove me onward.

In the darkness beyond the wall, the road to Narbo was a river of lighted torches. Shadowy shapes moved beneath, marching with a rhythmic tramp. Occasionally torchlight would gleam off armour, or briefly light the side of a massive ox-cart. A few hundred paces from the city gates, the torches flowed right and left, settling down into stationary, orderly clumps that grew and spread. It was like watching a city swiftly taking shape under the walls of the existing one. Perhaps the most terrifying thing about it all was the silence. The people on the ramparts watched quietly as the size of the threat became more and more apparent.

The Romans, though easily within hailing distance, made hardly a sound. Occasionally we heard an order briefly barked, or an ox lowing in complaint. There was the rhythmic thud of a mallet pounding away on something metallic, and once, incongruously, a dog went into a fit of hysterical barking that terminated in a sudden yelp. Yet overall, the thousands of torches simply seemed to flow over the ground, and halt at their appointed place. And all the while more torches appeared up the road.

There was no point in seeing more, so I pushed my way down the steps from the ramparts and went in search of a horse-trough in which to soak my tunic. Then I was going to bed. Caepio's army was here, and there would be no leaving the city that night, or any other night until the Roman army was gone - or Tolosa was.

The next day we were back on the walls again. His drunken highness, Vidnu Lymp'dic, wanted to see the Roman threat for himself, and both Madric and I wanted to give the army a closer inspection than was possible by torchlight.

Things did not look good. The morning was overcast, the sky the same metallic grey as the chain mail of the legionaries who worked on abates and support trenches, seldom glancing up at the walls of the city they were attacking. Several hundred paces away was an already completed Roman field camp, with a ditch and earthen walls topped with sharpened stakes. Within, I had no doubt, were legionaries sleeping off the effects of their forced march and preparing for their assault on the morrow. Quintus Sertorius was probably there too, beneath the red standard which marked the Praetorian tent of Caepio's headquarters.

While the legionaries seemed merely frightening, the artillery was terrifying. Rank on rank the catapults were lined up, with engineers swarming over their machines, tightening parts and fitting washer-bars into the bronze sleeves of the torsion engines while legionaries toiled like ants to add stone after stone to the growing pile beside each catapult. At a quick count there were well over five hundred of the things, ranging from little 'scorpions' with just the arms of the crossbows peeping over their protective *vineae*, to massive two-story high brutes capable of hurling stones of 300 librae*. Most were the standard one-talent** shooters - impressive by their sheer number.

Madric and I went to the ramparts, leaned our heads over and looked right and left. As we straightened up, Madric said the obvious. 'No wool-sacks. Sertorius must have told Caepio that some time ago.'

I nodded. 'Have you seen that section of the camp? Cypriot mercenary archers. I've no doubt that there's a contingent of Balaeric slingers here too. This is no impulse raid - it has been a long time in the planning.' I pointed with my chin. 'The towers are going up already. Caepio had pre-fabricated parts in those big waggons.'

Vidnu asked something, and there was a brief conversation in Gallic. Madric explained, 'He is asking what the towers are for, and how little men like the Romans intend to raise something large enough to come over the walls.'

'Look over there - those soldiers are already clearing a path. Combat engineers will fill the ditch, and those towers will be pushed right against the walls. You can get a maniple of 120 men a

*About 220 lbs (100 kg).
**A 'talent' about is 75lbs (33 kg).

minute over the ramparts with one of those things - and it looks as though Caepio has three. There will be other assault troops on ladders rushing the walls at the same time.'

Vidnu gave a huge laugh. It was intended to be heard over a quarter mile, and it was. The chieftain wanted everyone to know that he thought the Roman assault preparations were ludicrous. Out of the corner of my eye I saw some of the Roman engineers working on the catapults briefly lift their heads to look at us. Madric translated.

'And where will the warriors of the Tectosages be while all this happens? We are not women to wet our skirts with fear. Not against men who go to war like ditch-diggers instead of warriors. The first Roman to come near these walls is a dead man. We will hold these ramparts with our bravery and our blood.'

A breathy, whirring sound dropped Madric and me as though we had been felled by an invisible axe. A quarter-second later there was a sharp crack as something struck the rampart breast-work overhead. This was followed by a plangent, fading whistle. I found myself at floor-level looking closely at the toe of Vidnu's boot, and noted that the thread near the toe was coming unstitched. The Galatian had not moved a muscle. From this point of view he looked like a steel tower topped by a pair of nostrils. Contempt radiated off him like heat from a furnace.

'Um, ... the artillery is ready. Tell Vidnu to wear his helmet. He'll want to protect his head.'

The gigantic Gaul looked at me scornfully as Madric glumly passed on his words. 'Think you that Vidnu Lymp'dic is scared of these Roman ... engines? He is a man and a fighter of the Tectosages. In any case, were the Roman engines to hit him with even the smallest of their stones, even Gallic steel would not save him. He will face his enemies like a man.'

'I didn't say the helmet would save him. I said it would protect his head. Otherwise it will turn into a red mist with gooey bits.

With a helmet, his head will get knocked clean off his shoulders. Then we can go looking for it a few hundred paces away[*], and put it back with his body so that he can make a handsome corpse.'

Just to make the point, a couple of scorpion bolts whizzed by, the arm-long missiles briefly visible as they arced downwards to vanish among the houses behind us. A few paces along the wall, another catapult stone hit the ramparts with a resounding crack. It occurred to those around Vidnu that the Galatian's size and rich armour made him a particular target, and there was a gradual and discreet withdrawal until not a man stood within ten feet of the prince.

Madric and I sat with our backs against the breastworks, and our heads well out of the line of fire. He dug into the pouch on his belt and produced an apple.

'Bite?'

'Thanks.'

'What do you think?'

I crunched the apple and considered. 'Dawn tomorrow. Especially if the weather lifts, and it looks as though it might. It should be done and dusted by midday - all bar the screaming.'

Vidnu leaned forward to ask something and we both winced as, with a sound like tearing cloth, a scorpion blot ripped through the space where the Galatian's head had just been. Madric summarized our conversation to date. He did not get up.

Vidnu responded with passion. He waved his arm up and down the ramparts, now crowded with Gallic warriors. Some were jeering at the Romans, and others trying their skill with javelin and the bow. But even the height of the walls could not compensate for the distance and the effectiveness of the legionary defences. Nevertheless huge cheers every now and then suggested that the occasional hit was being scored.

---

[*]The Jewish historian Josephus relates exactly this happening to the man standing beside him at the siege of Jopata two centuries later.

'He's going on about engineering skill not being equal to warrior spirit,' Madric said wearily. 'How these walls are stone-and-timber, and the Roman catapults can hammer at them for months without making a dent. How one Gaul is worth ten Romans in a fight, even when that Roman is not balanced on the top of a ladder and so on, and so on.'

'Wool-sacks.'

Vidnu grunted an enquiry, and I elaborated. 'You haven't got any.'

The problem for the Tolosans was not their walls. These were massive - up to forty feet thick in places. It was the ramparts. Vidnu was perfectly correct to say that the Roman artillery could hammer away at the walls for a month and achieve nothing but healthy exercise. Correct, but utterly irrelevant. The Roman artillery would not aim at the body of the walls, but at the ramparts atop them. Here the breastworks were two or at most three feet thick, and the stone was already juddering regularly against my back as the catapults hammered against it.

The impacts would weaken the binding of the bronze clamps which held the stones together. Thereafter, each hit by one of the larger stone throwers would turn that section of rampart into an untidy jumble of rubble. By late afternoon, the ramparts would be destroyed, and anyone atop the walls would be visible from the knees upwards to the attackers. That's when the scorpions would start picking off half a dozen men a minute each (a scorpion can fire only one bolt every fifteen seconds, but it skewers three men with a single shot.) And that was why I had looked for and found Cypriot mercenary archers and Spanish slingers in the Roman camp. Once the men on the walls were exposed, the mercs would march up close behind the protective shields of the legionaries, and pour a rain of missiles on to any defenders who remained.

This would leave the Gauls with an unenviable choice - by clumping together they could raise a shield wall against the slings and arrows of the light artillery. But a single stone ripping through the group would cause havoc - and any such group would be a target for literally dozens of siege engines. But if the defenders spread into open order, the arrows would come at each individual from top, bottom and sides. The bowmen at ground level could, and would, form up into ranks over twenty deep. On the walls, maybe the Gauls could muster six deep. In any case, the Gauls did not have that many archers to start with, being of a more hand-to-hand disposition when it came to combat. Eventually the ramparts would be cleared of all but the most suicidal defenders. Then the siege towers would roll forward, and the legionaries would prepare to rush the now undefended wall with their ladders. Once a stretch of wall was taken, the end was inevitable.

The trick to saving the city would have been to make sure the ramparts were not levelled in the first place. Demolition could be prevented, or at least slowed down, by slinging sacks filled with wool over the stone facings of the breastworks to absorb or soften catapult stone impacts. But - as Quintus Sertorius had undoubtedly pointed out a long time ago to his masters- the Tolosans lacked the requisite wool-sacks. Perhaps because it was so long since the spring shearing that not enough wool was available, or more probably because the Tolosans only knew of fighting other Gauls. The enforced peace of the Roman hegemony after the Carthaginian wars meant their counter-siege craft was more theory than practice. Theory with a gaping hole in it.

'Tonight?'

'It has to be tonight. The weather has cleared, and the ramparts have been pretty much cleared as well. So tonight, I reckon Caepio lets his army rest, and tomorrow, when the sun is peeping over the horizon, directly into the eyes of anyone mad enough to still be on the ramparts, the Romans will come. And as they come over the east wall, we leave over the river wall to the west. By then everyone will have other things on their minds than stopping us. In fact there will probably be a queue to use the ladder when we are done with it.'

'So we'll do the temple treasury tonight.'

'We know that the guard schedule is not different in the evenings, but inspections are more frequent,' Madric supplied. He and one of Vidnu's bodyguards - much to the latter's frustration - had spent the afternoon watching the temple guards on shift. It was a pretty slipshod business. The guards only changed every six hours, and one of the pair had wandered over to the tavern and joined our two spies in a drink. His complaints about the schedule had provided all the information we needed on that front. Apparently the guards were unpaid citizens 'volunteered' by the temple authorities, and most of them considered the job a complete waste of time.

'No-one has - and I quote - so much as tried to piss in the treasury portico all the years that our guard had been doing the occasional shift,' Madric told us. 'The guards will be more edgy with a Roman army just outside the walls, but even with their ramparts totally demolished the Gauls still think Caepio will settle down to a siege. They were just upset at not being able to participate in the sally.'

'Talking of which, how's Vidnu?'

We turned to look at the giant Galatian, who was following our conversation intently, not understanding the words, but trying to read our faces as we talked. Every now and then he would give a threatening rumble, and Madric would hastily summarize in Gallic our strategy meeting to date. There was a tight bandage around Vidnu's forearm, stained with blood and other unmentionable substances. The whole thing looked disgustingly unhygienic, but I held my peace in the hope that blood poisoning might remove at least one problem from my life.

Tormented by the catapults, the Gallic defenders of Tolosa had attempted a sally during the afternoon. It had not gone well. As soon as the gates had been flung open to disgorge the pride of Tolosa's fighting force, the Cretan archers on the Roman side had reacted swiftly. They wheeled into files and trotted away from the column of Gallic warriors who charged blindly at the nearest siege engines. The Romans working on earthworks and trenches there evidently had shields and swords close at hand, and they even managed to throw a couple of pilums into the front ranks of the attackers.

These heavy Roman spears drove their long, narrow shanks straight through shields and scale armour, and well into the warriors behind, a fact which surprised and impressed many. The attack might well have faltered right there had not our own Vidnu played the hero. Bellowing like a bull in rut, he single-handedly charged the wall of Roman shields. He actually burst through, and started laying about him in all directions with a massive sword that - for all its golden scroll-work - technically resembled a metal tree trunk. With his own bodyguard and the Tolosans following, the Gauls scattered the Roman guards. These fled back several rows of trenches and warily re-formed their ranks.

The legionaries made no attempt to advance but remained watching as Vidnu and friends set about trying to destroy the Roman catapults. Inexperience had the warriors hacking at solid oak reinforcing bars, or slashing easily replaceable whipcord when they should have been breaking the delicate machinery of the windlasses. Nor had anyone thought to bring the little bottles of flaming pitch usually considered *de rigueur* for such occasions, since breaking one pot on a catapult usually reduces it to an instant bonfire.

Nevertheless, several dozen catapults were put out of action before shouted warnings from the walls told of cohorts in battle order trotting at the double out of the Roman camp. The Gallic warriors were comprehensively outnumbered, and each came to an individual decision about the best time to stop catapult demolition and head back to the gates.

That's where things went wrong in what had so far been an amateurish but basically successful excursion. The Cretan archers had lined up right and left along the path the retreating warriors had to take. They shot arrow after arrow into unshielded backs and sword sides and did it at very close range, so the hardened steel arrow points (selected for just such occasions) went right through most chain mail. When the frustrated and enraged Gauls turned to charge them, the unarmoured Cretans simply skipped away. As soon as the breathless Gauls returned to their retreat, the arrows started once more.

Soon the way back to the gates was littered with dozens of writhing bodies which the fast approaching Roman cohorts briskly finished off without breaking stride. Having been reluctant to leave the catapults with so many undemolished and then taking time out to charge the archers, the Gauls had left it too late for an orderly return through the gates. Instead there was a massive crush as increasingly panicked warriors tried to get within the walls even as the cohorts started cutting down the late-comers at the back of the crowd. Those at the rear (who inevitably included Vidnu) finally turned and put up a creditable rear-guard action which allowed the congestion at the gates to clear. Whereupon the city authorities, with considerably more pragmatism than gratitude, ordered the gates closed to prevent the Romans from forcing their way in with the retreating rearguard.

Ropes had been thrown over the walls, and Vidnu had been one of the lucky ones who was pulled to safety, arrows pinging off the stonework as he rose. Many others were less fortunate, and died where they stood. Overall the Gauls lost about two hundred of the thousand or so warriors who had made the sally. And many of the catapults they had damaged were back in action by evening.

To cap it all off, just as he reached the top of the wall over the gates, Vidnu had taken the arrow through his forearm which had elicited my present enquiry.

After a rapid exchange with Madric, Vidnu drew a dagger with his injured arm and slammed it point-first hard into the table. We made appreciative noises about how well the arm was functioning, and all tried to pretend we had not seen the large fresh bloodstain that spread across the bandage afterwards.

The plan of action was as follows. At moonrise, we would set off. I, Madric and Vidnu's retinue would head for the target house across the alley from the temple with the rope and the ladder. Once we had removed the tiles and slid down the rope into the temple, we would open the doors from the inside.

By then Momina should have rolled up in the cart containing Vidnu, who confessed he could do without hanging from any more ropes that day. On arrival Vidnu would take out the sentries and load the bodies into the cart while we escorted Momina into the cellars to find her statuette. Since the sentries were fellow Tectosages, I had hopes that Vidnu would merely incapacitate them rather than something more terminal. Though as Madric remarked, since Romans outside the walls were already killing off Tectosages wholesale, it hardly behoved the Roman within the walls to get squeamish.

We would board the cart with our booty (since we were taking the statuette, I was planning to also take a top-up reserve for my depleted retirement fund) and find a quiet spot alongside the western wall until the Roman army provided the ultimate distraction in the east. All going to plan, we'd be out of town before any unpleasantness reached us, having a late lunch and mapping out the rest of our lives in some tavern by mid-afternoon. That's the problem with plans. Reality gets in the way.

The wheels came off my cunning scheme even as we left the inn. We'd just finished dickering with the landlord over the size of

our bill when there was a god-almighty rumpus from the eastern
side of town. Alarmed shouts filled the air, and the sound of
running men from the street outside. I looked eastward and
groaned. 'Moonrise. The bastard is not waiting for sunrise. He's
gone with moonrise.'

'Works almost as well,' Madric agreed. Moonlight behind an
advancing army confused those throwing missiles at it, as the
shadows made it hard to get the range right. On the other hand
the same moonlight lit those facing it, and made them outstanding
targets[*].

Vidnu grunted a single word. Madric nodded. 'Treachery. That
works too. Chances are that some Roman sympathizer has opened
a postern gate. Easier to do that by night. Our prince here knows
his own people best. Maybe your Sertorius did a deal or two.
Offered lenient treatment for those rats prepared to sink a sinking
ship, if you know what I mean.'

'So forget the treasure house. Drive straight for the western
wall.'

Vidnu interpreted my tone rather than my words. An ungentle
pricking above my kidneys reminded me that the Galatian could
indeed use a dagger with his wounded arm.

'The prince feels we should stop at the treasure house, since it
is on our way.' Madric informed me. 'And he asks that you don't
make him press the point home, which is quite a cool pun, when
you think about it.'

'Ho ho. Momina, please, let's get those ponies moving.' From
the eastern ramparts a roar issued from thousands of throats. It
signified that legionaries were charging forward with siege
ladders. They would literally be at the walls in seconds. Somewhere in the shadows close at hand a woman started to wail. We

---

[*] As shown by the Athenians at Epipolae in the 5th century (Thucydides), the
Pontics in a night action against legionaries (Appian), and legionary v. legionary
at Bedriacum (Tacitus).

put our heads below the duck-boards of the cart and let Momina guide it into the throng on the streets.

With every able-bodied Gallic man heading east to fight off the assault, the men in our group would have looked decidedly odd heading determinedly in the other direction. But a woman apparently alone in a cart was totally unremarkable, and indeed a quick peek over the boards showed a few other women determined to get as far away from the assault as possible. Some carried children, and one pushed a high-piled wheelbarrow, though what she was expecting to achieve by this was beyond me.

The break-down in law and order which inevitably accompanies these occasions manifested itself about a hundred paces down the road. I had been cursing our slow progress and mentally urging Momina onward when she was unexpectedly bowled over backwards into the body of the cart. She lay still as a balding middle-aged man struggled to his knees above her, fumbling at his trousers with one hand and the hem of Momina's dress with the other.

In other circumstances it would have been comical to see how his expression changed as his eyes adjusted to the gloom and he found himself kneeling in the midst of a group of armed warriors. As the stranger opened his mouth to say something Vidnu's huge hand clamped over his face. There came a sharp snap as though someone had broken a broomstick over one knee, and the man went limp. Vidnu threw the corpse aside like a broken puppet, and without a word, Momina scrambled to the front of the cart to regain control of the reins. The whole incident took less than ten breaths. There was screaming also from some of the houses alongside us, which suggested that not all the menfolk were at the wall. Some looting and pillage was not going to wait for the Romans. Not that the Romans were far away. There was a discordant clanging mingled with the shouting behind us now, as though thousands of demented blacksmiths were in competition. The

Galatian retinue murmured at the sound of sword beating on sword, and like hounds straining at a scent they swivelled their heads to look eastward. A faint glow in the night sky marked the first roofs to catch fire, and I thanked the stars for a windless night.

We turned into a side street and Madric stuck his head out of the side of the cart. 'Hey, up! We're here. Already.'

'Weren't you meant to tell Momina when to turn?'

'Apparently she knew.'

'Told you she was following us the other afternoon.'

'You might want to hurry,' Momina informed us with unusual terseness. 'I've got to get this cart turned around, and I can't do it in that courtyard.'

As we scrambled from the cart, pulling the ladder after us, I saw what she meant. My (evidently deeply flawed) plan had called for Momina to drop us off alongside the house across the alley from the treasure-house and then turn in the courtyard opposite. A courtyard now occupied by a waggon and a family frantically piling it high with their worldly goods. 'Probably a hell of a crush at the river gate by now,' murmured Madric.

'And a Roman picket waiting to mop up the departures,' I grunted as we trotted with the ladder towards our target house. One stroke of luck was that the front door gaped open, the inhabitants evidently fled. A neighbour took time off from her hasty evacuation to call something, but fell silent when one of the Galatians turned on her with bared teeth and sword.

To my unease, Condrusix was one of our party. He showed remarkable initiative when getting the ladder upstairs proved tricky. Of course, if one does not have to worry about damage, the quick way is simply to smash through the ceiling and hoist the ladder through the gap. Nevertheless, just in case the Galatian held a grudge, I made sure that I was the last to make the wobbly passage over the dark alley to the treasure-house roof.

We had planned to lift the tiles quietly, but Vidnu's bodyguard had evidently decided that the time for subtlety had passed. The crash of their forced entry would have woken everyone in the district, if everyone in the district had not been awake in any case. There was shouting and an occasional shriek from the main road, but this had nothing to do with us. I kept my ears pricked for the clatter of hobnails on stone - the distinctive sound of legionary *caligae*, very different from the soft thump of Gallic boots. So far, nothing. But the smell of smoke was stronger in the air, and the clanging, shouting and screaming ever louder and closer at hand.

One of the Galatians slipped through the hole in the tiles, and there was a scratching noise as he secured the rope to a roof beam. Below the temple was a pit of blackness into which I stared with foreboding.

'Pot,' I muttered, and the Galatian charged with the task understood my accompanying obscene gesture. He thrust the head of a torch into the neck of the small pot of smouldering charcoal which we had taken from the inn. A few waves in the air, and the tarred wool burst into flame. The idiot dropped the torch so close to where the end of our rope dangled to the floor that for a moment I thought the thing would catch fire. One of the other warriors evidently thought so as well, for he shimmied down the rope at a speed that surely skinned his palms.

As he landed and kicked the torch clear, a wraith-like, tattooed figure materialized from the shadows behind him. In the moment it took me to realize what I was seeing and shout a warning, the apparition had struck the Galatian firmly between the shoulder-blades with something in his fist. Faster than I could see in the flickering torchlight, the warrior whirled, drawing his sword as he turned, and stabbed the tattooed man so firmly that the blade stood two hand-spans out of the back of the wiry body as it silently folded over the sword.

The Galatian warrior stood over the corpse as one by one we

slid down the rope. As my feet touched the floor, the warrior dropped to his knees, and then slowly toppled, hitting the flagstones face first. Madric rolled the body on to its side, while I examined the small copper knife. It looked antique, such as the knives they take sometimes from pre-Etruscan graves. The tip was bent, for the knife had naturally bounced from the warrior's chain mail, but it carried a bloodstain the size of my little fingernail.

'Poison,' grunted Madric in disgust, 'get rid of the foul thing'. He turned, undoubtedly warning the others to watch out in case there were further Druids on the premises, while I quickly wrapped and tucked the venomous little blade under my belt. A bit of insurance never comes amiss. Torch in one hand and sword in the other, I headed for the doors, noting the iron brackets and the heavy oak beam held them closed. Beside me, Madric whistled softly.

Gold. When you suddenly noticed it, it was everywhere.

Liber VII

Somehow I'd had the idea that the gold would be lying about in untidy heaps like the fake treasure on a pantomime stage. Instead, there were racks stretching up towards the rafters, rather like the library I had seen in a rich customer's house. Each rack was stuffed with loot. The torchlight that danced across golden goblets chased shadows along the rims of jewel-encrusted kraters and rested, gleaming softly, on torcs, and golden shields and helmets which had surely never seen a battle.

There were boxes too, neatly stacked, and when I pried one open with my sword I saw that it was packed with golden Greek tetradrachms, each stack in a little wooden compartment, and each coin enough to feed a workman's family for a month. The next box contained silver. Not coins, not ornaments, but simply slabs of silver resting in a bed of straw. The racks and boxes stretched backwards into the gloom, and I remembered that this was but one of several such treasure houses in Tolosa. No wonder Caepio had seen fit to make a detour from his march against the Germans. In front of me was a Grecian muscle cuirass, mounted like a trophy on a crossbar, and a silver helmet with a splendid horsehair crest above. Though fantastically expensive, there was a functionality about the kit which suggested that it had been stripped from the corpse of some Greek officer, perhaps in the very raid on Delphi which had brought back the statuette and the curse that now lay over all this treasure.

Thinking of the statuette finally reminded me of my duties, and picking up the torch I proceeded to the doors. With an effort I levered the oaken bar off its brackets. The doors immediately crashed back, landing me flat on my backside as I cursed Vidnu for his impetuosity.

'Bloody oaf,' I muttered, and yelped in shock as I saw the sloping sides and purple crests of legionary helmets. Armoured men forced their way inside. At the sound of my voice, the nearest soldier turned on me, his face smeared with sweat and smoke, and his teeth bared in a bestial snarl. I opened my mouth to say something, but his shield was already rising as he punched at my face with the boss. I knew that trick, and skipped to my right rather than to the left, where the blade of his sword flickered out from behind the shield like a striking snake. Behind me there were shouts of confusion and the clang of sword on sword as Roman and Galatian went straight for each other's throats.

It might have been possible to get some sense through everyone's heads right at that moment. There seemed just over a dozen Romans in the store room, and every man present could come out with more gold than he could safely carry, and still there would be thousands of pounds of the stuff left. What were we fighting for? Stepping in, I chopped the edge of my hand across my attacker's face, and felt his nose break with a crunch. As the man staggered back, I grabbed his horsehair plume and banged his head hard against the door jamb, rapping him firmly on the skull with the inside of his own helmet.

Then I stepped back, opened my mouth to shout, and for the second time that evening went over backwards; this time over that triple-accursed oaken door beam. The fall knocked the wind out of me, and the stunned legionary recovered first. He lunged, stabbing downwards and his sword point skittered off the flagstones as I rolled. He moved in for the kill, and one of his comrades stepped up behind him, eyes also fixed on me. This second legionary's head seemed suddenly to jump off his shoulders into the darkness, and my attacker had barely time to throw his shield across his body before Condrusix's sword scoured a deep cut through the wood. As I scrambled to my knees I saw two more legionaries run towards us, shouting.

There were fighting men in clumps across the room, the bodies vague in the light of torches hastily dropped as the fighters leapt, twisted, slashed and stabbed. Already several bodies lay inert or thrashing weakly on the ground, and the legionary whom Condrusix had beheaded suddenly realized he belonged among them. The standing corpse buckled at the knees, hit the floor and lay still with blood fountaining from his headless torso. Despite their numbers, the legionaries were getting much the worst of the fight.

This was a broken field play, where legionaries accustomed to fighting in the ranks had to watch their backs and flanks against Galatians who were not only practised at this form of fighting, but very, very, good at it. The sword of Condrusix was a whirling arc of silver as he parried, twisted and then unexpectedly lunged, taking a man under the chin so hard that I heard the 'clonk' as the upward-driven sword exited into the back of the helmet.

A swinging shield caught me struggling to rise through the tangle, and I staggered back to see a legionary lunge his sword right at my unprotected chest. The tip actually touched my sternum when the sword dropped, the soldier's amputated arm still firmly clutching the hilt. Condrusix gave me a wild grin that changed to an expression of shock, and he reeled even as the legionary behind him stepped forward and stabbed again. That brought the Roman close enough for me to drive the little copper dagger deep into his thigh, right where the large leg artery curves towards the groin. Swinging my leg around I kicked the man hard behind the knee, and wrenched the sword from his hand as he fell. Bellowing with berserk fury, I then charged at my fellow Romans with murder in mind.

It was probably all over in less than a minute, though it is hard to measure time in such circumstances. Apart from Condrusix, the Galatians had not lost a single man, though one was holding a bloody flap of skin up against where his cheek had been. Incredibly, he seemed to think it was a huge joke. Madric grunted as he finished heaving the oaken bar back into place to seal the doors.

'We've got a problem,' he announced. 'The street is swarming with Romans.' No-one replied. Most were leaning on their swords, sucking in air with huge gasps, or when they had the breath to comment, buffeting a comrade on the shoulder to remark on an especially fine bit of sword play. Black blood spread in ever-widening pools beneath the corpses. Madric shook his head, and pushed out a lower lip, impressed.

'Eleven. Taken out by four Galatians. And you my friend. You got at least two, apart from that fellow you poisoned back there. Lucky I advised you to keep that knife, eh? By the way, have you figured out whose side you are on, because it's looking a bit, you know, ambiguous?'

I wiped a forearm across my sweaty face, only to discover that the sweat was a layer of someone else's blood. 'Mine. I'm on my own sodding side. Against the rest of the bloody world, and the Gods too, by the look of it.'

Madric nodded. 'Mount a torch on that bracket over there would you? It's time to play *capsarius*.' He dragged his pack from where it had dropped between the racks of treasure, and produced a fistful of bandages and a small, flat box. This box, it turned out, contained a set of small, curved needles and catgut. I watched in awe as the Gaul briskly stitched and bandaged various injuries, starting by sewing back the injured Galatian's cheek.

'You brought along a medical pack?'

Madric did not look up from his needlework. 'All the way from Rome. Surprised I haven't needed it before now, but I reckoned it was well worth bringing along. In case everything did not go to plan tonight. Some plan.'

He stitched some more, his subject remaining stoically still. 'By the way, I hope you aren't just standing around looking all heroic and decorative. We've got Galatians here who do that so much better than you. You're meant to be working on getting us out of here.'

I nodded. 'Already on it. I'll need a white ribbon. And you know how you told me Galatian daggers are sharp enough to shave with?'

'Leave that cart alone!'

The legionaries rushing towards the cart and the small, brown-headed girl driving it, stopped in their tracks. They swung around to where an officer stood on the treasure-house steps. He was clad in the expensive armour of an aristocrat, with the white ribbon of a military tribune knotted under the pectorals. A silver helmet sat firmly on his head. 'She's with me. You men get over here, now!'

'Aaaat the double, you filthy creatures. In files! In files. You aren't rushing a whorehouse to visit your mothers, you ignorant bunch of swine. Pretend to be legionaries!'

This last came from the *optio* in bloodstained chain mail who stepped from between the bronze doors, the rest of his squad barely glimpsed in the shadows behind.

The voice of command acted on the legionaries almost at the level of instinct. In seconds there were two rows of ten men standing stiffly at attention before me. Behind them Momina waved cheerily from the waggon. Other legionaries entering the street saw an officer delegating a work squad and warily backed away. They had better things to do.

I turned languidly to Madric, who stood at attention, quivering with eagerness. 'Optio, I want that cart loaded from the temple. Take the boxes of coin and silver bars, and a couple of decorative items, cups and the like. I fancy a dinner set.'

One of the legionaries in the street protested. 'But Sir, we were told to leave the treasure houses alone. On pain of death.'

Well, well. Not everyone had followed that order, though the 'pain of death bit' had turned out to be extremely accurate.

Strolling down the steps I coolly looked over the objector. Madric followed at my heels. 'Optio, take that man's name and unit. I'll want a word with his centurion later.' I leaned forward, very close to my victim, who stared to the front, his gaze firmly fixed on infinity. His jaw muscles were bunched, and he flinched as I purred softly in his ear. 'It looks as though we have a Scipio Africanus here, optio. At the very least. A man who knows better than his officers. Who do you think you are - Thersites?'*

Wisely, the man stayed silent. Losing interest, I turned to my optio. 'Two squads - yours bringing material from inside the temple, and these fellows here, loading the cart. And no chatting now. The sooner the cart is loaded, the sooner everyone can go about their business.'

After I had walked a few steps I added in a low voice that was intended to be overheard, 'Oh, and if a box should fall and break, don't check too carefully what happens to the contents. The lads here have earned a small bonus.'

And that, I thought as I strolled towards the waggon, should considerably incentivise my impromptu work party.

'You forgot to get a man to guard the waggon, Lucius,' Momina reproved.

'Eh?'

'To look after Vidnu.' Momina pointed with her chin to where a surly-looking Vidnu stood leashed to the cart by a short rope running from his bound hands. I smirked at him and received a murderous look in return.

The priestess murmured, 'I wouldn't upset him - he's only pretending to be tied up.'

Hastily, I turned and yelled at Madric to delegate one of our

---

*Thersites - voice of the common man in Homer's *Iliad*. Killed by Odysseus for pointing out that his 'betters' were acting like a bunch of blood-crazed adolescents and it would be better for everyone if the Greeks just went home. His was not a popular view in the ancient world.

men to guard the waggon and 'our Gallic prisoner'. There was a brief silence while Madric worked this one out, and then one of the Galatians came scampering from the treasury at such speed that I hoped the real legionaries in the second work party failed to note the numerous wardrobe problems with his kit.

Momina took the man aside for a briefing in rapid Gallic while I watched the first squad of grunting legionaries load a crate on to the waggon. Then the little priestess fell in alongside me. 'Come on.'

'Where are we going?'

'Into the treasury, silly. Did you forget what we came for?

'Seriously?'

'Come on.'

And she was off, leaving me trotting at her heels and feeling slightly foolish. Madric looked up as we approached. I explained to him.

'The lady wants to see inside, and maybe take a souvenir of the time that she was held hostage by the Tolosans. She feels they owe her something for the scare. After all, we got to her only just in time.'

The legionaries exchanged knowing looks. I had heard that a few Roman women had been caught in Tolosa when the city rebelled - merchant's wives, the family of the fort commander, people whom the legionaries might have been told to keep a look-out for. Momina played up to the occasion, making it look as though the booty she planned on seizing lay under the tunic of her rescuer. She practically dragged me from the leering gaze of the soldiers into the deeper shadows of the treasure house.

Once out sight of the work party, Momina became all business. Taking the torch from my hands she headed through the gold-laden racks towards the basement, making her way along the aisles with the familiarity of a man walking to his own bedchamber by night.

'How did ...?'

'... I know what was going to happen? It had to go that way. As soon as I saw the legionaries arguing about how to break in the treasury door I backed the waggon into that smelly alleyway.'

'There's only one way to get out of a street full of Roman soldiers, and that is to be Roman soldiers. Roman officers like to dress as Greeks* and pretend they are Alexander the Great, so I was sure you would find something suitable in the booty. And the legionaries who charged in would supply the armour for the men. So really, it was just a matter of waiting for the doors to open again.'

'And I thought I'd been so clever. A pity this Greek was so small. My ribs are killing me.'

'He was just fourteen, the poor boy. At least his helmet fits.'

The helmet I was carrying reflected Momina's arm and the torch she held, so for a moment it looked as though she was a manaed** painted with incredible accuracy on the chased silver itself. 'Bit of a bucket, isn't it? With those cheek-plates and nose-guard. No wonder no-one could tell if it was Patroclus or Achilles in that armour ...'***

'Ahhhhhh.'

Momina had ignored my rambling, and stopped by a set of shelves that looked no different to any other set of shelves. She stood on her tiptoes and reached up to pull a little wooden box toward herself. Within were a number of votive figures, all

---

*While legionary armour was (roughly) homogeneous, the only rules for an officer's kit in this period appear to have been that it should look suitably martial, and bear a ribbon depicting the wearer's rank. That a white ribbon denoted a military tribune adds a useful titbit of information to our knowledge of Roman military designations.

**Female follower of Bacchus who celebrated arcane and gruesome rituals by night.

***A famous case in Homer's legend, when one Greek hero impersonated another by wearing his armour.

statuettes in silver or gold. She selected one and held it high.

Then she turned on me.

How to describe that feeling? It was like being drunk, yet still able to think clearly. Like falling, yet with feet solidly on the ground, feeling like a child awed by grandeur, yet safe as a bird under temple eaves while a mad tempest roars outside.

It was still Momina. At least, it had the form of Momina and that form had not changed a bit. Yet if I could have commanded my limbs, I would have fallen on my face before her. Not in worship, not in fear, but simply because the sensation of being in her presence was too powerful to bear. There is no way to describe it, any more than to describe colour to a man blind from birth, or touch to someone who cannot feel. There's also no way that anything mortal can experience that intensity and survive for more than a few seconds. She looked at me, and her gaze struck the wind from my lungs, and my face felt as though the flesh was peeling from my skull.

'You have done well,' she said, quietly in a voice that filled and became the universe. I felt the shifting of spirit from body, the colours in the torchlight were impossibly, nauseatingly rich, the touch of armour and clothing on my body too intense to bear, the falling sensation increased - and she was just Momina, prosaically tucking the little golden figure into her robes, and smiling at me impishly as I staggered back, and for the third time that night landed on my backside in a perfect pratfall.

Momina giggled and held out a hand to help me up. 'So you've met my Lady.'

'I never want to do that again,' I said hoarsely, and noted without surprise that my hand was shaking too much for the priestess to take it.

Outside, the street looked monochrome, sounds were muffled, and smells were subdued. Madric was telling me something, and I merely looked at him blankly. Up the street, a Roman officer was directing men trying to contain a flaming building by breaking apart the sheds alongside it. My work party was gone. On each side of the waggon, Vidnu's men were standing at what I presume they thought was attention, each looking anywhere but at their leader bound to the back of it.

'... Any more and we'd break an axle.' Madric was saying. He shook his head as I staggered off, and he turned instead to report to Momina.

He and one of the bodyguard caught up with me as I entered the tavern through a door hanging off its hinges. There I dully noted a stink of spilled wine, blood and faeces within. Something writhed on a table as I pushed by, and seized a wineskin by the neck.

The raw, acidic taste of Gallic wine brought my senses back with a rush. What lay on the table was a Gallic serving girl. The men who had raped her had not bothered to tie her hands, but simply pinned her wrists to the table with meat skewers. One breast was a mess of ruined flesh from which blood slowly pumped. She was still conscious and watched me with hate-filled eyes as I told Madric and the bodyguard.

'Help her'.

There was a canvas awning which had been used to shield outside patrons from the autumnal wind. I wrapped this in my arms as Madric gently freed the girl.

'Get wine, bread, supplies,' I said over my shoulder, 'Anything that looks worth little but has bulk.' I bundled up the canvas in my arms. 'And carry that girl to the waggon.'

'That girl' had raised herself to a sitting position, and her face contorted as she flexed her fingers. As the bodyguard approached, she stood shakily and pointed one of the skewers at him. The man backed off as Madric said something quickly and reassuringly in Gallic. The girl looked at him, then suddenly drove the skewer hard into her own stomach. Appalled we watched her double over, legs kicking spasmodically. The bodyguard stepped toward her, and she vomited a gout of blood over his feet.

Uselessly, we stared at her naked back, and then I said softly again to Madric, 'Help her.' I left the room as his sword thudded into her exposed neck.

Outside the street was a maelstrom of noise, flame and men running and shouting. 'Be quick,' Momina told me. 'We've got about a hundred heartbeats.'

That was enough to get the crates spread with the canvas and loaded over with wine-skins, sacks spilling apples, bread rolls, onions and cabbage and atop it all, a small barrel of butter. We were preparing to move off when a maniple of legionaries headed by a centurion came trotting in files out of the smoke and formed up in front of the treasure-house.

'You're late,' I told the centurion as he came over and, after giving a dubious look up and down at me in my armour, saluted. 'What happened?'

'Gauls. Gauls happened. May I ask, Sir, who in Hades are you?'

'I'm the man who has been taking time off from his job to keep your temple treasury safe for you. Some legionaries got in before we arrived, but my men chased them off. Your lateness will be noted.'

The centurion had been trying to inconspicuously edge sideways and had reached the point where he could politely crane his head back to see inside our waggon. The market produce within reassured him. 'Not completely going to plan this evening, Sir.' ('Tell me about it,' I thought), 'Those Gallic buggers are fighting like fanatics.'

'You didn't think they'd just let Rome take over their sacred treasures?' I asked dryly. 'Now I'm officially handing custody of the building over to you. I promised I would be back with supplies and I'm already late. They probably think I've been looting.'

The centurion stepped up, and looked hard at my face.

Fortunately with that Greek helmet on my head and the only light coming from the flames leaping up across the street, I could have been Romulus reincarnated, and he would have been none the wiser.

'Who are you?'

There was a pause as I regarded the centurion stonily. After a few seconds the man mentally replayed his question and rephrased it.

'From which officer am I receiving custody of the treasure house, Sir?'

'Caius Lusius. I've just got here, but I can see that my uncle is going to have to work on sorting out discipline when he takes over. Some of the lower ranks are too familiar for my taste. Now get about your blasted business, man, and leave me to mine!'

The centurion went rigid. He gave me an icy salute and stalked back to his maniple, while beside me Madric gave a sigh of relief. He asked, 'Who's Caius Lusius?'

'Marius' nephew. A nasty little shit-squirt. He'll be coming up to Gaul soon to check things out for his uncle. You get to hear lots of gossip while running an upper-class brothel, and none of that about Lusius is good. Hopefully by the time he gets here, I'll have encouraged a few centurions to hate him.'

'He won't have a problem with the men being familiar - rather the opposite,' Momina murmured. Madric glanced at her questioningly, but at that moment she got the waggon moving, and getting out of the burning city alive took all our attention.*

There was no point in heading for the river gate now. We'd simply be caught in a crush of panicked Gauls and Roman predators. Instead we turned eastward, and went along those streets where the *pax romana* was already established, and running red

---

*Caius Lusius did indeed arrive in Gaul as scheduled. While there, he summoned a winsome young soldier to his tent one night and attempted to rape him. The outraged man stabbed Lusius to death on the spot.

from corpses into the gutters. Looting here was noisy but methodical. Squads went from door to door, smashing their way in, and
emerging with booty and screaming or sullen captives. The booty
was loaded on to a cart, and the newly-acquired slaves tied in a
long coffle behind it. Anyone who showed the slightest sign of
resistance was instantly cut down.

One carter, a legionary with reddened bandages around his
shoulder, gave us a cheerful wave with his working arm and
nudged his vehicle to the side to let us pass. Momina waved back,
rather to his astonishment.

'You going out, Sir?'

'Yes, we got what we came for.'

'We're getting there. Do us a favour Sir, and take a string of
slaves back to camp. They're to go to the quaestor as booty for
sharing out later. The army might like to keep that one.' He jerked
a thumb at bearded warrior with a bloody scalp whose arms were
tightly bound behind him.

'You think he's better than my arena fodder?' I pointed out
Vidnu, and the cart driver laughed. 'Our one's not gladiator bait.
Judging by the workshop he was defending, he's a master
carpenter. If the treasure stories about this place are half-true,
we're going to need lots like him for boxing the stuff.'

'How about I make very big wooden man-root, and you put it
up bottom hole?' enquired the carpenter with a snarl.

The carter laughed. 'And he speaks Latin too. You should have
heard him curse when we tied him. You might want to cut his
tongue out if he won't learn manners. Don't need a tongue to
carve wood.'

The coffle of slaves came in handy when we reached the gate
picket. By then we had dropped in with several other carts loaded
with booty which blended into an irregular stream of vehicles
bumping down the road to the Roman camp. Like ours, all the
other carts had strings of captives tied to the tail, some wailing,

but most too shocked by the sudden turn of fortune do do more than stumble along. Slowly the nightmare screams from the city became distant, and our way was lighted by torches instead of flaming buildings. The night air was suddenly cold on my clammy skin. As it became clear we actually might live through this, my body began shaking gently but insistently, and my knees wobbled so much I could barely keep walking.

'Pull over by that side road,' I murmured to Momina. Unnecessarily, as she was already guiding our ponies toward the verge. Someone from the cart behind called out sympathetically as I smacked the axle of our waggon in frustration with the flat of my sword. Madric called to one of the bodyguard, who clambered into the cart and tossed down the barrel of butter. Another of the bodyguard moved down the coffle, warning the prisoners to be silent, viciously cuffing any who questioned him. I began methodically collecting the nearby torches to light our work.

'There will be a gap in traffic in about five hundred breaths,' Momina told Madric. 'Can you be done by then?'

'Knotting wrong with axle or wheel. What you do?' Naturally a carpenter would know. Vidnu straightened up, and the rope around his wrist slipped off as he moved cat-like into the shadows. He reappeared alongside the carpenter, and talked softly and urgently into the man's ear as he stealthily cut his bonds. The carpenter said nothing, but immediately slid under the cart to help Madric with his work.

Vidnu gave me a long, hard look and backed silently out of the torchlight into the darkness. He had been very upset by the death of two of his retinue, and had only been prevented from going back and storming the treasure house single-handed by the information that his comrades' bodies lay in a box in the waggon, well-caulked to stop tell-tale blood leaks and packed together with their swords and armour. That I had killed Romans to avenge Condrusix had impressed the giant Galatian almost as much as the recollection was disturbing me.

'Now?' asked Momina quietly. One of the bodyguards began quietly snuffing the torches we had gathered, plunging our section of road into darkness.

'Now,' I agreed, and Momina clicked her tongue to set the waggon rolling silently down the side road, the usual squeal of the axle temporarily greased away by a thick layer of butter. We went as quickly as silence permitted, breath held in expectation that at any moment there would be an accusing shout from the road behind. But when I looked back, the cart that had been following us was heading past the intersection towards the Roman camp, and no faces were turned in our direction. A hundred paces more, and a welcome turn in the road had taken us out of sight, and after a while our path dipped towards the plain in front of the city, and into the friendly woods around the ruined fort.

Without needing instruction, two bodyguards took off like greyhounds to scout the road ahead, and I peeled off into the bushes to be heartily sick. I shakily wiped vomit from my mouth and scrambled after the waggon and its tail of increasingly-confused Tolosan prisoners. A haunting recollection would not leave my mind, displacing even the memory of the still bodies of Roman soldiers slain by my hand on the treasure-house floor.

This memory was of the peaceful Italian countryside by night, and a girl looking at me earnestly with firelight shining in her eyes. Her words came back as clearly as though they had been spoken only moments ago in my ear. 'When we get to Gaul, we'll hire a waggon. When we leave Tolosa, that waggon will contain all the gold it can carry.' Did she know? Had she known all along that it would go like this?

It turned out that I also was a true prophet. As predicted - before the midden hit the windmill - the eighth hour of the following day saw us sitting wearily down to a late lunch at a tavern to discuss our plans for the future. We were by now far enough from Tolosa that news of the city's fall had arrived only an hour or so before us. Our captives had been freed, each with a small cash donation, and instructions to find themselves homes with relatives in the countryside. Madric informed me that some of the men without homes or families had departed with the intention of joining the Cimbri and visiting on Rome the grief the legions had brought on Tolosa. Some of the women in the same predicament attached themselves as auxiliaries to our little band. None of the Galatian warriors raised the slightest objection to this.

The innkeeper had decided that we were Roman deserters. The Galatians had ditched their Roman armour and helmets, and retrieved their own gear from the waggon. Nevertheless, the martial air, short haircuts and crudely shaven faces screamed 'Gallic auxiliary on the run'. Army deserters are extremely desperate and ruthless men, and the recent misfortunes of the Roman army in this part of Gaul had spread fear of them throughout the countryside. Our terrified host kept rushing about offering us wine, food and slave girls 'on the house' in the hope that giving us everything beforehand would stop us destroying the place when we left.

'So we're done,' I said, stretching my legs with relief. I wore a clean tunic, and after being carefully bathed by a trembling tavern wench, I no longer stank of wood-smoke and blood. It was a wonderful feeling to be clean, undamaged and heading out of danger rather than into it.

'You've got your statuette, Momina. I'll assume that the girlish squeals and groans from next door while I was being bathed mean that Vidnu has got his mojo back. And we are all obscenely wealthy.'

'A happy ending,' agreed Madric. 'For us, at least,' he added bitterly, and his face twisted as though the wine had soured in his mouth.

Momina said nothing. She stared at her plate like a child expecting to be whipped after her meal. Her gaze would not meet my eyes.

'Momina? It's okay. It's over. You can go back to Greece and be a priestess, and never see a corpse again. They'll greet you like a heroine, won't they?'

The priestess smiled wanly. 'I can, I will, and yes they will. You're wrong about the corpses though.'

She came to a decision. 'It's you I'm scared for, Lucius. Are you a good swimmer?'

I wasn't. At that moment I decided to become one. 'Momina? Tell me what you see.'

She grinned. It took an effort and looked ghastly. 'I see you in Asia Minor in your villa near Ephesus. You are middle-aged, and sitting in the sunlight beside the pool of the atrium. You are wondering whether to exercise one of the horses in your stables or whether to remain to discuss the affairs of your estates with the manager. Or maybe you'll just relax and watch the morning sun on the sea. You are enormously happy and completely content.'

'But ...?'

'Right now, this is one of the times when you have to choose about something. It's very big decision, and I can't tell you how it works out because everything depends on you.'

The good cheer around the table evaporated, and I came down to earth with a bump. The Galatians caught the changed mood, and stopped to look at us. Vidnu paused with a chicken drumstick halfway to his mouth.

'I'm not going to like this, am I?'

'The thing is, despite everything, you love Rome.'

'It stinks, it is terminally corrupt, it's ruled by thieves and thugs and everything worthwhile in its architecture, art or literature we stole from someone else. It tells you something when our proudest civic feature is a sewer. No-one has anything like the Cloaca Maxima*. Love Rome? I despise it. But yes, it's home, and I'm happy to be going back.'

A long pause.

'Aren't I?'

'This is about curses. Lucius, curses happen. If I drop this cup, do you blame gravity if it falls to the ground and breaks? Curses are like that. They just work and it does not matter to them what they work on. If there's an avalanche in the Alps, it does not matter if there's a village in its path. Or if the village deserves to be there. It's an avalanche, and its coming down, and that's it. This curse is like an avalanche, a big one.'

'You mean the gold we took? It's cursed? I thought ... .'

'That Aphrodite and Apollo would turn aside the Furies, and make our waggon hold just metal and stones? Without a male-volent and unsleeping supernatural force riding along with it?'

'Well, that would have been nice.'

'Oh, they did. That gold is purified. The jewels are without taint. That's what can buy you your mansions in Ephesus. Your share will get you everything you ever want for the rest of your life.'

'Um ... why Ephesus? I'd prefer Rome. Somewhere on the Caelian, perhaps ... .'

Momina gulped. This was the bit she did not want to get to. 'There won't be a Rome, Lucius. The Cimbri take it apart, brick by brick. Ephesus stays safe.'

I sat and gaped at her. No Rome? 'Impossible. We always come

---

*An epic and ancient edifice, originally built to drain water from the marsh between the Palatine and Viminal hills where the forum now stands, the *Cloaca Maxima* became Rome's sewer *par excellence*. Even today, almost three thousand after it was built, it still carries away the excrement of modern Romans. Had it any other function, the *Cloaca Maxima* would be praised in song and art for its millennia of service as a public good that has probably saved more lives than all the world's saints combined.

back. After Hannibal, after the Allia*, we always come back. We're Roman.'

'Not this time. Rome has the gold, Rome has the curse.'

'But you said ... .'

'That the gold you took was purified. It is. The rest stays cursed. Believe me, Apollo and Aphrodite could stop an avalanche more easily than they lifted even this fraction of the curse. Why should they even try to stop the rest? That gold belongs in the temples of Delphi. When the statuette was taken the treasure was cursed. It will destroy whomever gets it, and now Rome has it.'

I tried to interrupt, but Momina was merciless. 'Your Italian allies hate Rome. They'll rise in rebellion in less than a generation, curse or no curse. And when the Cimbri have done with Rome, the Samnites will come from their hills, and with them the Lucarnians, and the Transpadenes. They'll methodically eradicate everything the Germans have left, and no-one will try to stop them. Rome will not be even a memory.'

'There's got to be a way to stop it. Jupiter ... .'

'Not the King of the Gods himself can turn aside the curse. But you can.'

---

*In the early fourth century BC the Gauls under Brennus defeated the Romans at the battle of the Allia and sacked Rome.

Liber VIII

The inn seemed very quiet. There was a gentle stamp and whinny from our ponies outside, and a stray breeze bumped a shutter against the wall. A ray of sunlight spread a bright rectangle over the table, hiding the faces of the Galatians in shadow. Momina's words floated in the air like dust particles in the sunlight as I struggled to understand what she had said.

'... Now wait. You said that the curse can't be averted.'

'It can't.'

'And whoever has the gold is accursed.'

'Mm hm.'

'So the only way to stop Rome from being cursed ... .'

'Is to stop the gold from reaching Rome.' This last was an interjection from Madric, who was evidently eager to show that he was paying attention. I had another consideration in mind.

'What about Caepio's army?'

Momina shook her head. 'It has the gold by now. Nothing can be done for it. Taking the gold set the Cimbri moving, all the way from their homelands, and they can't be stopped. Not until Caepio's army is destroyed.'

'No, that's not right. The Cimbri have been moving for years, decades. Caepio took the gold last night, this morning even.'

Momina looked puzzled. 'So?' Then her brow cleared. 'Things don't work in a straight line as you ... you Romans think. There's cause and effect, always. They just don't always happen in that order.'

Madric shook his head like a dog shaking off water. 'Momina, exactly *what* are you?' Vidnu heard the intensity of the question, lifted his head and growled warningly. It was clear that the lifting of his geas had not lessened his protectiveness towards the priestess. For once the mercenary did not back down. He snarled right back. Abruptly I realized that Vidnu was no longer Madric's employer. In fact, Madric could probably hire a medium-sized army of his own if the urge took him that way.

That put another thought into my head, a thought with ... implications. 'Vidnu, Madric. Stow it. There's things I need to know here. Momina, you are suggesting that the Tolosan gold might be, let us say, um, diverted on its way to Rome?'

The priestess gave a neutral nod.

'And that would save Rome and her army?'

A decisive shake of the head. 'Nothing can save the army. But Rome itself, yes. Yes, it would.'

Madric looked from my face to Momina's. His jaw dropped slightly even as his bushy eyebrows climbed.

'Lucius Panderius. Are you proposing to steal the gold?'

'There may be a way.'

'All of it? All that gold? Okay, I say gold, but there's silver, and precious stones and, man, there's probably fifty, no a hundred waggon loads like ours. What are you planning to do? Pick them out of Caepio's pocket? Oh, I forgot ... .'

Madric was hitting his rhetorical stride. '... There's a Roman army guarding the stuff. Hello? You remember the Roman legions? The guys who beat Hannibal, and more recently conquered Greece, Spain and Africa. You remember, Lucius. You were there for some of it. You want to steal a hundred waggon loads of gold off the Roman army? Are you batshit insane?'

'You put it so eloquently,' I murmured, still lost in thought. My mind was questing down another line of enquiry, and not liking what waited at the end of it.

'That curse.'

'Mm?'

'It's not negotiable is it? I mean don't the intentions of the person taking the gold also matter? That's got to count for something.'

'Absolutely not.'

'So let's get this straight. Let's assume that we steal the gold. All the gold.' I paused to let Madric have a choking fit. Intrigued, Vidnu asked him a question, and was yet more interested by Madric's answer. The two embarked on a rapid-fire question and answer session. Under cover of their voices I asked Momina quietly, 'Can we do it?'

Equally softly she breathed, 'Yes.'

'And if we do, apart from having Rome and every bandit under the sun after us, we get cursed by the gods?'

'That's about it.'

'Or I go to Ephesus.'

Momina nodded. 'Or you go to Ephesus.'

Late September is a busy time for a shipping agent. There's only a month to go before the authorities declare the *mare clausum* - the 'closed sea'. Thereafter the Mediterranean weather gets even more treacherous than usual, and going to sea in a merchant vessel becomes certain death rather than merely attempted suicide. You can't claim insurance on a cargo that goes down during the *mare clausum*, so anyone with goods to ship before winter makes the arrangements in late September or early October. Also, this year was particularly busy. With the current situation in the province, those who preferred the certainty of being robbed by shipping fees to the chance of being pillaged by Germans were sending their moveable assets to safety.

Consequently, finding a shipping agent in Narbo was a matter of making a few quick enquiries. Thereafter I went to the back of the *horreum* [warehouse area - ed.] on the river side of the city wall and kept an eye on the pavement as I walked. The shipping agents - both of them - were situated on the Cardo Maximus, on opposite sides of that road. All the better to keep an eye on the competition, I assumed. Actually, the agents did not seem to compete much.

Beneath the feet of bustling pedestrians the mosaic on the pavement outside the *negotiatum* of Philostratus advertised shipments and voyages to Spain and Massalia only. The only other agent in town was Gnaeus Quintus Fabius. His name advertised him to be a Roman citizen, and appropriately he advertised shipping to Rome, Africa and *totium mundum ulterio*r - 'to all the world beyond'.

Both the name and the barbaric Latin suggested that Gnaeus Quintus Fabius was a Gaul. His family had probably been given citizenship in return for helping the general Quintus Fabius Allobrogicus in his campaign of some two decades back. A campaign of which Madric might have some traumatic childhood memories. That was when the Romans had spanked Madric's tribe hard enough to make them stop raiding Roman traders in Gallia Transalpina. Perhaps Vidnu had the right idea. Just be identified with a nickname. You can learn a lot from a man's real name.

Today, for example, I was Marcus Afer, Roman man of means, enquiring about events I had set in motion eight days previously. At that time the shipping agent Quintus Fabius had been away, and my transaction had been handled by his *institor* - the slave who ran the business as his proxy. Now the *instito*r took me through the premises to a back office, which turned out to be a half-enclosed balcony directly over the harbour with a refreshing breeze and a view.

Quintus Fabius was a skinny stick of a man, balding and peering rather short-sightedly at a papyrus bill of lading - one of a precipitously large pile on his desk. He welcomed me effusively, and took my arrival as an excuse to break from work and join in partaking of a well-diluted beaker of some nondescript wine.

'Your wards should be here within a few days,' Fabius told me, 'Assuming they were as ready to leave Rome as you say.'

'Oh yes,' I assured him, 'They don't like Rome, and it appears that Rome has little liking for them.'

'Yet from your accent, you are a native Roman. You must excuse my Latin, by the way. I'm aware that my own accent is as thick as a bullock's hide.'

'Actually, it's better than your advertising led me to believe.'

Fabius laughed. 'A mistake by the man doing the mosaic. I got a discount for that - and since bad Latin makes the local Gauls trust me more, I have never bothered to correct it.'

'My wards come from the frontier. They grew up in a military colony, and spent as much time with their barbarian slave maid as with their father. Their Latin has a distinct German accent, which makes them rather unpopular in Rome right now. And they are a bit, um, unconventional for Roman tastes. I'll be frank. There was a minor scandal.'

'Ah ... .'

'Precisely. They need closer supervision. As I am all the family they have left in the world, I have decided that they should join us in Narbo.'

'And what do you do in Narbo, Sir? Is it business that brings you here?'

I took another sip of wine. It really wasn't that bad. A pity that our morning was going to go downhill from here.

'Narbo is a new town. Business is booming. In a decade or so, it is going to overtake Massalia as the entrepôt for trade between Gaul and the rest of the world. Assuming Caepio beats the Germans for us, of course.'

'Jupiter make it so,' murmured Fabius, and tipped a splash of his wine on to the paving stones as an offering to the deity.

'So I want in on the ground floor. I plan to take a partnership in a business and help it to grow.'

'An excellent plan. What business are you thinking of going into?'

'Shipping. As an agent.'

To give Quintus Fabius credit, he hid his reaction well. His steel-grey eyes narrowed somewhat, and he went still, but when he spoke his voice was light and relaxed. 'Shipping eh? It can be profitable, but there's not much room for competition.'

'So I understand. You had competition on the Narbo-Rome route, but the business burned down. And your competitor had a nasty accident when he tried to rebuild.'

Fabius put down his wine. 'What do you want?'

'It's what you don't want. You don't want competition, and I want to go into the shipping business. It's logical that we should be partners.'

'Give me a name.'

'Why, my own, Marcus Afer. And my friend Valerius Titus on the city council can vouch for me.' (He had better – we had paid him enough.)

'Valerius. Yes, it would be that corrupt bastard. Would it be a reasonable guess that you are not going to take 'no' for an answer?'

'Please, Quintus Fabius. This is not a shake-down. It's a real business proposition. I will buy my way in. With cash.'

'Valerius Titus is not enough protection for you. My own connections are better.'

'Wait .... '

'Are you a good swimmer, Marcus Afer?'

Quintus Fabius was good. I could swear that he had given no signal whatsoever, and apart from his *institor* the front office had been empty. Yet two brawny types with 'ex-legionary' stamped all over their ugly faces came abruptly shouldering through the curtains that separated the balcony from the rest of his business.

'This is a huge mistake.' Ungentle hands lifted me from the couch.

'Indeed it is,' said Quintus Fabius walking back to his desk.

'The Gods go with you, Marcus Afer.'

Any further contribution to the dialogue on my part was prevented by a ham-sized fist slamming into my stomach. As I doubled over, gasping, the second thug casually rabbit-punched me to the floor. A hard kick to the head almost caused me to black out.

'A good swing now,' I heard Fabius say as I was lifted into the air, swung back, and launched over the balcony rail into the filthy waters of the harbour below. It was a fair guess that my offer had been rejected. Come to that, even more rudely than I had expected. I only just missed a fishing boat before hitting the water, or I would have gone into shipping more literally than originally intended.

Later that night Quintus Fabius came awake. There were the usual gentle sounds of the night in his country villa - a soft wind rustling the yellowing leaves of the beech trees, the distant bark of a dog in some farm compound, and the soft breathing of the slave girl beside him in the bed. Yet none of those things had awakened him. Instead the gentle tapping of a knife blade on the bridge of his nose raised him from peaceful slumber to the stringencies of a cruel world.

Fabius was one of those lucky men who can go from deep sleep to near total awareness in a very short time. Which was just as well, as on this occasion his life depended on it. Without opening his eyes he said quietly, 'I keep my money in a strong box in my office in town.'

A voice chuckled, 'Oh, I seriously doubt that, you know. But ask yourself, is money everything?'

The girl stirred. 'Who are you talking to Quintus?' she asked in a sleepy voice.

'Let the girl go. She's nothing to do with whatever this is.'

The girl sat up, and saw the shadowy figure sitting beside her lover on the bed. The faint light seeping into the room showed her pale shoulders rising as she drew breath for a scream which never emerged. A huge hand clamped firmly over her mouth, and the girl was lifted effortlessly from the tangle of blankets.

'Where did you get that monster?' asked Fabius of the huge shape which he saw outlined briefly against the door frame as Vidnu exited the room. The girl was tucked under one arm, her frantically kicking legs a white blur in the darkness. Muffled sounds of feminine indignation slowly faded into silence as the girl was carried off across the atrium. Fabius used the delay to put two and two together. 'This is about my visitor this morning? Well, yesterday morning now, I suppose?'

'Come now. You knew that already. Or we'd be speaking Gallic, instead of Latin. My colleague is very upset with you. He nearly had his brains bashed out against the prow of a fisherman's skiff.'

Fabius continued to put two and two together, though the mental arithmetic brought him little joy. 'There was a bodyguard at this door?'

'And don't forget to mention the other three sleeping in a dormitory opposite the kitchens. Well, they were. I've received a strong request to drop them into the harbour from a height which guarantees them about an even chance of survival.'

'And this is the moment when I say that you will never get away with this.'

'Aha! The cue for my evil chuckle. Of course we will. Domitius Junius Farsus is on board, and your patron Aulus Macarinius sends his regrets. That's the two most powerful men in town. Isn't corruption great? You've been bought and sold, boyo.'

'What do you want?'

To Madric's annoyance I now broke into the conversation. Fabius jumped slightly as I spoke. He had been unaware of my presence until then.

'As I told you earlier - a share in your business. We're now taking a lot more and paying a lot less. Buying your protection off did not come cheap. And there's your habit of making guests play Icarus over the balcony. That you have to pay for.'

'Ah yes,' chuckled Madric. 'The defenestration discount. Make it large enough and you get to keep your teeth.'

At that moment Vidnu re-entered the room. In the darkness his huge bulk did indeed make him look like the monster from a child's nightmare.

'Here's an interesting fact. Did you know that, using just his bare hands, our large associate here can pull a man's arm right off at the shoulder? Last time he did that, he stuffed the arm down his victim's throat. Got it in all the way in to the elbow. Now isn't that a heck of a way to die?'

'Okay. I'm intimidated.' The quaver in Fabius' voice showed he was not joking. 'Just tell me what to do. I'll do it. Whatever it is.'

'Why don't you start by apologizing?'

'Marcus Afer. Most respected Sir. I deeply and with all my heart regret having done you violence. I humbly beg your forgiveness.'

'No, don't be a fool. You're meant to apologize to me. Next time you have him chucked off a balcony, make sure that I'm there to see it.'

'Oh, thanks Madric.'

With Quintus Fabius in an accommodating frame of mind we lit the lamps and I produced the paperwork. Madric had found us a jurist who had drawn up the terms that afternoon. It was short notice, but the man had been well paid - on Fabius' denarius.

My new partner scanned the contract with an expert eye.

'You're actually buying in ... um, these are even reasonable terms. Very reasonable terms.'

'Considering the circumstances,' I agreed drily.

'Oh indeed, for this amount I might have considered ... .'

'Next time you should listen to what the man is offering before you throw him off a balcony,' said Madric who had wedged himself into a corner on some cushions. 'Just because you do business like a starving lamprey does not mean that every one else is a natural predator.'

Fabius gave the Gaul an amused look. 'Ever worked in the shipping business? Everyone, but everyone, is an unnatural predator. The esteemed Afer here is not the first to try to shift me out. He's just the first that has made a decent offer. You'd be surprised how many slick Roman gangsters think that the yokels in Gaul are a pushover.'

We took our leave as the dawn was breaking. It started as an amicable parting, though the atmosphere changed markedly when we went in search of Vidnu and found him *in flagrante delicto* in the vestibule with Fabius' former bedmate. A sarcastic comment by Madric had the Galatian at his throat, and I had to separate the pair while Momina did the same for Fabius and his slave girl. For a while the small room had more shouting, screaming and shoving than centre stage at a Greek drama, and it took a while for everyone's emotions to cool.

'I'll thank you all never, ever, to show up at my home again,' Fabius told us coldly. Vidnu had partly redeemed himself by offering an exorbitant sum for the slave girl, and she and a pathetic little sack holding all her belongings now sat in the back of the waggon recently occupied by Fabius' thugs. Madric, in high dudgeon, had opted to walk back to town. As they were ransomed back to their employer the ex-legionaries gave me dirty looks to which I responded cheerfully.

'Get used to me lads. I'm your new boss. And I have a long memory.'

'So come to the office around the sixth hour, and I'll show you around the business,' Fabius told me. 'Unless you think that your busy night deserves a day off?'

'I'll be around in a ten-day. We're off to drum up some new custom.'

The new custom was standing by the banks of the river Atax watching gloomily as mud-smeared legionaries worked in the shallows to extract charred and battered chests from the gutted wrecks of a string of burned-out barges. The work was going slowly, as there were a goodly number of the chests and they were all extremely heavy.

'They do say, Sir, that this treasure is cursed.'

Minucius Postumus Pompelo swore passionlessly. After a frantically busy night and two weeks of unrelenting toil he was too bone-weary to feel any emotion. Well, any emotion other than a desperate longing to go to his tent and sleep for a week.

'The treasure, Centurion? It's me. I'm cursed. Of all the tribunes in the entire army, it's me that gets the job of hauling this golden nightmare back to Rome. Tell me one thing, just one thing, that's gone right since.'

'Well ... .'

'Perhaps the fact that it has only rained twice since we set out? Once for all the first week, and once for all the second? How about the fact that every legionary knows what's in those chests, and what's the point of setting guards if you and I have to spend all our time watching the guards, since they are just as larcenous as the rest of this cohort of thieving bastards? And if you even *think* of telling me *quis custodiet ipsos*, I'll personally have you crucified.'

'So, we spent our time getting the ox-carts out of each and every one of the string of mud-wallows that passes for a road in these parts, but I'm consoling myself that when we reach the Atax, the barges Quintus Sertorius had arranged for us would be waiting. Then we load the treasure onto the barges, and just float down to Narbo without a care in the world.'

The centurion gave an angry bellow which jolted the tribune out of his self-pitying soliloquy. 'You! Guards! Arrest those men on the crane! Get away from that chest, you sons of swine!'

Ignoring his commander, the centurion strode furiously along the river bank, his vine-wood rod of office raised threateningly. The crew of the crane backed away from their apparatus and tried ineffectually to look innocent.

'You think I wouldn't see you dropping that thing from five feet up to see if it would burst open? You gang of thieves - you disgust me!' There came the vigorous smack of vine-wood against flesh. The crew cowered away from the furious centurion as the duty guard squad came jogging down to take the men into custody. The centurion turned on them with a roar. 'Not all of you. Not all! You, you and you, get back to guarding the chests at the stockpile. Run!'

Minucius Pompelo covered his eyes with a shaking and soot-stained hand.

'A hard night?'

The tribune turned in surprise to see that a newcomer had come to stand alongside him whilst the little drama at the river bank played itself out. Unlike the legionaries and himself - sweaty, smelly and muddy after a fortnight on the road - the stranger smelled of fresh pomade. His tunic, though simple and plain white, was expensively made of Egyptian linen, crisply ironed, and the assemblage topped off with a Leuconian *cucullus** one of the finer hooded cloaks of Gaul. I looked and smelled as though I had stepped straight out of my chambers after a hot bath. The truth was somewhat different. Like Minucius Pompelo, I too had suffered a rough night. He had been up since moonset dealing with a Gallic raid that had taken down a picket line, sneaked up to the barges, and used olive oil in jars stoppered with burning cloth

---

*This *cucullus* cloak is the ancestor of the cagoule, cowl and modern 'hoodie'.

to set the transports aflame. I had been up all night organizing and leading the Gauls on that raid.

It had been a tricky job co-ordinating arson by a mob of vindictive rustics and skilled take-downs by Vidnu's commandos. The objective had been to achieve maximum destruction with minimum casualties and by and large we had succeeded. Vidnu's men, accompanied by the most promising villagers, had done most of the actual damage, but the others had done a fine job of keeping the Romans busy. We'd had a splendid time around the seventh hour of darkness, ducking random javelins and dancing around squads of confused legionaries, many of whom were wearing chain-mail over their birthday suits. All to a backdrop of flaming barges that lit the night and sent occasional walls of heavy smoke across the river bank.

Getting the Gauls from their village had been easy enough - they recognized Vidnu and were grateful for his help in getting them grain to survive the winter. A chance to hit back at the soldiers who had brutalized their village had likewise been greeted with enthusiasm. But getting the villagers to move in silent co-ordinated groups had been sheer murder - though nothing compared to the strain of getting them to break off a combat they thought they were winning. Beneath my elegant tunic I was burned and bruised, and my fresh-scrubbed appearance had been hard-won in freezing water a mile upriver with the help of a handful of sand. Nevertheless, the sight in daylight of the blackened and still-smouldering barges gave me the warm satisfaction of a job well done.

So I was stealing the gold. Personally I blame Atilius Regulus. Perhaps Atilius Regulus blamed Horatius Cocles. Horatius, you will recall, was the man who held the bridge against the Etruscan hordes, and saved our infant republic. Manly stuff, standing at the end of the bridge and taking on all comers hand-to-hand while the senators demolished his escape route behind him. Personally I've never understood why the Etruscans did not just put archers around Horatius and his two companions and turn them into patriotic pincushions. Maybe they did things differently in the old days. But anyway Horatius, bless him, set the precedent, and we Romans are big on precedent. It goes like this. As a Roman, you get to lord it over Italy. You get the protection of laws and tribunes, and the power to choose which aristocratic idiot will mismanage this year's campaigns. In exchange, if need be, you die for Rome. Without complaining.

Atilius Regulus, along with a lot of his army, was captured by the Carthaginians a hundred and a half years back, during the first Punic War. The Carthaginians were by this time getting rather tired of fighting the Romans, because another of our national traits is that we never give up. 'Peace talks' are defined by the Roman senate as letting the other side discuss how to surrender. We had sent army after army against the Carthaginians, and frankly, they were getting sick of it. So when the Carthaginians captured a Roman general, they rightly figured he must be a big wheel back home. Regulus was told to present some really rather reasonable peace terms to the Roman senate. If the senate agreed to make peace, Regulus could stay in Rome with his wife and family as a free man. If the peace offer was rejected, Regulus was to report back to Carthage for a horrible death.

Regulus did as promised, and presented the peace terms to the senate. He also argued powerfully and convincingly against making peace. In a way he was right. Rome went on to win the war on her own terms, conquered Sicily from Carthage and destroyed that city as a naval power. And Regulus, as agreed, took himself back to the Carthaginians who put him to a horrible death.

That's the thing. As a Roman, you pray that you'll never have to live up to that standard. But you also pray that, if push comes to shove, you will. It's not that if you fail you can never again look your fellow Romans in the eye. Because if necessary you can move to, say, Ephesus and never see another Roman again. Sure, you can live without other Romans. But if you are a Roman you'll never live with yourself. It is how we are, and that's about the size of it. Perhaps they put something in the water.

I did not know it then, but almost at the time I was speaking to Pompelo, a hundred miles further north a man called Marcus Aurelius Scaurus was talking to a young Teutonic leader called Boiotrix. The Cimbri had turned southwards once more, and met the outliers of Caepio's army. The inevitable clash had led to another Roman defeat, not a crushing setback, but enough to leave young Scaurus, the consul's legate, in enemy hands.

The Teutons did not expect their prisoner to walk into their camp like a conqueror. Nor did they expect him to confidently warn Boiotrix to turn back before he reached the Alps lest he and all his people perish. Boiotrix expected prisoners to do a lot more grovelling, and pointed out the required etiquette. Scaurus laughed in his face. Under the circumstances, this was suicide and Scaurus knew it. He too died horribly - but so bravely that it shook the confidence of the German leaders. *Requiescat in pace*, Aurelius Scaurus[*]. When one lives among people like him, what are you supposed to do? If the gold had to be stolen, stolen it would be, and damn the consequences.

'Did someone drop a candle?' I enquired innocently.

The centurion came up to loom over my shoulder. 'Shall I chuck this man out of camp, Sir?'

'Not until he tells me if there's a bath-house within an hour's walk of here.'

'I rode. My horse is parked out of sight until you lot promise not to confiscate him.'

Pompelo scrubbed a sooty hand over his face and yawned

---

[*]The heroic death of Marcus Aurelius Scaurus is described in the *epitome* of Livy bk 67. Young Scaurus was a relative of the corrupt Roman general whom Lucius praised in earlier chapters.

wearily. My jaw creaked as I suppressed a yawn in response. 'What do you want?'

I smiled brightly. 'To let you know that all your troubles are over. Didn't Sertorius tell you? I'm Marcus Afer, shipping agent. Just say the word, and it becomes my job to get the Tolosan gold from here to Masallia.'

Pompelo's eyes narrowed suspiciously. 'How do you plan to do that? I was told to contact someone called Quintus Fabius - only after I got to Narbo.'

'Oh indeed. Fabius is my partner. He sent me out to see what's keeping you. Turns out it's a bit of a problem with the barges. Was it a Gallic raid?'

'Maybe you should have him flogged before we chuck him out,' suggested the centurion bitterly. Even allowing for his trying circumstances, I was fast going off the man.

'Letters of introduction?' Pompelo was feeling less vindictive against the universe.

Introductory letters from Quintus Fabius and two members of the town council vouched for my identity and integrity. Both types of letter had been expensive. Pompelo read the letters through carefully. Then he whistled for his orderly. 'While I'm sending a messenger to Narbo to check you out, let's retire to my tent and discuss arrangements. Centurion, have you got things here?'

'I'll keep the bastards working Sir. Permission to behead anyone who seriously pisses me off? It would help.'

'Denied. Call me if anything urgent develops. Meanwhile, feel free to flog away until your arms ache.'

Minucius' tent was of woven and waxed cloth, a pleasant change from the leather-hide tents shared by the average legionary. I caught a glimpse of a neatly squared-off camp bed and working desk before Pompelo emerged dragging a chair and a small trunk.

'Sorry about the trunk,' he told me. 'You'll have to sit on that. I need the chair. For my dignity, you understand. It's hard enough keeping the respect of the men as it is. At least the rain has stopped, so we can sit outside.'

After the usual polite discussion, we established that we had no connections in common. Pompelo was from Placentia, one of our fortress towns on the river Po, and knew few people in Rome. I knew no-one in Placentia and could hardly have admitted it if I did. This was mildly embarrassing, as the usual way of doing business with another Roman is to find out what mutual acquaintances we have in common, and then judge our man by them. Still Sertorius knew and trusted Quintus Fabius (a fact duly noted for future consideration) and as Pompelo knew of Sertorius, that gave us a link, tenuous as it was.

'So how are you planning to get the gold to Narbo?' Pompelo enquired as we moved to the business phase of the conversation.

'By waggon. You've still got the waggons here that brought the cargo this far. We'll use them the rest of the way.'

'That's back-breaking work and will take forever. It took two weeks to get this far. The road is in atrocious condition - especially as the waggons are very heavily loaded. One pothole and we snap a wheel or an axle.'

'The road gets better as you approach Narbo. We'll get it fixed anyway.'

'Tried that. First tried to conscript the local tribesmen into it. That failed. The few of the buggers we could catch ran away at the first chance they got. Then I offered cash, and got no takers. The opposite in fact - more workers left. I'm sure that some of the potholes were deliberately dug just to annoy us. I've had to put out cavalry patrols to stop it.'

'Ah. I've got connections with the local tribesmen. They'll be more co-operative if we arrange to pay them in grain, because that's always welcome before the winter. I can set that up as well. You should have contacted me earlier.'

Pompelo thought of another objection. 'The chests. We can't take them in the waggons, because the boxes are burned, broken and damaged. We're dredging treasure right out of the river as we speak. Some chests were totally destroyed. It was already hard enough keeping the legionaries and locals from stealing the gold when the boxes were secure. When the treasure is loose, or boxes are dribbling coins out of the seams, it will be impossible. That accursed raid last night screwed things up - just as I thought my troubles were over.'

'But your troubles are over. You have local talent on your side now. We always keep a large stock of boxes handy in our warehouses. You'll be surprised what some people think makes suitable packing for a cargo at sea. And standard-sized boxes fit more easily in a cargo ship. I've recently acquired a new carpenter. The man's a genius but doesn't want to stay in Narbo. So I had him make a large reserve of shipping boxes. It's almost as if the Gods foresaw this problem and had the answer prepared.'

'Security has to be paramount.'

'It will be. No-one wants that gold in safe hands more than I do.'

So it was arranged. The treasure would remain in a vast stockpile while suddenly co-operative Gallic tribesmen repaired the road between the camp and Narbo. Meanwhile several unloaded waggons would go to the city, and return with the custom-made boxes. A gang of slaves had been churning these out from a privately rented warehouse for the past two weeks under the supervision of our Tolosan carpenter. As I had claimed to Pompelo, the man was a genius.

With the road repaired, and the treasure securely re-boxed, it could be at the docks within eight days.

'We've arranged for a secure warehouse to be rented right on the dockside. It's usually used for bonded goods, such as wine and spices. You'll seal each box with your personal seal as it's packed right here in camp, and we can check the seals any time up to and after loading. Just to be doubly sure, Quintus Fabius has arranged for the goods to be moved by ships from Ostia. We've made arrangements with a shipper called Lentulus Baebius. He once told me he'd make a fleet available to me if I asked him. His ships will be here any day now.'

'In fact,' I smiled fondly, 'they will be carrying my wards from Rome. They're coming to Narbo to stay with me. A lovely pair of girls. I've missed them.'

Pompelo nodded. 'Caepio has made arrangements for the ships to be secure. You'll see more when we get to Narbo. Meanwhile, the Gods be praised, it looks as though the weather is lifting. We might even see some sunshine soon.'

Somehow I was fairly sure we would. The Gods be praised, indeed. Many people forget that, as well as being ruler of Olympus, father Jupiter is a weather god. It felt good to have him on our side.

Our team was now scattered in and about Narbo. Momina, for example, had made herself at home at the local shrine of Aphrodite (an offshoot of the large temple of Aphrodite Phyrenea which lay a day's ride away*). Whenever we met she gave me occasional gentle reminders about things I had forgotten, and which she could not possibly have known about in the first place. When bluntly challenged on this, she smiled cheerfully and remarked cryptically, 'People talk a lot more than you think. It's not hard to keep track of things around here.'

This was true. I liked Narbo. The place had a raucous, boom-town feel to it, an atmosphere helped by the large number of hard-drinking ex-legionaries who had settled there. The culture was more Roman, and had a harder feel to it than the slightly

---

*According to Strabo, this ancient temple was 63 miles from Narbo.

claustrophobic domesticity of Baeterrae. On this occasion Momina and I were relaxing in the *Golden Dragon;* a tavern not far short of being a brothel. The sounds and the feeling and the smells of that place on that sunny afternoon often came back to me in the months that followed. A memory of something lost, something that, until it was gone, I so took for granted I was barely aware I'd had it to begin with.

A memory of how Surisca the bar girl, her hair piled up in a Greek hair-band, had swung her quivering backside to the tune of a castanet as she danced tipsily, wantonly in the smoky room, noisily keeping time with herself by smacking her reed-pipes with her elbow. We'd worn wreaths of violet, with yellow flowers and melilot entwined with dark, velvety red roses as we nibbled on little cheeses dried on the tavern's rush mat awnings.

'There's lots of taverns and fast food joints,' remarked Momina. 'Are you here for the floor show, or can we go somewhere quieter?'

We compromised by going to the garden out back, where mulberries hung purple above baskets of waxy, red autumn plums, chestnuts and apples. I reclined and took a swig of *vin* very *ordinaire* straight out of the jug, and a lizard winked at me from his lair in the cracked wall.

'Plenty of places where it's easy to eat and drink on the run, in Narbo. Less easy to find somewhere to relax when the chance presents itself. Have some more wine. No? What, you want to wear garlands only on your tomb?'[*]

Momina grinned. 'Business,' she reminded me.

'Note the clean tunic. I've made a deal with a local washer-woman that guarantees clean tunics every morning and even a whitened toga for special occasions. And a daughter, ahhh, such a

---

*The poem *Copa* attributed to Vergil describes this scene very closely - right down to the name of the bar-girl. This suggests that the Panderius papers might have enjoyed a limited circulation prior to being buried.

daughter! Hey!' Momina had interrupted by throwing a bread roll at me.

'Look, I use my after-hours socializing to keep an ear to the ground. She knows a lot of legionaries, my washer-daughter does. You'll be reassured by the general feeling that if the Germans make it as far as Narbo, the Narbonese plan a warm welcome.'

Momina sucked a grape off its stem. 'So did the Tolosans for Rome.'

'Ah, but Narbo has the sea to escape by, and German siege craft is vastly inferior to Roman. And yes, they have wool sacks for the walls. I asked specifically. Any chance of reconciling Vidnu and Madric?'

Momina shook her head, making the flowers on her wreath wobble gently. She seemed unworried that ever since the spat at Fabius' house, Gallo-Galatian relations had taken a nose-dive. I shrugged. 'Well, they do say that amateur generals discuss tactics and strategy, while veteran commanders talk logistics. By that count, our dysfunctional little team still makes up a command unit comparable to a modern Hannibal's. The barbarian contingent may be having a private snit, but work goes on apace.'

'Madric never really liked Vidnu. For a mercenary, he doesn't take orders well,' commented Momina. 'Fortunately, these days Madric and Vidnu seldom meet, which is probably just as well. Madric's the one giving the orders down at our factory, keeping the workers churning out our wooden boxes. Now that the pattern is established some of the brighter slaves are supervising the work as foremen. Alborius seems to be enjoying adapting the ships.' Alborius was our ex-Tolosan master carpenter.

'Ship, singular. The one he's already done is a merchantman. The one he should be adapting right now is called a shipping lighter. It's a boat, not a ship. That's what will actually carry the gold in the harbour.'

Momina put her wine cup to the side. She had not even tasted the wine. In the time I had known her she had often held a beaker in her hands, but had actually never taken so much as a sip. Another oddity to mull over.

'Having any trouble keeping to the security specifications? That nice Minucius Pompelo had rather a lot of them, didn't he?'

'None of which would have been shared with a random priestess of Aphrodite. But I'm not even going to bother asking how you know anyway. No, all going well there. Let us now praise Roman efficiency. Pompelo has established a secure area around the waggons. The Cretan archers whom I suggested he urgently requisition from the main army have turned up. Sixteen of them. Six are permanently on guard. They've orders to shoot anyone other than designated workers who step over our little fence. We erect that with twenty feet of grass clear from the waggons any time the waggons are not moving.'

'Each Cretan is paired with a legionary, chosen at random from the ranks each morning. The legionary has orders to cut down the Cretan if the archer himself decides to wander over the fence. Workmen who enter the secure perimeter undergo a body search on leaving. Meanwhile the legionaries have been ordered to declare any gold on their persons. There's random searches and a publicly proclaimed death sentence for any other gold found on a legionary or in his kit. Gold-lust is rapidly on the wane among the ranks.'

'And the gold is moving smoothly towards town.'

'I'll pretend that was a question. Once the waggons are on the move along our newly-repaired highway, no-one boards or leaves the vehicles other than the waggoneers. Who get searched as soon as they step away from the waggons. At some random point during each day's journey, Pompelo and his centurion randomly check waggons. They like our solid wooden crates and look to make sure they remain unbroken, and the seals which he has personally set on them stay intact.'

'Vidnu's done a great job organizing the roadworks, but naturally I'm taking care that Pompelo never knows he exists.'

I bit viciously into an apple. 'I contributed my pension to make sure that tribe could scrape through the winter. I organized the sabotage that had slowed Pompelo's waggons, and organized the raid that destroyed his barges. Then I negotiated terms for the road repair crews. Terms generous enough to guarantee that the tribe - who had faced starvation a month ago, you remember - can now look forward to a comfortable winter. And what do I get in return? When they don't ignore me, the tribesmen regard me with amiable contempt, and treat Vidnu as reverently as a god. Where's the justice?'

Momina kept wisely silent, though she muzzled her wine cup as though suppressing a grin. 'Still it's good to have the hulking lout and his merry men along for the ride. Not that it was anything to do with my charm and persuasion. How did you get him to help?'

'I told him it would be a nice thing to do. He has a very kind nature.'

This I roughly translated as: Momina had told Vidnu that he was helping me, so Vidnu was helping me. When it came to the priestess, the Galatian princeling was as obedient as a well-trained puppy.

'It boosts his prestige, and Vidnu is always looking for ways to do that. Being the man who stole the Tolosan loot off the Romans would do wonders for his reputation back home. I'm afraid you'll rather get written out of the script.'

'So you told Vidnu he would be saving Rome in the process?

'No, he's worked that part out for himself.'

'Yes, I feared he would. That lout has remarkable perception. It's one of his many annoying traits. And he's okay with saving the empire?'

'Ummm, I may have mentioned that Galatia is going to need

Rome badly in a few years. There's a large and powerful kingdom called Pontus next door. The new king is a predatory type, I'm afraid. Charming character though. You like Sulla, so you'll like him. But Vidnu, well not so much.' *

'So, in order to preserve his future kingdom, Vidnu runs the road crews and bangs heads in the background.'

In fact, with the tribesmen filling potholes instead of digging them and the clement autumnal sun fast drying the ground, the surface of the road to Narbo had rapidly become as smooth and firmly rounded as an Amazon's buttock.

'He's sad about losing his little slave girl though.'

'Such ingratitude by the girl, but such excellent judgement of character. How's Vidnu taking it?'

Apart from his growing feud with Madric, the only cloud on Vidnu's horizon was that in a fit of generosity, he had freed his little slave girl. She, with astonishing indifference to her obligations as a freedwoman, had gone straight back to the household of Quintus Fabius.

'Poor Vidnu sulked, muttered and moped for an afternoon. Then he found a Tolosan widow with an amazingly large chest. But he still glares furiously at your friend Quintus Fabius whenever he sees him.'

'I know, but seeing him is something which our Fabius has the good sense to do as rarely as possible. I'm not that keen on Fabius myself right now.'

'Honestly Lucius, I don't think he minds.'

The coolness between myself and my business partner was because my charming wards had arrived from Rome with the cargo ships sent by Lentulus. (Fabius' discreet but unsuccessful attempts

---

*Under King Mithridates VI (the great) Pontus began building an empire which at its greatest extent stretched from Armenia to the Adriatic. As Momina pointed out, Roman intervention alone prevented Galatia from being conquered and destroyed. Galatia eventually joined the Roman empire as an ally.

to discover how I had arranged for this to happen provided me with a certain degree of amusement.) The girls had been introduced at a soiree arranged at Fabius' villa, and to my evident chagrin, the older Afera (known to her friends as 'Beauty') had developed an immediate rapport with Quintus Fabius.

As I complained to Momina, 'It's not just that they both take a kind of perverse pleasure in annoying me. I'm beginning to think that they really do like each other. An odd pair, but your Goddess has notoriously poor taste in these matters.'

'But Minucius Pompelo looks just right next to your, um, younger ward. Does he call her Afera minor?'

'As a Greek, you may not know that children of my imaginary brother automatically bear as their names the feminine of our patronymic,' I pompously informed Momina. 'But to avoid confusion, she told Pompelo that she likes to be known as 'Wonder'. Pompelo seems convinced that it is an entirely appropriate name.'

'So here I am, like the jealous father in one of your Greek comedies. I'm trying not to look foolish ...'

'... and failing,' interjected my companion helpfully.

'... as my two wards flirt shamelessly with my business associates. I have to make almost daily trips out to the waggons to check on the progress of the gold towards Narbo. That's not helping. From the smirks I get from the workmen when I get back to the city, it's obvious that Beauty and Quintus Fabius make the most of my absence. Meanwhile Wonder insists on coming out to the waggons with me, and then occasionally stays overnight as the guest of Pompelo 'To see this amazing Gallic countryside'. So I get the soldiers sniggering behind my back as well.' I tipped the wine jug, but it was empty.

'So in fact ... .' Sympathetically, Momina pushed her wine cup over for me to finish.

'So in fact, it's all going rather splendidly.'

Inevitably, the tangled romances in my household led to

midnight assignations. The most memorable of these happened a few nights after my tavern conference with Momina. The location was a ridge near Quintus Fabius' home on a pitch-black, cloudy and moonless night. We were to start loading the gold on to the ships the next morning.

For his secret rendezvous, Quintus Fabius had slipped quietly from his house wearing a rough cloak and the coarse brown tunic of a slave. He carried no torch, for his single meeting with Vidnu's men had given him a singular appreciation of their abilities. He suspected, with good reason, that Vidnu's bodyguard currently divided their duties between watching his front door and the tent of Minucius Pompelo.

For the same reason, Fabius' discreet message had requested a meeting, not with Pompelo himself, but with the centurion who was Pompelo's second-in-command. It was a pity therefore, that all these precautions were in vain. A highly-interested Galatian stalked unseen in the shadows some twenty feet behind the nervous Fabius. The centurion who Fabius was meeting, far from lurking stealthily at the lip of the ridge near the villa, advertised his presence to the world with a continual hacking cough audible hundreds of paces away.

The centurion was wrapped deep in a *pallium*, the military cloak of the upper ranks. His breath whistled through mucus-clogged airways, and the voice which emerged from the shadows of his hood was an almost indecipherable rasp.

'Damn you Gauls, and your God's damned country. I'll swear you've killed me with your rain. If this is not as urgent as you say ... you are dead as well.' He broke off for another round of coughing, while Fabius looked around urgently.

'It's important that the tribune gets to hear of this at once. I'm a loyal Roman ... .'

'Out with it!' growled the centurion, 'Or I'm back to Narbo and a hot fire.' The centurion's dark form shifted as he moved to turn away.

'It's Afer. He's not who he says he is. He's a renegade called Lucius Panderius. I was suspicious when he turned up, and even more suspicious when I found that he knew about shipping the gold even before I did. He's up to something. You can't trust him.'

'You know this how ...?'

'His ward. She's looking for a husband, and is sweet on me. I turned on the charm and got it all out of her. He sent her to spy on me, and it backfired on him. I'll bet that other girl of his is spying on your tribune as well. He should be warned. That's the kind of man this Panderius is - the kind of man who would prostitute his own wards for his personal advantage.'

The centurion paused thoughtfully. 'What should we do?'

'Arrest him. He's got a factory by the river where he makes his crates. For Jupiter knows what reason, he's stockpiling empty amphorae there as well. Find his slaves and torture information out of them. Someone has to know what he's up to. He has got to be after the gold.'

There was a short silence. The only light was a lamp glimmering from the gates of Fabius' villa several hundred paces away. The centurion was a shadow among shadows as he leaned over the drop.

'How far is it to the bottom here?'

'Eh? I don't know. Twenty feet maybe? Why?'

'This girl. We can take her. She'll tell us more under a whip,' the centurion wheezed. 'She'll talk.'

'No!' Fabius sounded alarmed. 'She's a woman and a Roman citizen. You can't harm her. She's helped us.'

'She's a spy. And we are at war.'

'She's told me all she knows. I swear it. Pompelo would never let her get hurt. He's a gentleman.'

The centurion gave a harsh laugh that ended in another coughing fit. 'So you are as sweet on her as she is on you? You've been struck by Cupid, eh? A fool for love?'

'May Cupid strike you with lust for a diseased mongrel - if that cough does not kill you first. I've done my duty, and informed on Panderius. Deal with him. Just stay away from his ward.'

Fabius turned to go, and strode face first into the chest of the Galatian bodyguard who had moved behind him. I pushed back the hood of my cloak and enquired in a cough-free voice, 'Are you any good at flying, Quintus Fabius?'

Liber IX

'So how are you feeling?' I enquired solicitously, perching myself on the edge of Fabius' bed. 'The doctor says a shattered forearm, some cracked ribs, and a sprained hip. It could have been worse.'

'I could have died!' Fabius spat at me.

I gave him the old line, 'Non fui, fui, non sum, non curo.' which means roughly - 'I didn't exist, I did, when I'm not, I won't care.'* I may have put a certain stress on the 'I won't care' part.

'Look Fabius, you can't go around presenting yourself as the victim here. See it from someone else's view for a moment. A man comes to you with a perfectly reasonable business offer. You toss him from your premises with egregious violence. You didn't even wait to find out if he can swim - which was important, you know.'

'Nevertheless, that man, still in good faith, not only does you no harm in return, but negotiates the shipping deal of the century with the Roman authorities. And you get a full share for doing nothing. You repay this poor fellow by seducing his ward and making him the laughing stock of the town. And then if that were not enough, for good measure you go behind his back - the back of your partner - and try to get him arrested.'

'Take a few breaths before you reply. Actually, remember that you can still take a breath because we are tolerant people. It might hurt your ribs a bit, but that's a reminder, you see, about ingratitude and um, how far tolerance can be stretched. Here's another reminder. See this charcoal brazier? Such unsteady legs. If this brazier were to fall, right on this rug here, your entire bedchamber would go up in flames. And you, with your damaged hip, won't be able to crawl to safety. Seriously, you won't. I guarantee it.'

'On the bright side you have your very own Galatian bodyguard outside the door to see that you come to no unnecessary

---

*A line by the Philosopher Epicurus. Yet another indication that Lucius was both more aristocratic and more highly educated than he likes to appear.

harm. Are we clear so far? A nod will suffice.' Fabius nodded, but the look in his eyes came close to incinerating the bedchamber right then by spontaneous combustion. The man was far from cowed.

'So here's what happened. You went out on a love-lorn tryst to meet my ward. In the dark, you slipped over the ridge. By the grace of the Gods, your fall was broken by some thorn bushes. Praise be to Aphrodite, protector of young (or in your case, early middle-aged) lovers.'

'Now you need some peace and quiet. Some bed rest while you recover. No-one is to come or go from here without our knowledge. The effort here has to be on your part, you understand? You have to convince us of your good intentions. If it seems you are not concentrating on making a full recovery and doing nothing else - well, whoops goes the brazier. Oh, and I'll make sure that faithless ward of mine is in the room and dies with you. That should sink your reputation so low that there won't be a single respectable Roman at your cremation. Though of course, you'll be pre-cremated in any case. Think of the money our partnership will save on funeral expenses.'

'I'm trying to say, Fabius, that I'm very angry. Angry and disappointed. My colleagues are not sympathetic people, and I've had to concede a lot to them just so that you have the privilege of hating me from that comfy bed. Trust me. Right now it is very much harder to keep you alive than to see you dead. So play nice, okay?'

Leaving the sickbed, I made my way to the room which Fabius used as his office while at home. This was a commodious room, since like most Romans, Quintus Fabius did not greatly distinguish between home and work space. Annoyingly, my partner's injuries meant that I and Fabius' *institor* actually had to run the business between us. This took time and focus away from the primary task of getting the gold shipped.

Being busy also made it harder to keep the peace in our little team. With the return of Vidnu and his bodyguards to Narbo, friction had increased between the Galatian chief and Madric. Vindu treated Madric as a lackey, though with the statuette retrieved, the mercenary's service was done. Madric now treated his ex-employee with indifference bordering on contempt. This drove Vidnu to dangerous explosions of rage requiring diplomatic interventions from myself and Momina. Furthermore, as Madric frequently pointed out, Vidnu had not paid him for his services claiming (with some truth) that Madric had already enriched himself enough.

As I pondered the ramifications of the Gallic cold war, Beauty slipped into the room to offer a steaming herbal tisane. 'So you were listening at the door then? Relax. The threat was for his benefit alone. Neither of you will be harmed.'

Beauty smiled mirthlessly. 'You are a lying bastard Lucius. I didn't want Gnaeus to be hurt in the first place, and you agreed he wouldn't be.'

'Gnaeus? Oh, yes Gnaeus Quintus Fabius. Well, it came down to hurting him or killing him. When we read his letter to Pompelo, Momina and I were the only ones wanting him alive. Fortunately Momina is a majority all by herself.'

'How did you know about the letter he sent to Pompelo? Gnaeus loves me (I think) but he has me watched every moment. There's no way I could have got a warning out.'

The words 'even had I wanted to' hung unspoken in the air. What a pleasant little household Fabius ran - riddled with distrust and spies being spied upon. I smiled at Beauty without answering her question. It would hurt her feelings to know that she was the decoy. Fabius would have expected me to plant a spy in his household. So I had sent him Beauty, who more than met his expectations in every way. But, infatuated with that girl's Teutonic good looks, Fabius had paid little attention to the slave girl whom

Vidnu had freed. But that same girl was being extremely well paid to give her close attention to Fabius.

'So even telling Fabius my real name was not enough to get him to trust you?'

Beauty shook her head, sending her blonde tresses tumbling on her shoulders. 'Fabius does believe I am your ward though. You won't tell him otherwise? Seriously, Lucius, he and I might have a future together. If you will let us.'

'Beaut, really, I'm honestly pleased for you. I'll be out of town in less than ten days, and then you and he can go somewhere new and start a new life. There will be money, I promise you.'

The girl smiled at me hopefully, her blue eyes sparkling. For a moment she looked as though she would hug me. I smiled back. I really did like Beauty. 'So do you still want me to drink that tisane?' I asked.

Beauty looked crestfallen. 'Am I so bad at this?' she pouted plaintively. Actually she was. But anyway, I knew my German girls. After I had injured Fabius, nothing on earth would have got me to touch that drink.

For all its out-of-town facilities (such as handy drops to hurl miscreants over), Fabius' villa being up in the hills was a nuisance. The next stage of the gold-loading operation was due around midday, and I didn't want to miss it. Apart from anything else, the timing had to be exact.

Back within the walls of Narbo I sought out the small barracks which the city authorities maintain to accommodate soldiers in town on detached duty. Marcus Pompelo could have parked himself with any one of a number of leading citizens anxious to ingratiate themselves with a rising young officer, but he had chosen to stay at the barracks. He claimed it was close to the city gates and the camp which his cohort* had set up on a newly-

---

*At this point the Roman army was transitioning from the use of the maniple as the basic military unit to the larger cohort. From this report by Panderius, it harvested field.

'What are you still doing here?' I asked him, approaching the officer as he stood in conversation with his squad leaders.

Pompelo answered with a predictable, 'Eh?'

'The sacrifice?' I prompted impatiently.

Pompelo stood pat on his previous 'Eh?'

'Gah!' I made an impatient gesture. 'Fabius' accident has thrown everything out of kilter. You did not get the message?'

'Message? Accident?'

'Aha. We have progressed to whole words. You know that Quintus Fabius went for a midnight walk last night, and took a bad fall?'

'He did? Is he all right?'

'It could have been much worse. Anyway, it's left everything at sixes and sevens. You'd better come with me or you'll be late.'

'What sacrifice?'

'A bull to Poseidon. Didn't Fabius even tell you that much? We aren't putting a cargo like yours aboard ship without first squaring things with the God of the Sea. He gets a bull, and you are dedicating it to him.'

'I don't have a toga ... .'

'Yes you do, courtesy of this laundry I have an arrangement with. You can get dressed in the office at the warehouse. We've borrowed a slave who'll give the garment pretty folds in all the right places. We'd better get moving. My priestess says it has to be done before noon.'

'Your priestess is doing it? Isn't she a priestess of Aphrodite?'

'It's under the auspices of the main temple of Poseidon in town. But I prefer to keep things in-house as much as possible. There may be all sorts of rumours about what we brought from Tolosa, but there's no sense in making them official. Not until the

---

would appear that cohorts existed as an administrative unit for a short time before they were deployed on the battlefield.

gold has actually been shipped off.'

'Do you think Poseidon can do something about the curse?'

'Oh, you heard about that did you? I've no idea. That's not my department. But we always give Poseidon a bull if the cargo is above a certain value. I believe the ships' captains make their own arrangements as well. Now we'd better hurry.'

There was a small group already waiting in the warehouse as I hurried Pompelo to his impromptu changing room. The tribune gave most of his attention to the garlanded bull which stood placidly beside an attendant who was hefting a double-bladed bronze axe on his shoulder.

'The bull seems to be taking it well,' Pompelo remarked.

'Opium in his feed.'

'What's that your Sybil is chanting? I thought it was Greek, but I can't recognize a word.'

'It's archaic. Just like the Roman Lupercalia with its verses in language so old that no-one knows what they mean any more. Keep to the old forms, I say. Gods like tradition. You know, things like the principal celebrant at a sacrifice showing up on time?'

Pompelo took the hint and trotted off to get himself dressed and purified, and I headed off to take part in those bits of the ceremony which we wanted completed before Pompelo turned up. I hadn't mentioned that Momina had strong connections with Apollo, or that Poseidon had been in charge of the oracle at Delphi until he handed the duty off to his divine nephew. *

Once our private preliminaries were done, we waited to form the standard procession which Pompelo would lead to the altar. He duly appeared, looking somewhat flustered.

'Why do I have a garland on my head? Aren't I supposed to cover my head with my toga?'

Momina took Pompelo in hand with that disarmingly cheerful confidence of hers. 'Oh, that's the Ritus Romanus. We are using an

---

*Thus confirming a report which we get from Pausanias in his *Guide to Greece*.

older form than the ceremony established by father Aeneas. I'm not allowed to be present for that one. Did you do your ritual wash?'

'Yes. You do know that my toga has not been Gabinated?'

'We don't need it tied back in a Gabine knot for the Ritus Graecus. You only need one arm free.*' Momina took Pompelo's arm in a proprietary manner. 'Just do as I say and you'll be fine. But remember to repeat the words of the ritual *exactly* as I say them, or we will be at this all day.'

Pompelo nodded. He knew the drill. It's the same in any Roman sacrifice. Everything has to go exactly according to script. One tiny slip and you have to do the whole thing again. It is particularly important to get things right first time when sacrificing to Poseidon. Other Gods don't mind a bullock, but Poseidon has to have a bull, and no-one likes being around an agitated bull when the opium wears off. The beast starts getting second thoughts about the fellow with an axe standing next to him.

The hired chorus began singing the opening invocation, so Pompelo moved like a trouper to the head of the procession and led us through the *praefatio*, the opening ceremony. In this he again washes his hands, and spills some wine before explaining to the Gods why he wants their attention. Momina fed him the required words, and fortunately Pompelo's Greek was good enough to repeat the bite-sized phrases accurately. Our priestess was using Greek which was ancient at the time of Homer, so while Pompelo could pronounce the words, he could have had no idea what he was saying.

Again, he needed a bit of help with the immolation of the victim. In the Roman rite, the attendant removes the ceremonial

---

*The 'Gabine knot' held together a Roman toga (which usually had no fastenings of any kind) so that those performing the rite could use both arms freely - something not usually possible with a toga, where the left arm otherwise has to be kept crooked to keep the thing from falling off.

cloth covering the bull's back and runs a knife along the victim's spine while the celebrant pours a bit of wine and then dusts on the *mola* - the salted sacred flour which the town's Vestal Virgins prepare every September the 15th.[*]

Instead, for this ritual Momina showed Pompelo how to sprinkle water on the bull's brows, and gently smooth on the *mola*. Now the victim was the property of the God. Turning to the trident-bearing statue of Poseidon we had set up for the occasion, Pompelo carefully repeated Momina's prayer word-by-word. As he finished, he turned to the bull. To the surprise of no-one who knew Momina, the bull bowed its head unprompted, consenting to the sacrifice. Usually the nodding is accomplished with the help of a little pulley attached to the bull's nose ring. The attendant had been indignant and frankly incredulous when Momina had told him to leave it off. This attendant (known as the 'pope') now limited his astonishment to a slight widening of the eyes as the bull dipped its shaggy head. Hefting his axe, the attendant turned and formally asked, 'Agone?' Do I strike?

Pompelo studied the docile beast with the eye of a military man, and shifted to where jetting arterial blood would miss his toga. 'Agere,' he said. 'Go for it.'

In the Roman ritual, the beast would be stunned by a hammer. Here, the attendant brought his axe down firmly and neatly to sever the spine just where the bull's neck joined the body. As the animal buckled, a second attendant seized the neck and pointed the head skyward. (Sacrifices to the gods of the underworld are pointed downward.) A knife was swiped deftly across the bull's neck artery, and after the first spurt, the blood was neatly caught in the *patera* (sacrificial bowl). Later this, together with choice cuts of meat, would be taken to the harbour, and there consecrated to the waters of Poseidon's native element. The cloying, coppery smell of blood filled the courtyard.

---

[*]From whence comes the modern expression 'Holy Moly'.

Behind me Madric muttered approvingly, 'Steak dinners this week.'

The ceremony over, Pompelo took the opportunity to run a check on security. By now the town was abuzz with rumours of what we had brought in from Tolosa and security was necessarily tight. The warehouse itself was in a block isolated from other buildings. Legionaries had established guard posts at each cross-roads around the warehouse and no-one was allowed on to the streets which ran alongside the warehouse walls. This included the legionaries at the guard posts, who were picked at random each evening, and ordered to watch not just the street but also the legionaries in the two other guard posts in their line of sight.

At my insistence, other guards were positioned on the roofs of any buildings from which a ladder could be stretched over the roadway to the warehouse. These guards not only watched the road, but also the guard posts. A soldier was punished if he came within ten feet of the warehouse without good reason (and apprehending a malefactor was more or less the only acceptable excuse). At least twice a day Pompelo and his centurion entered and checked the warehouse carefully, and repeated the check twice at night. All visits were performed at random - basically when Pompelo felt like it. (Which caused a certain amount of disgruntlement on the part of Feranius, as I discovered Pompelo's centurion was named.)

The crates made for transporting the gold were cubes of solid timber planking four feet on a side - bulky and heavy enough that lifting and carrying them required serious equipment. Smuggling them out of the building was practically impossible. Pompelo had inspected the contents of each crate before it was nailed shut and marked with his personal seal. Just to make life more difficult for anyone who did sneak into the warehouse, the crates were placed one atop the other in stacks twice the height of a man, with wide aisles between the stacks so that any damage to the side of the crates would be immediately evident.

Finally, the contents of the warehouse were the responsibility of 'lonely Marcus' - the guard on a twelve hour shift inside the building. There was a metal cage with a good view of the premises, and each 'lonely Marcus' was locked inside it and fed by Pompelo when he came around on his inspection. If the guard saw anyone but Pompelo and his centurion, he was to raise the alarm immediately.

Transport was by a team who loaded one crate at a time on to a waggon. Once the team had loaded the waggon, they were searched. A squad of legionaries was to accompany the waggon with the men twenty paces away, fore-and-aft while the waggon covered the two hundred paces along the sealed-off and guarded street to the section of the docks cordoned off for loading.

As the waggon reached the loading bay on the dock, the squads would wait until the cases had been inspected for damage and the seals checked as intact. Thereafter chains would be attached to the crate, and it would be lowered on to a specially modified lighter which would convey it to the cargo ships waiting offshore.

The lighter was a flat barge on which a customized platform had been raised in the middle. The purpose of this platform was that once a crate had been lashed to it, that crate was in plain view from ship and shore at all times. If any rower left his place and approached the crate, he was to be apprehended and punished by the soldiers on the guard boat which followed fifty paces behind. The rowers were not the usual men employed for the job, since - if my experience with Lentulus Baebius was any guide - such men were closely linked with the local criminal fraternity. Instead we were using Gallic river-men imported specifically from the interior.

When the lighter reached the cargo transport ship, chains were again attached to the crate which was lifted by an on-board crane (usually used for loading and unloading grain). As the crate dangled in the air, a workman and a centurion visually checked that the seals and the crate were intact. Then the crane would deposit the cargo directly into the hold, which was sealed off from the rest of the ship. The two workmen in the hold wore nothing but loincloths and were carefully supervised from the deck at all times. The cargo ships and their crews had been kept in isolation since they had arrived from Ostia, and those aboard had no idea of what they were loading. I reckoned most could make a pretty good guess, but there was nothing to gain by confirming their suspicions. For no reason could the lighter remain alongside the merchantman for more than the period it took to unload the cargo. Were there any problems with the winch or the loading, lighter and cargo were to return immediately to the secure dock and try again when the problem was resolved.

Work would stop as soon as it became too dark to see perfectly, at which time the duty centurion would seal the hold, and set up his sleeping quarters atop the hatch. Through the night two guard boats would circle the cargo ships in a constant orbit to ensure that no-one and nothing left the ship.

The cargo ships were anchored about a quarter-mile into the Lacus Narbo, the lagoon which lay to the west of the city into which the river Atax drained. This lake provided a perfect port, being linked to the sea by just a single channel and protected from storms by the land on all sides. As a special treat for any would-be pirates, the authorities of the port at Massalia had provided Pompelo with two triremes. These shark-like warships waited at the narrow channel leading to the sea, one beached off-duty and the other floating at instant readiness on the water. Once the cargo was fully loaded, the little convoy would be escorted to Massalia, where the cargo would be checked once more, and then the gold would be taken onward to Ostia and Rome.

Pompelo saw all this and pronounced it good. He was a truly decent young man, and I was racking my brains to find a way to have him exonerated from blame should my plans succeed. On the bright side, at worst he would be alive to face charges in Rome. If he remained in Gaul then, according to Momina, he was be doomed along with the army of Caepio.

Rumours filtering back to Narbo told us that the main Cimbric force was now at the river Rhone, and getting larger every day as further warbands joined the main body. The Roman army was moving to intercept the Cimbri if they crossed the river, and a battle was expected within the next ten days. In short, we should finish loading the crates just before the decisive battle for Gaul, and possibly for the survival of Rome itself, was fought out in the north. If the gold reached Rome, Momina solemnly assured me, the Cimbri would be at the city gates before the Saturnalia, and by this time next year cattle would graze beside the ruins of the Capitol. The stakes were very high.

Once I had conducted Pompelo around the site, the first waggon was loaded, and we watched it trundle to the docks. Loading went without a hitch, and we stood at the quay staring at the lighter as it pulled slowly toward the cargo ship. The afternoon had that translucent autumnal light which sometimes marks this time of the year. Colours seemed somehow washed-out, the summer's dancing reflections and rich contrasts of light and shade replaced by a steady, fragile light that swiftly faded to dusk. We got almost a dozen crates loaded in that time.

Thereafter I politely turned down Pompelo's invitation to a soldier's supper (grilled pilchards with olives, I recall) and instead made my way back into the warren of lanes in the warehouse district. Re-emerging with the hood of my Gallic cloak pulled over my head, I boarded a small merchantman anchored a hundred or so feet further down the wharf from where I had started.

The shadowy shapes of two of Vidnu's bodyguard were visible near the bilges, one wrapped in a heavy blanket, but still shivering violently, while Momina patiently scraped a layer of grease off the muscular and tattooed body of the other. She looked up from her labours as I arrived, and then got back to work as I squatted beside her.

'So far, so good,' she assured me. 'It's going to be a busy few days, but Vidnu reckons everyone will manage just fine.'

I blew out a sigh of relief, and asked the question that had been on my mind for those parts of the afternoon when I had not been in a funk about being caught and beheaded at a drumhead court-martial. 'How did the second sacrifice go?'

Momina looked thoughtful. 'Depends. Overall, good, I think. It's an interesting curse. It applies to all the treasure as a whole, and also to each and every individual bit of it.'

'So ... ?'

'So if you take the whole treasure, you are doomed by the curse. If you take even one tiny bit of the treasure, the curse duplicates itself for that part of the hoard, and you are as doomed as if you had the whole lot.'

'Um ... that's not helpful, Momina.'

'Well it is. The second sacrifice went well. The cost of breaking the curse for a single item is two bulls. You see, blood has a higher value than gold for some gods, especially the cthonous gods, but Poseidon rather likes the stuff too. So you are effectively buying the treasure off him.'

Momina kept scraping away at the well-greased warrior and talked to me over her shoulder. 'So a single gold coin from the treasure costs two bulls, but so does a one-talent gold bar. If you pick your treasure carefully, you should be able to make an excellent profit. It will take time of course.'

I looked closely at the shivering warrior, and he stared stoically back. 'Do these men know that once we are done Vidnu plans to kill them to keep this secret?'

Momina wiped her sigil on a hank of wool and resumed scraping. 'No he doesn't. And looking for a reaction from these men is a total waste of time. They really, really, don't know Latin.'

'Okay. If possible, I'm going out for one of the runs tomorrow. It's one thing to practice, but the real thing should be something else.'

Accordingly, the afternoon of the following day saw me holding to one of the wooden piles under the quay. Dust fell from between the thick planks above as the gold waggon trundled to a stop. The cold of the water was already making itself felt through the thick layer of grease on my otherwise naked body, and the stench of putrid garbage floating a few inches from my nose almost made me retch.

A shadow grew darker upon the water as the hull of the lighter approached the wharf. The timbers shivered gently as the vessel bumped to a halt, and there was the usual nautical scampering to and fro as ropes were secured and the lighter made ready for its next load. A blond head silently broke the water a few feet away, and the Galatian's questing gaze locked on to my own. Seeing me, the man nodded, his bearded chin dipping into the water each time. A raised hand, two fingers outstretched in the benediction of the bull and the Galatian was gone, silently paddling between the piles towards our merchantman further down the dock.

As the gold was loaded above, I worked equally busily below. There was a lot to be done in a limited time. Firstly, two water-filled amphorae had to be taken from the pile stacked below the rancid waters of the dock, and lifted under the barge. Being underwater, the water-filled amphorae were relatively light, but bulky and cumbersome. Fortunately, everyone on the team had spent hours drilling on the required sequence of movements.

There was a sort of underwater see-saw fitted to the underside of the lighter, and I located the components I needed by touch and practice alone. Opening my eyes in the polluted soup of the harbour was probably a recipe for enduring blindness.

I wedged the two tightly-stoppered amphorae into their customized holders on one side of the see-saw, and a strong push on my side brought amphorae and counter-weight past the point of equilibrium. A tight grip on the amphorae was needed to stop them thudding against the lighter. (The boat was padded at this point for just that reason, and the crew of the lighter had been well paid not to comment on *anything* out of the ordinary, but there was no reason to give them things to wonder about.) Then I hitched the counterweight to a catch attached to the lighter's bottom for just that purpose.

The first part of the job completed, there was just enough time to pop up under the wharf to quietly gasp some air into myself. Then as practised time and time again, I slipped under the boat, pulling my way across the hull until my fingers grasped the edge of a space which none but our little group knew existed. Helped by the grease coating my limbs, I wiggled, fitting my body into the groove our master carpenter had made in the lighter's hull. My body now lay at an angle, feet down and chest pressed into the deck above. My head was mostly outside the water beneath the boat's raised central platform. Because the top of the platform was above the waterline, and we had waterproofed the sides, the boat floated with a hole in the middle*. The top of this hole was covered by the planks of the platform, and through a crack in these I saw the bulk of the treasure box being lowered into place just above my face. The little slot felt remarkably claustrophobic, and must have felt even worse for the larger-bodied Galatians.

At least the bulk of warriors' bodies would help to keep off the cold seeping into every bone and muscle in my body. I reflected that we might want to change the shifts more often.

Fortunately, as the lighter was sculled out into the waters of

---

*Rather like the hole in the middle of a child's swimming ring, though much smaller in comparison to the rest of the boat.

the lagoon it hit a warm current. This came and went as we moved along. A particularly cold patch caused me to squeeze out my bladder; quite uninhibitedly since if anything, urinating into the harbour probably raised the purity of its water.

After a slow count to six hundred, it was time to get slowly and carefully to work. Under the raised platform was the catch that opened the hidden trapdoor exactly under the treasure box. Again I blessed the fate (or God and Goddess) which had delivered the master carpenter into our hands during the sack of Tolosa. With the trapdoor open, the crate was now directly above. This crate and its fellows were the main reason why Vidnu's villagers had embarked on that highly dangerous raid on Pompelo's camp. Destroying the barges had been useful, but at all costs, the original crates that the gold had been packed in had to go. Those original crates did not have the clips within the base that our improved versions carried. Clips which, when pressed here, and here, caused the bottom of the crate to swing smoothly open, revealing a tight-packed layer of straw through which the bottom layer of treasure was already starting to sag.

I wrestled item after item out of the packing case, letting each sink swiftly into the waters of the harbour. The trick was to prevent straw from falling into the water and appearing in the lighter's wake. This had proven almost impossible, so the ever-provident Madric had come up with a fine meshed net that stretched halfway down the hull. This thing was yet another pain, as it accumulated all sorts of trash apart from straw, and its foul contents had to be emptied about every third trip. Nevertheless, this crate was emptying steadily, and now contained little more than straw and packing slats. After dozens of trips between dock and cargo transport, there lay beneath the placid surface of the Narbonese lagoon a golden trail worth hundreds of millions of denarii. I had worried enough about this becoming visible from shore to insist on the lighter taking a different route to the cargo transport every day 'for security', but also because the Galatians who usually did the gold-dumping had complained that the direct route left them pushed for time.

Once the crate was empty of treasure, there was an uncomfortable reach back over the shoulder to unhitch the counterweight. As it swung down this no doubt did horrible things to the balance of the lighter and the stroke of the rowers. They had to wonder what was causing it. Still, these men were Tectosages personally vetted by Vidnu himself, and Vidnu had assured the rowers that completing the job without incident would lead to great wealth. But, just as the amphorae balanced the counterweight, Vidnu's promise of riches was balanced by the very sincere promise that any loose talk or suspicious behaviour was a short and direct route to a horrible death. So the rowers kept rowing, and smoothly adjusted their stroke to account for the now accustomed shift in weight and drag.

In fact the counterweight somewhat more than balanced the amphorae, which is why it had been so hard to stop the amphorae thudding against the lighter when they were loaded. With the obstruction of the trapdoor removed, the release of the counterweight lifted the water-filled amphorae smoothly and precisely into the now-empty crate overhead. A few swift moves were all it took to deftly wedge the amphorae into place. When lifted, these amphorae would cause the crates to swing with sufficient momentum to convince those ashore that they retained their weighty cargo. Of course, those on the ship unloading the barge would have known otherwise. But they had been kept carefully ignorant of what they were unloading or how much it should weigh. Security can be a wonderful thing.

Now it was a matter of winching the counterweight back into place, dogging shut the clips so that the crate would look intact for its visual inspection by the centurion, and then quietly slipping the trapdoor closed. There had been two occasions when for some reason or other a crate had not clipped shut properly, and one where an amphora had been discovered to have a tell-tale leak. In each case, the Galatian under the boat had used option B, which was to tie the entire crate to the boat with hooks provided both within the packing crates and inside the trapdoor for just that reason. When the crate failed to lift off the deck, Lentulus' crew (as instructed) reported problems with the winch or a water-swollen knot on the lashings holding the box in place. Then, as regulations ordered, the lighter returned to the dock - beneath which our carpenter had been hurriedly dunked to sort out matters.

It was hair-raising stuff. Robbing one crate would have been childishly simple. And just one would have left us all comfortably off for life. But this robbery had to be done over a hundred times, crate after crate, every time without a hitch. A rational man would have bet heavily that something would go wrong at least once. And I was betting my life the other way - that each and every theft would go perfectly right every time. One mistake and the whole operation would be exposed, my life forfeit and Rome flushed down the sewer.

The lighter bumped alongside the cargo ship, and my crate was hoisted out of sight. There was no outcry in the time that it took for the 'treasure' to be stowed in the hold along with several hundred other amphorae of seawater; so it would appear that this run too had gone smoothly. All that remained was not to die of cold as the lighter sculled back to the dock. There my replacement would be waiting with two more amphorae to take up treasure-dumping duties.

It was just as well that Marcus Pompelo did not understand archaic Greek. He fondly believed he had sacrificed his bull to Poseidon to get safe passage to Rome for the treasure. But instead of asking that the treasure come safe to Rome, our little ceremony had basically given the treasure to the sole possession of Poseidon, God of the Sea, and god of the harbour into which the gold was now being systematically deposited.

It's standard army procedure. If you have a problem that you can't handle, make your problem the problem of someone higher up the chain of command. Our group could not lift the curse on the treasure, so we could not have it - even if we could imagine a way to spend so much gold within a hundred lifetimes.

Rome could certainly spend the treasure, but would be powerless when Fate delivered her bill at Rome's gates ... together with a hundred thousand Cimbric warriors.

Poseidon was an elder god, older brother of Jupiter and absolute ruler of the sea, just as Jupiter rules the sky, and the third brother, the dark Lord of Many whom we do not mention, rules his shadowy domain of the dead. Poseidon could handle the curse, and probably spank the backside of any minor god who objected too strenuously. By accepting Pompelo's unwitting sacrifice, Poseidon assented to taking the gold (did I mention that gods have this odd fondness for gold and blood?).

Once we had dumped the gold, I really hoped the curse was no longer our problem. What happened next, curse and Sea God could sort out between them. The argument would be that Momina, Vidnu and I were not taking the gold. We were acting as agents to transfer it to a more competent custodian who had accepted the ownership bestowed by Pompelo, its previous keeper.

And we were doing so with the blessing of father Jupiter - who had a vested interest in the survival of his favourite city - and the goodwill of Apollo and Aphrodite. It was my firm belief that things were going smoothly simply because with four major gods on the case - and all on our side – we would have to seriously screw up for our enterprise to fail. Of course, there was one minor problem. Like princes, the Gods can be more focussed on results than rewarding who had achieved them. Jupiter and company did not want the gold to get to Rome. Once our group had achieved this, our fate became irrelevant in the great scheme of things.

My confidence, and the mild euphoria of having done a successful run, both abruptly dissolved when I nearly died on the way back to the merchantman for de-greasing.

'One bar of gold is not worth your life,' Momina told me afterwards as she scraped my shivering and puking body clean of grease. 'And shut up Madracaera,' she added before the latter had said a word.

I had taken from the treasure a solid gold ingot about half the length and thickness of my forearm. Trusting to my new-found swimming ability (I had been practising regularly in the waters of the Atax whenever I'd been out of town), I'd tried to carry the treasure to our ship. Since our Galatians swam like bricks, we had supplied air-filled bladders under the dock to help them get to and fro. In my exuberance I'd decided to dispense with these supports.

Do you know how much even a half-ingot of gold weighs? Enough to take you straight to the bottom. In the case of the harbour, this began only three feet or so beneath my toes. There, slime covered mud, and that mud sucked like a starving piglet. By the time I had thought to let go of the ingot, I was stuck solid to my knees and panicking. No amount of kicking or twisting could free me, and in fact only served to wedge me in tighter. For what seemed like an eternity I thrashed in the water, eyes tight shut, and my throat straining for air.

Finally, inevitably, I had to open my mouth as my pain-wracked lungs forced me to breathe. It would be nice to recall that at this point I properly commended by soul to the Gods, but in fact I went to my death like a rat in a trap, struggling madly with hardly a rational thought in my head. Barely had a cupful of the vile harbour water entered my lungs before a powerful hand closed around my throat. There followed a few moments in which it was uncertain whether my head would be pulled off my shoulders before my legs were pulled from the mud. (My neck later let me know it was a close-run thing). My last conscious recollection was a ghastly sucking feeling as my lower limbs came free, and of opening my eyes as I surfaced, there to confront the blue, stony and distinctly unamused stare of Vidnu.

The Galatian chief had been dispatched by Momina who had 'felt you would need help'. Vidnu partly revenged himself for having been sent on this errand by only releasing my throat long after I had succumbed to unconsciousness from asphyxiation. His excuse was that coughing and splashing would have alerted those on the dock above. Sure. Suffocating me was a bonus for the Galatian swine, and even worse, we both knew that I now owed Vidnu my life.

Somehow the giant Galatian had also retrieved my ingot, and I stared at it moodily as Momina went about restoring me to health with businesslike efficiency. 'I hope that thing *is* worth my life. Any chance that Vidnu will accept it and consider the slate wiped clean?'

'None whatsoever,' contributed Madric. It was unusual for him and Vidnu to share the same space these days, and it generally led to a shouting match when they did. But my misfortune had put the mercenary into a cheerful mood.

'That's a major *officium* you're stuck with there, and our giant friend knows it, blockhead though the pig-headed tyrant might be. Owing someone your life is a big deal. You are going to have to work hard to get this one off your back, I'd guess. Sooner you than me. Anyway, we need the ingot. Operating expenses, you know?'

The annoying Gaul had a point. We had been spending money like water ever since we had left Rome, though admittedly we'd also been acquiring impressively large amounts of the stuff. It also helped that Rome, through Pompelo, was paying us well to transport the gold we were actually stealing. But we had expenses too - such as the merchantman I was now aboard, and of course amphorae and lots of bulls.

Madric occasionally expressed reservations about what bull consumption in sacrifices was doing to the provincial herd. As he remarked, if we kept this up, there wouldn't be a bull left in Transalpine Gaul to sire next year's calves. As I remarked in reply, if we didn't keep this up, there wouldn't be a Transalpine Gaul for next year's calves to be sired in. A fair chunk of the waggonload of gold from Tolosa had gone in buying my way into Quintus Fabius' business, buying off town councillors, building our customized crates, and acquiring the workshop, the carpenter's slaves, their food and housing. Furthermore for our different purposes, both Vidnu and I wanted a large reserve to take home afterwards.

So we were paying our day-to-day expenses with Poseidon's treasure. This worked because we could lift the curse with a sacrifice, and buy off Poseidon with another. It seemed Poseidon liked blood even more than gold, and we could supply the blood with bulls. As Momina said, each wanting what the other can supply is what all trade is based on. If we salvaged gold worth more than two bulls then we came out ahead, especially as we were selling a lot of steak to local butchers. My ingot would buy well over a dozen bulls and probably pay us through to the end of this job. But financial freedom had cost me dearly in personal obligation.

Officium is not a debt as such. A Roman can owe thousands of denarii and duck his creditors to little more than the amusement of his peers. But a man who fails to honour an *officium* is less than scum. He is a non-person. Rome runs on *officia* - the idea that if you do a man a favour, he owes you the same or better. Don't repay those favours, and your contacts dry up, friends stop calling and business deals fail. If you really want to bug a Roman, do him a favour he can not repay. That makes him your client. Even if a client can't return a favour, he must, so to speak, pay interest on it by providing whatever goods and services he can, when and as required. He also has to publicly proclaim his obligation and consequent loss of status. Every Roman understands the wry comment, 'I hate you, because you have done so much for me.'

Madric was right. Vidnu had me for a client and he was not going to let me off the hook lightly. Even as Momina carefully wrapped me in a warm towel, I was considering how to endanger Vidnu's life just so I could save it.

The opportunity came sooner than expected, on a day which should have ended in celebration. It was a cold and cloudy morning on the last day of September. Momina, Madric and I stood side by side at the harbour edge and watched the cargo lighter sculling back to the docks for the last time, seagulls fluttering in its wake as always, vocal in their displeasure at the lack of food or scraps.

Beyond the lighter, the leaden daylight showed that once loaded, the gold transports were wasting no time. Already they were unfurling sail and making a start for Massalia even as the last crates were secured below decks. One escort trireme waited outside the lagoon, the tip of its sail rolling slightly in a light swell. The second trireme remained behind the transports, sail down and ready to fight with its oar-powered ram at a moment's notice.

Gnaeus Quintus Fabius was there for this special occasion, propped on crutches with Beauty in solicitous attendance. Beyond his shoulder came Pompelo deep in conversation with a stocky officer with a vaguely familiar gait.

'Well,' said Madric, misreading my sudden change of posture. 'You did it. Rome may never know or appreciate it, but you've served her well these last few weeks. I'm glad it's over.'

I glanced out over the harbour. Was it imagination, or was there a golden shimmer in the water, starting at the docks and ending where the transports had been moored? So much gold, so many problems. The sacred gold had ruined Delphi, devastated Tolosa and demanded the sacrifice of a Roman army. It had dragged Momina half-way across the known world, and turned my comfortable life upside down. It was Poseidon's problem now.

Surely our part was over? Momina had her statuette; Vidnu had regained his manhood. Madric was immensely rich, and he and Vidnu had refrained from killing each other. There was gold enough left over for me to either start anew with my Temple or live out a comfortable retirement. So why this feeling of impending doom? 'It's over,' I agreed firmly. 'And thanks to the Gods for that.'

'Over? Oh no. Thanks for getting the gold sent on its way, Lucius Panderius. Your Gallic friend is correct - you have done well. I have no idea why you took it on yourself to do it, but I suppose Rome should be grateful for your energy and initiative. But over? Oh no. We have several hundred thousand hairy Cimbri to dispose of before we can say anything is over. In fact, the fun is about to get properly started!'

It took a lot of self-restraint not to jump out of my skin at start of the interruption. Nor did I throw back my head to howl with despair at the end of it. Putting an arm around Madric's shoulders to stop him from bolting, I turned with forced and friendly casualness. It probably looked like a death's head, but I managed a smile and put an amicable tone into my voice.

'Oh, hello, Quintus Sertorius.'

Liber X

Sertorius and Pompelo stood side by side smiling at me benignly. 'I suppose I should be upset with your little deception,' Pompelo said with mock indignation. 'But Quintus here explained that you are Sulla's agent, and that you're operating undercover in Gaul. Well, you got the gold safely off, so you can stop pretending to be Marcus Afer. I did wonder how you knew to arrange such comprehensive security. It seemed well beyond the capacity of a mere shipping agent. I suppose you do this sort of stuff all the time.'

'And we've just picked up those Tolosan refugees you warned us about. The city council have probably not had time to question them yet, but its pretty clear that they were in town to cause trouble. A rough-looking crowd, even for Gauls. It's good to have them in custody, especially with things coming to the crunch with the Cimbri.'

'The big fellow takes a lot of restraining, so just as well you drugged his wine. Good work that. It would have been a real job taking him or the rest of them alive, and we would certainly have taken casualties. And we need every man we've got. Still, it was a useful exercise for the men.'

I nodded, and tightened my grip on the shoulders of the squirming Madric. 'Cornelius Sulla would want me to do my duty for Rome, so I just did the job I saw in front of me*. Was the information I've given you enough, or do you need me to make a full report?'

---

*Neither Sertorius nor Pompelo saw anything odd in Panderius' actions because, if he saw the need a Roman above a certain rank was simply expected to take charge of a situation on his own initiative. For example twenty years later, Pontus unexpectedly attacked Rome in Asia Minor. A Roman youth studying rhetoric in Rhodes awarded himself command of allied forces in the area. Despite his limited military experience young Julius Caesar performed competently until an official general was sent from Rome to replace him.

'Oh, I look forward to hearing about all your adventures in Gaul,' interrupted Sertorius bullishly, 'Including exactly what stopped you getting out of Tolosa with me. I'll want to hear all about that. And you owe me for two horses that I got for you to escape on that you didn't use. I donated them to the cavalry for you. You have their gratitude.'

'But a full debrief will have to wait until we are back with the army. There's an amphora of imported wine in my tent and you are formally invited to share it with me later. Consider it a reward for helping to ship off that gold. A good job that. But it's also advance payment on work still to be done. We've got a fight on our hands. It looks as though the Cimbri really mean to invade Italy this time. They are mustering to cross the Rhone, so it's time for proper soldiering. Any day now's the big battle. That will be something to tell the grandkids, won't it? I'll be heading back to the army today. Look me up when you get in with your cohort.'

'My ... um?'

Pompelo chipped in. 'We thought of it as soon as you volunteered for a combat post. Your ward probably told you. I have been marked for a staff position - mainly thanks to the smooth despatch of the gold. I'm not saying I'm happy missing out my first major battle ... ,' Pompelo paused, 'but being posted to the staff of Mallius Maximus is a huge career opportunity. And you're a veteran. I suspect the men will be happier with you than with me in any case. Feranius, my centurion - well, your centurion now I guess - was telling me you've quite a reputation. '

'Anyway, he's got the men packed and on the road. You can catch up with them in a few hours on that horse of yours. Wish I could afford one like that. He's a beauty. '

'He is, rather. Well, I won't be off immediately. I want a last consultation with my priestess. She seems to have wandered off somewhere.'

'No problem. We've left you a cavalry escort of twenty men.

Veterans from Narbo. They're waiting at the Three Fountains tavern by the west gate.'

A thought struck me. 'You've called up allied tribesmen to serve as auxiliaries, of course. Those with treaty obligations?'

Sertorius smiled indulgently. 'You have been out of things. Anyone who can walk and hold a spear has been called to the standards. There's an awful lot of Cimbri to fight. I mean, we call them Cimbri, but there's Teutons and all sorts mixed in there. Every man we've got, you understand?'

'Oh, that's clear. So that will include Madracaera, here. He's Allobroges, and an ex-auxiliary. Your call-up applies to him?'

'Well, certainly.'

'In that case I'm appointing him as my orderly. Welcome back to the eagles Madric.'*

The subject of my salutation turned on me indignantly. 'Lucius, you son of a dog! You ... .'

'Now, that's insubordination to your tribune,' I broke in calmly. I turned to Pompelo. 'Marcus, can you detail two of your guards to escort my orderly to my quarters to pick up my things? Then get your men to take him to the tavern where he can await a suitable punishment. If you will excuse me now, gentlemen, things have been moving fast enough for catching up to be required. I have a priestess to consult.'

'A warning would have been nice. You know, not even anything specific, but something like, I don't know, how about "Lucius, just as you think you've got out from under the hammer, you'll find that you've been stabbed in the back - figuratively speaking - and please prepare yourself to be literally stabbed through the front

---

*A confusing comment. The eagle only became the official standard of each legion a few years later. So either the *aquila* was already unofficially considered the senior totem of the army (which is quite possible) or Panderius has let slip a remark based on his extensive later military experience.

next week"? A man likes to brace himself, you know?'

'You own the merchantman you're standing on right now,' Momina reminded me. 'Set sail before sundown and you'll be safe. In a month's time you can have that estate in Ephesus.'

'No I can't!' I raged. 'I'm in the army now. Called up to the standards. Well, I volunteered for them, if you believe Pompelo and Sertorius. A man can duck and evade the draft, but once he's conscripted, he's in. And I'm in. That's why a warning would have been appreciated. Given due notice, we'd have been elsewhere when Sertorius came calling.'

'So you'll deprive Rome of a few billion sestertii of gold, but not the services of one tribune?'

'That's not fair, and you know it. And yes, dodging enrolment is questionable perhaps, but it's not desertion. Now I've got a cohort to command - damn them. Actually, they are damned, aren't they?'

Momina looked at me with big, solemn eyes. 'Lucius, if you go, you might die.'

I sighed, stopped pacing and sat down heavily. 'Momina, what happened to your powers of prophesy? Seriously, you didn't see this coming?'

Momina shivered in the clammy autumn air and pulled her *stola* more tightly about her small shoulders.

'When you meddle with the great powers, it clouds things. I can't predict what the Gods will do, and well, Lucius, the Gods are rather on your case at the moment. We've been playing fast and loose with an awful lot of cursed gold. It looks as though it's got you, Madric and Vidnu and his men. I'll have to pay too, I think. But I don't know how just yet.'

'Vidnu wasn't cursed. He was betrayed. Just as I was set up. Humans, not gods, did this.'

Momina shook her head. 'You think it was carelessness that dragged you into the mud under the wharf the other day? The curse is malign, Lucius. It might work through humans, but it's still the curse.'

'Damn. So we didn't get around it. What about Aphrodite?'

'What about Aphrodite?'

'We've served her well. Surely she can help if you ask her nicely. What else are gods for?'

Momina sighed. She looked grey and drawn. 'I didn't know what was going to happen, Lucius, but I've had the feeling something bad was coming. I tried and tried, and I couldn't see what. It doesn't work if you force it, but I couldn't help it. So all I would have been able to say is that things might well end badly. Should I have said that? It wouldn't help. And you did good, really, despite everything.'

'And this is our reward? How Aphrodite rewards her followers?'

'Um, Apollo and Aphrodite have done stuff for us I think, but if you are a follower of Aphrodite, your actual reward is knowing that you have done her will. If that's not enough for you, then you are not a true follower; so why should she care what happens to you?'

Ah, yes. That's the Gods for you. They get you coming and going.

'We slipped up somewhere, Lucius. Handled some unpurified gold, maybe had a small error in the rite. I don't know. I wish I did but anyway, we're cursed. The past few days ... it's like going blind. How do you stand it?'

Seeing Momina like this shook me. Her cheery confidence had carried us all, and more than we realised, we had come to depend on her.

'So we're fucked?'

'What? Oh ... yes, well, no. Maybe. Really, I think we've been let go. Lachesis no longer has our threads. That's the best the Gods could do for us.'

I pondered this. 'Lachesis is one of the Fates. She's the one who determines every person's lot in life, and measures out how long it's going to be. When we get to our predestined end, her sister Atropos cuts the threads. But ... we don't have threads? Is that even possible?'

'I think so. It has to be why I can't see ahead. If our future is predestined and there's a curse making sure we actually don't have a future, then Apollo might remove our threads. It's a huge blessing, or even worse than the curse. You and I are off the map. We make our own destiny.'

'But we are free of the curse? That's a relief anyway.'

'Oh no. Nemesis is still after you. But now there's no guarantee she'll catch you. It's not predestined. Nothing is now, for you. That's why I'm not sure going to fight the Cimbri is such a good idea. Under the circumstances.'

So it came to this. I could abandon my cohort and desert from the Roman army. Which might improve my chances immensely. Or it might not. As Momina had explained, it was the curse that was the problem, not conscription. Running would not help, Nemesis - or at least the curse she embodied - would simply work on other ways to get me. At least on the battlefield I could see Nemesis coming. And if one has to go, it's no bad thing to go down fighting. Perhaps the only nice thing about a battlefield is that there's any number of people that you can vent your frustration on. But there were things to be done first.

'Can you come along with me for a couple of hours, Momina? At least there is one bit of today that I'm really going to enjoy.'

They had shackled Vidnu's wrists to his ankles with heavy iron manacles, and put him behind bars for good measure. These seemed perfectly reasonable precautions. When the giant Galatian saw us, he bellowed like an outraged bull, and strained so hard at his bonds that it seemed as if the veins in his bulging arms would burst through his skin.

Momina spoke to him quietly and reassuringly, and put a

slender hand through the bars on to the warrior prince's tattooed shoulder. It calmed Vidnu somewhat, but he nevertheless gave me a look that caused me to wonder if they had made the cage thick enough. We were not in the town prison, but in a stone building outside town. It served as the supply depot when the ex-legionaries of Narbo fancied gladiatorial games to supplement the town's regular festivals. They had put Vidnu in one of the bear cages.

His men were in the dungeons below. After all, the guards at the local prison dealt with the occasional footpad and a lot of drunks, but the organizers of the games regularly deal with desperate and dangerously well-trained men. Vidnu and company were certainly in the latter category.

'The decurions [town councillors -ed] were going to torture you for information and then execute you,' I explained through Momina. 'Fortunately you've been closely watched by a Roman agent - me - and we already know everything about you. Then the councillors were paid a huge sum of money to transfer custody to that agent. Um, that was your money, but since the alternative was that you get tortured and executed, I thought you wouldn't mind.'

There was an ominous stillness on the other side of the bars. Vidnu looked at me with a slight frown. His undivided attention was disconcerting, and definitely scary. I took a breath and continued. 'Officially, you are now in my custody. You are being shipped off to Rome where you and your men are going to fight and die in a gladiatorial combat celebrating the improbable victory the council and I very sincerely hope Caepio will win over the Cimbri.'

Vidnu's lip curled, and I went on remorselessly. 'Unofficially, you are going to escort Momina here back to her temple, where she will see to it that the statuette is properly restored to wherever it's meant to be. You are going to swear to do that, and swear by everything you hold holy. Losing the ability to get a hard-on will be the least of your problems if you should disappoint me. I will make it my personal business to track you down, in this world or through the Underworld if need be. By now you should know me well enough to be sure that if you renege on your oath, I *will* find a way to make you eat your own testicles.'

'After you've seen Momina safe home, well then feel free to come back and take your revenge. You'll actually be a welcome sight. I'm off to fight for Caepio's army, and seeing your ugly mug afterwards will mean I've lived through the experience. By then, neither you or anything else is ever likely to scare me again. Oh, and remember this. You saved me under that wharf, and I've saved you now. We're even. This time in a fortnight, one of us will be a free man, and the other probably be a corpse. But until then, I've purchased you and your men.'

I pushed my head against the bars and stared right into the Galatian's bloodshot eyes. Behind me, Momina translated my precisely enunciated words. 'You might be a great warrior and a prince of the Galatians - but never forget this. Right now you are the legal property of Lucius Panderius, Roman military tribune. Vidnu, I *own* you.'

It was at times like this that Madric would have come in handy. The ex-mercenary and now reluctant conscript to the auxilia was currently under guard at the tavern, and someone had to deal with a bunch of block-headed officials to get Vidnu and his lot properly crated into cages and sent as cargo to Ostia.

Fortunately my recent experience helped. My persona as a shipping agent also stopped the officials from being too obstructive or demanding exorbitant bribes for the paperwork. Largely out of consideration for Beauty, I had asked Pompelo to keep my real identity a secret from all but his men and the town council. So for the moment my former employee still had a sporting chance of seducing and marrying Quintus Fabius as the ward of the (by then probably deceased) Marcus After - and as a bonus the customs clerks gave us the benefit of the doubt with the paperwork.

Once officialdom had been dealt with, there was unofficialdom to be sorted out. This came in the form of the captain and crew of my merchantman. The mariners needed updating on the extempore arrangements for releasing Vidnu and his men from bondage without massacre and mayhem at sea following immediately afterwards. That Momina would be a passenger greatly reassured the captain, who looked uneasy enough to otherwise have simply dumped the cages and their human contents overboard as soon as he was out of sight of land.

Far more than threats and promises from others, Momina tends to have an effect on people. Before long, the captain was offering to give up his cabin for her. If Vidnu got Momina safe and sound at her temple in Greece, at least one thing would have turned out right. What happened thereafter was not my problem. In fact I had no plans for anything after next week. Being marked for death can be remarkably liberating.

Nevertheless, it was hard to fake cheerfulness for the cavalry recruits at the tavern and I abandoned the pretence altogether on the stairs up to the room where they were holding Madric. I dropped the little flagon of wine on the bed next to my freshly appointed orderly, who treated me to a sullen glare.

'Here. Drink up, but don't overdo it. We're having a quick meal and ride in an hour. But I wanted this chat first.'

In reply Madric stared at me, and then at the wall, unspeaking. Dirty looks seemed to be a speciality of former colleagues today.

'Look, I understand about Vidnu. He offered you mortal insult on a couple of occasions. Drugging his wine and turning him in to the authorities was a typically sneaky Gallic retribution. We'd done the job, so why not? Besides, eventually someone, somewhere was going to translate Lym'p'dic for Vidnu, and who wants to spend the rest of his life waiting for a large Galatian to explain the dangers of mistranslation?'

'But Madric, you didn't think. If Vidnu and his men get tortured and executed, that would mean that we too are doomed. If Vidnu and the boys stay alive, no curse has yet done its thing and we have a chance. Yes, we dealt with enough cursed gold to be under its effects, but man, we have powerful allies too. Whose side are you on?'

'And Madric, why did you have to betray me also? Really? What did I do to deserve that?'

The Gaul sighed. 'I think I'll have some of that wine after all.' He un-stoppered the flagon with his teeth and drank deeply. Then he looked up at me with the sheep-dog expression on his face particularly pronounced. 'Nothing personal tribune, it was just business.'

'Business? You wanted my money? Man, you have a fortune of your own.'

'That's kind of the point. I need a large fortune. A very large one. Mine and yours, plus Vidnu's would about do. Then I wouldn't have to mess further with the stuff still under the harbour.'

'What do you want to buy? Sicily?'

Madric sighed. 'Lucius, you're a Roman.'

'I've noticed. But thanks for pointing it out.'

'Shut up. Um, with respect, *Sir*, just bloody schtup for a moment okay? My tribe got levied of all its young men for Caepio's army this year. Some were just twelve, and the recruiting officers took them as bum-boys for their own pleasure and to serve the army, not to serve in the army, if you get my drift.'

'And so it begins. I was in Spain when I was a kid of seventeen, pretending to be twenty. In the auxilia I spent a lot of time helping the civil authority, and I'm not proud of what I did and saw. For your education, here's a quick run-down of life in a Roman province. For a start, forget justice. If the Romans fancy a house or someone's daughter, they just think of a reason to tax or fine the householder high enough that he pays with all his savings or his daughter's honour. Then they take the house anyway.'

'If anyone objects, the army comes calling and explains that what people have to put up with gets ever so much worse if they won't put up with it. Even so, it's taken nearly a dozen rebellions to explain this properly to the Spanish. Do you think they keep rebelling because they think they can win? For a hobby? It's because the Roman administration pushes people to the point where they have nothing to lose, and after that, they just keep on pushing regardless.'

'You've seen those shits in the senate, the silks and purple they wear to impress each other, and the games and gifts they give the people as bribes to win elections. You are a Roman. You're hardly taxed at all, no matter that you complain bitterly about it anyway. The Roman rich don't get their money from you. Come live in the provinces, and see what real taxation is. I've known men who fought alongside the Roman legions for almost a decade - men who now have to decide whether to feed their children or pay taxes just so that some fat Roman aristo can have a plate of sugared lark's tongues set aside as an optional dessert.'

'There's men who pay everything they own, and are taxed a fortune the following year on assets they don't have. They pay that year's taxes by selling themselves into slavery, because that's the last asset they have left. And their new owners torture them, just to make sure that they didn't hide a little nest egg somewhere so their wives and daughters don't have to sell themselves the following year.'

'So do you really think I was taking that treasure to save Rome? As far as I'm concerned the Romans can go screw themselves, and that includes you, Lucius Panderius, much as I like you personally.' Madric took a long, angry pull of the wine flask.

'There's provincial governors, quaestors, to stop that sort of abuse.' I pointed out, and Madric responded by spraying wine across the room.

'Provincial governors. That's a joke. They say that a Roman governor needs to make three fortunes off the provincials. One to repay debts from money spent bribing his way into the job, the next for buying off jurors when he gets prosecuted for thieving and corruption while in office, and the final one goes towards bribing his way to his next promotion.'

'Now let's say we get an honest governor. He doesn't handle taxes. That's done by the tax companies, the *publicani*. The senate tells the *publicani* how much money to raise for Rome, and they get to keep any surplus. And there's never been a tax-company that didn't find a surplus. And here's the thing. If the governor objects to how the *publicani* raise the revenue, the *publicani* will prosecute him. For malpractice. The tax-companies are all owned by members of the equestrian order. And guess who sits in judgement of governors in malpractice cases? The equestrian order. The same men get to be not just the accusers, judge and jury, but they're also the perpetrators of the crime in the first place.'* Madric spat, and the aroma of sprayed wine gently filled the air.

'You want justice from a Roman court? Then buy it. Rome's as rotten as a month-dead dog and you can buy anyone from a laurel-wreathed consular to a penny whore, the only difference being that the whore might have some lingering morals. Now, I'm not saying that the Cimbri are any better, and I'll help Rome defend my homeland because pillage and rape is no better if its done honestly instead of under the guise of Roman law. But I want my Allobroges to have a chance, see? And so, when the Romans try their Spanish tricks in Gaul - and they will, they will - I want my

---

*Madric is not exaggerating. Exactly that happened to Lucius Panderius' old commander, Rutilius Rufus. For attempting to rein in the excesses of tax companies in Asia Minor he was tried and condemned - for the very extortion he was trying to prevent.

people to have the money to purchase honest verdicts, the financial resources to legally screw any profiteering bastard to the wall by buying the judges and the jury that try him. And do it again and again, and still have money to pay ever-rising taxes for a few decades. It's not that much money when its being poured into the bottomless pit of Roman greed.'

'So where can the Allobroges get a fortune large enough to choke even the Romans? Exactly.' Madric wiped his mouth with the back of his hand and looked me in the eye. 'Oh, I'm sorry for what I did. But only because I didn't do it properly. How did you figure out it was me? I mean, how did you figure it out so fast? I reckoned it would be that girl you'd suspect, Beauty or that prissy Quintus Fabius. They've tried before. You should have been half-way to the Rhone before you figured out who was behind it all. But the moment you heard that Roman officer speak, you had me in a death grip. Why?'

'He was friendly.'

Madric burped, but with a questioning tone to it.

'As soon as Sertorius spoke, I knew something had come unstuck. That meant either a mistake, bad luck, or betrayal. If there was going to be bad luck or a mistake, it would happen while we were getting rid of the gold, not immediately afterwards. So that left betrayal. If Quintus Fabius, Beauty or anyone else had figured out what was going on, Pompelo would not have been smiling, he'd have been furious and the first to speak.'

'So someone wanted us out of the way, but either didn't know or didn't want it known that we've removed the gold from Roman custody. Since both Beauty and Quintus Fabius knew we were leaving town almost as soon as the gold transport ships did, they had no reason to do anything but sit tight and they'd be rid of us.'

'No-one told Vidnu about Sertorius, for obvious reasons. So if someone from our group had contacted him, that left Momina, and you. And the moment I grabbed you, you looked remarkably shifty. The pulse in your neck was hammering away, and your skin was clammy. Your body language showed that you were nowhere as near worried about Sertorius as you were about me - so you basically informed on yourself.'

Madric nodded. 'All it took was a couple of letters. To Sertorius, to say that you'd finish shipping the gold today and wanted to be back with the army as soon as possible after that. Which is noble and heroic of you, by the way. The army lost a lot of officers in that clash with the Cimbri a fortnight back. I knew Sertorius would be keen to have you with the troops. He was eager already, back in Tolosa. Then telling the council that a bunch of Tolosan refugees were in town to cause trouble should have got them arrested and executed. Let's face it, Vidnu so richly deserves execution. He's a treacherous, murderous, raping, torturing amoral pig.'

I nodded. 'A Galatian prince, in fact. Apparently you have to be like that to survive in Anatolian politics. They write it into the job description.'

'Didn't expect that they were planning to question him, though. That was a bit gratuitous. Those guys on the council have way too much time on their hands. You'd think that with the prevailing emergency they'd have better things to do than put some rebel refugee on the rack. It could have turned out nasty for us. Vidnu would have had no reason to keep anything back. Ach, I was not thinking straight, even as you say.'

'Madric,' I said patiently, 'It's the curse. On the one side we have various gods, who have a mild interest in looking after us - though less now that we've served our purpose. Even Momina's prophesy is getting cloudy. On the other hand we have Nemesis. We've technically done enough to avoid direct retribution, but the curse is like poison - handle it enough, and some rubs off. You didn't think about Vidnu being tortured and implicating us because the curse made your anger, fear for the future and lust for revenge skew your thinking.'

'This coming battle is the key. No matter what, there will be blood enough spilled to placate the Furies. Caepio's army is the sacrifice, and we are part of it. Momina reckons if we go willingly to the sacrifice (and with the gods' help, live through it) we come out the other side free and clear. Let's find a chance to put some offerings on the altar of Apollo and Aphrodite before then, eh?'

'You or I can run from this fight. But we can't outrun fate. Now, it's up to you. We can go downstairs for lunch, and then ride out. Or you can hop out that window by yourself. I've called off the guard. If it helps you to decide, my and what remains of Vidnu's share of the gold have been moved somewhere safe. Vidnu had some expenses. Your share took some finding, but Momina helped. She is not very happy with you right now. That should worry you even more than anything Vidnu might do. He has errands to run, but you are on his 'to do' list; bet on that. Actually bet your life on it.'

'So, survive the Cimbri and we'll tell you where your gold is. If you want the gold under the harbour for your people, good luck with parting Poseidon from his loot. Or if you want to cut your losses, scoot out of that window and face a hard, cruel world - including Nemesis and Vidnu - on your own. We'll be keeping your cash as damages. Vidnu's not the only one with hard feelings. Do the Cimbric hordes still look so bad?' Or are you coming downstairs?'

Here's a thing about the Roman army. If you are watching from the outside, say for example, from the walls of Tolosa, the legions look like a huge, impersonal war machine. A great, grey tide of mail-clad legionaries moving with practised skill to methodically crush all resistance.

Get on the other side of the lines, and things look very different. From an insider's point of view, any Roman army is a collection of emergencies about to gang up to form a crisis. At least one unit is generally missing, late or in the wrong place. Morale is either fragile or suicidally high, and discipline among temporary conscript farmers is always a problem[*] with ours currently fretting as much about the harvest at home as about the Cimbri. Then there's always a shortage of something, be it cavalry, rations, or hobnails for legionary boots. After just one afternoon in camp, it was clear that our particular shortage was in leadership.

I had spent as much of the journey as possible with my new cohort, and when one of the legionaries became ill, I'd made a point of putting him on my horse and marching with the men - my feet and legs could use toughening anyway. We all ate the same rations, but these were much better than regular army fare because Quintus Fabius sent extra treats by pony express. (Beauty now owned my share of the shipping business and was both an active and sleeping partner in the enterprise.)

Overall, the men seemed basically happy with the change in command, and the misanthropic centurion who served as my second-in-command hated me no more than he despised everyone else. The same feeling of cautious goodwill was absent from the rest of the army. In fact it was two armies, since Roman consuls come in pairs and each Roman army is always led by its own consul (or if one consul can't make it, a proconsul). So one army was led by proconsul Quintus Servilius Caepio, and the other by consul Gnaeus Mallius Maximus.

Mallius Maximus was not even supposed to be here. We should have had the other consul, Rutilius Rufus. I've fought under the command of Rufus in Africa, and found him an excellent leader apart from his odd liking for Caius Marius (who, like the oily bum-sucker he is, can make a favourable impression

---

*Though changes were afoot to make the army more professional, it would take a huge upset to accelerate the pace of change. That upset was still two days away, so Panderius' fellow soldiers were mainly peasants and small-holders.

on his betters). Caepio had used his aristocratic connections in the senate to make sure that Rufus stayed stuck in Rome.

After all, Rutilius Rufus was smart, skilled, experienced and highly capable. Caepio was dumb, unskilled, inexperienced and highly incompetent, so he wouldn't want Rutilius Rufus showing him up, would he? So we got Mallius Maximus, who possessed all of the qualities of Rufus apart from intelligence, skill, experience and competence. And to further damn Mallius Maximus, the idiot so favoured Marius that the men in camp mockingly called him 'Marius Minimis'.

Mallius was a 'new man' - the first of his line to be appointed to the consulship. He'd gotten elected only because an unbroken series of military disasters had rather shaken the commoners' trust in aristocratic leadership. On the other hand Caepio was a Servilius, and his father had been consul (and had botched a war in Spain so badly that his men mutinied), and Caepio's father's father had been a consul too. And so on and so on through almost half a millennium of military incompetence. If the family of Mallius did well, in a few more generations the Servilii Caepiones might consider inviting one of his descendants to dinner where they would sneer gently at the man and patronize him a bit. But for now Caepio literally regarded Mallius as beneath contempt, and conducted operations as though his colleague either did not exist or would unhesitatingly follow his social superior.

Mallius, on the other hand, regarded Caepio as 'the stinking and degenerate remnant of a family line that would have bred out generations ago if their women hadn't been humping slave boys on the side.'* Just as Caepio made no secret of his disdain for his colleague, Mallius did not shy from expressing his opinion of Caepio. In fact he shared the above opinion with a dinner party to which I was invited the evening that our cohort arrived in camp.

*A rather ungenerous crack at a family that would in 160 years time produce the Servilius Galba who would (briefly) be emperor of Rome in AD 69.

The rest of the *contubernium** were present as well, including Mallius' own sons. So it seemed certain that Mallius' opinion of Caepio was as well-known to his soldiers as was the fact that Caepio quite honestly couldn't care less what Mallius thought about him or about anything else.

In short, I reflected, after leaving the dinner early to take my centurion's side in a billeting dispute involving the men, each part of the army felt that the other part was led by an ignorant and pig-headed incompetent. And each part was right. My glance over the ramparts uneasily followed the line of the river towards the village of Arausio. The camp's position was abominable - and totally indefensible if we were to be beaten in the field. I had mentioned the point before dinner in my most diplomatic and circum-locutory manner. The reply was a patronizing lecture about how battles were not won by hiding in camp. Thereafter, all through dinner Mallius had made heavy-handed jokes about people fighting the African war while running backwards. Idiot.

If Rome relied on competent generals to win her battles, we'd still be besieging Veii twenty miles from the Capitol, as we had been doing when Brutus established our Republic. It is not the generals, but the legionaries who have made Rome great. Time and again the Roman legionary has been led into an impossible position and fought his way out of it by sheer stubborn bloody-mindedness and a total failure to recognize that he had actually been beaten.

That's one thing to be said for both legionaries and their officers. Romans have no reverse gear. If the Cimbri won the coming battle, Rome would raise more armies and come back for a rematch. And if need be another army after that, and others after that. Once the Cimbri crossed the Rhone, as long as there was a

---

*A Roman general shared his quarters with friends, advisers and the scions of allied families, in theory to give the latter the benefit of first-hand experience of Roman officers on the job.

legionary standing anywhere in Italy, Asia, Africa or Gaul, the war was not over. And eventually, once the Cimbri had been beaten back, the Romans would follow them to their homes and burn those down too. It may take a generation, or six, but Rome never forgets or forgives. You could ask the Carthaginians about it, but there aren't any Carthaginians any more.

It took the rest of the evening to get my cohort shifted from the semi-swamp just within the walls to which an incompetent *Praefectus Castrorum* had idly assigned them. Threatening and wheedling got the cohort safer, drier quarters just off the camp's via Praetoria. My effort was not out of deep concern for the men - well not only, as they were not a bad bunch, for Samnites - but because when push came to stab it was essential that these men should care for me.

The weather had turned again, and we enjoyed the drenching showers and overcast days which traditionally welcome October into this part of the world. The heavy rain swelled the Rhone to a brown flood, causing Caepio to condescend to shift his army to the same side of the river as the rest of us. Madric had mixed feelings about this.

'It's Caepio's lot that sacked Tolosa, and took the gold from the temples, right? So it's his army that's doomed. Well, we're in Mallius' lot. A completely different thing entirely. Now if Caepio just kept his army on the other side of the river, and if the river kept rising, we'd have a perfect solution all round. The Cimbri wipe out the blood debt of the curse, we've saved Rome, no-one can cross the river and no-one else gets hurt.'

'Apart from the forty thousand poor sods that Caepio's led to their deaths.'

'Pffft. Romans. Lots more where they came from.'

My 'orderly' was sprawled on a camp chair helping himself to another beaker of wine. While smart and militarily subservient when anyone else was present, Madric tended to relax more than somewhat when we were alone. Much of his time was spent avoiding Feranius. My second-in command loathed Madric with a passion and regularly found reason to allocate dirty jobs to him, usually followed by a good walloping afterwards since the job was never done to his satisfaction.

'There's a man who's going to end up with a javelin between his shoulder blades the minute we advance on the enemy,' Madric pointed out with gloomy relish. 'I've a bet with the boys of III maniple as to who gets to take him down. He cracked young Pullacus' ribs with that damn vine stick of his the other day. Sodding bully.'

I took back my beaker and said nothing. While publicly unaware of the incident, I had quietly reached an understanding with Feranius. If any other legionary were to suffer a similar level of injury, my centurion and his vine stick would discover the hard way that the story of Pavonius and his peacock fan had not been exaggerated.

'You might get your chance soon,' I observed to Madric. 'According to Mallius' scouts, the Cimbri are already over the river. We arrived today, they arrive tomorrow. So we don't have long to enjoy the charming facilities here. So bugger off and let me sort out my armour.'

'Aren't I supposed to be doing that?'

'Trusting you with my gear means trusting you with my life. So, perhaps not. Anyway, I always and every time do my own gear. If a strap snaps or a buckle breaks at the critical moment, there's no-one else to blame. Not that there should be any problems. This stuff is top-of-the-range Gallic workmanship.'

The cuirass on a stand beside my cot received a rap of my knuckles. 'Bull-hide leather faced with bronze, and a Gallic helmet of tempered steel. None of that brass crap. And a short sword with perfect balance in a customized and tailored baldric. You're looking at five year's wages for a skilled workman right here. The armour practically dresses itself. A perfect fit.'

'Yeah,' commented Madric sourly looking over the panoply. 'I see you made it as different as possible to the stuff you wore at Tolosa. Never mind, you'll still make a beautiful corpse.' And on that cheerful note, he took his leave.

The morning did not so much dawn as gloomily seep into a camp that had already been busy for an hour or two. Breakfast - fetched to my tent by Madric, the ever-helpful orderly - was some form of spicy beef hash and fresh-baked bread, washed down with a beaker of well-watered wine. Despite my cheerful assurances, the cuirass actually took some getting used to before it was properly settled on shoulders and hips. Just as the thing was in place a messenger arrived with a summons to the Praetorian tent.

There was something of a crowd in there - over a dozen military tribunes, the *primus pilus* [chief centurion -ed] and the *praefectus castrorum*, who sent me a sour look of recognition across the throng.

There was Mallius himself, gorgeously bedecked in bronze armour, and his sons beside him standing at attention, the younger looking as martial as a prototype beard and acne would allow. Addressing them animatedly were what at first appeared to be the leaders of the Gallic auxilia. It took a moment to realize that even Gauls were not dumb enough to go bare-chested in this dank, misty excuse for an autumnal morning. Yet bare-chested the body-guards of these chieftains were, and with physiques that immediately put me in mind of Vidnu. Their swords were subtly different too. No Gallic sword had a dragon-head pommel such as that which one of the chiefs was wearing. This sword was oddly slung further around the hip, in such a way that it would slant across the wearer's lower back when he was on horseback. With a shock, I realized that these men were Cimbri. More precisely, ambassadors and their bodyguard.

'Negotiations?' I muttered the query to young Pompelo alongside of whom I eventually squirmed through the crush. He nodded.

'They were waiting at the Porta Principalis when it got light. No-one saw them arrive. The mist lifted a bit and there they were.'

'Not very subtly telling us that they know exactly where we are, and that they even know where the main gate to a Roman marching camp is, and they can find it in the dark. Do we have any idea at all where the main Cimbric army is?'

'Very close. We've sent out scouts. They didn't come back. Can't see much from the ramparts with this accursed mist.'

'Probably they're up to two miles away from us, east of the river. They arrived at least four hours ago.'

Pompelo gave me a startled look. 'Who's been talking to you? What evidence do you have for that?'

'A load of shit.'

'Eh?'

'As a late arrival, let's assume you were not stupid enough to locate your tent downwind of where forty thousand Roman soldiers have been emptying their bowels for a week? Me neither. Yet on the way here there was a distinct odour of crap in the breeze. The sort of thing that a very large army with poor toilet training might dump into the fields if the men were expecting a battle in the morning. The breeze is from the north-east, so either Caepio's army has relocated again, which I first thought, or the enemy army has arrived, which is what these ambassadors suggest.'

'They come in peace,' murmured Pompelo sardonically. By now a number of those nearby were giving us dirty looks and starting to mutter, so we dutifully shut up and listened to the speeches. The Cimbric side was translated by a middle-aged slave whose wistful looks at our armoured ranks strongly suggested that he was a former legionary captured in one of our nation's earlier clashes with the Cimbri - possibly when they slapped our legions around at the Noreia about a decade ago.[*]

Basically, when their speeches were stripped of their fine phrasing, the Cimbri were asking Mallius and Caepio to step politely aside so they they could go and pillage Gaul. It seemed that the self-sacrifice and courage of young Scaurus and the ferocity of the Roman response to date had unsettled the barbarians to the point where they were uncertain of taking on Italy itself. Then, when Caepio moved his army across the river, he had camped aggressively close to the barbarians. This was because with his normal incompetence, Caepio had not properly scouted the terrain. In the foggy weather he had not the slightest idea that the Cimbri were there. But the Cimbri did not know that. To them Caepio's camp had been an aggressive move which made Rome seem raring to get into the fight.

Mallius launched a long counter-argument which involved detailing all Rome's military victories since before the Hannibalic war. The general gist was that Rome was unbeatable, so the barbarians had better not try. This stirring declaration was somewhat weakened by Mallius' rather pusillanimous admission that he was not going to sacrifice his army to defend Rome's allies in the region. So Narbo and the province was off-limits, but anyone else in Gaul was fair game. (Madric would be indignant but unsurprised to hear of his Allobroges being thrown to the wolves in the name of realpolitik.)

As for Rome standing aside to also allow the rape of Spain, well, Mallius was prepared to put it to the senate while the Cimbri passed the time plundering what was left of Gaul north of the Rhone. Part of me winced at this un-Roman betrayal of friends and allies. The other parts cheerfully pointed out that this meant that no-one would be trying to kill me today. Maybe the curse of Tolosa

---

[*]When a fortuitous storm saved the Romans from annihilation. Thereafter the Cimbri had withdrawn and spent the intervening years pillaging northern Gaul.

had been stayed after all.

That, naturally, was the moment when a messenger burst without ceremony into our little gathering, and breathlessly announced that the mist was lifting. It revealed that Caepio's army had left its tents and was about to launch a full-scale assault on the Cimbric camp.

Liber XI

What happened to the Cimbric ambassadors after that, like much else of that morning, remains a total mystery to me. Did Caepio attack the Cimbric camp out of jealousy because the ambassadors had come to Mallius and not to him? Or did he launch his attack out of spite because Mallius did not invite him to the negotiations? Or did Caepio think that because some of the Cimbric chiefs were with Mallius, this was a great time to attack their camp?

In other words, did petty spite and envy overcome Caepio's military judgement, or was there never any sound judgement to be overcome in the first place? A dumb question really. What genius, when heavily outnumbered, attacks with just half the available force?

These questions rushed around inside my head as I, like almost everyone in the tent, promptly abandoned the conference and rushed off to get our men into battle order. Mallius hastily instructed us to get stood to, and wait for further orders. Feranius, who might be nasty but was also highly competent, had established our cohort's stand-to position in the intervallum. He would be mustering the men now, so I headed there at the run.

All Roman camps have a wide space between the tents and the ramparts, and this is called the intervallum. The intervallum is there because Romans fight best when formed up in their ranks. Sometimes there's no time to form up outside the walls, because the opposition have taken the initiative and come into the camp itself. So you want a clear space to deal with the gate-crashers because fighting among tents is plain messy. Furthermore, every Roman marching tent is saturated with lanolin oil. This - theoretically - keeps the thing waterproof, but it is a good idea to keep oil-saturated material well away from items such as the flaming arrows which nasty-minded individuals like to shoot over the ramparts.

Finally, and more frequently, a Roman army occasionally needs somewhere to form up in battle order within the walls before marching out of the gates or manning the ramparts. Deployments directly from tent to battle line seldom go well as individuals get lost, arrive late and generally confuse things. So being Roman and methodical, what we do is designate a 'stand-to area' for each unit. Then, when the trumpet sounds, everyone drops what they are doing and rushes to take their place in the ranks. There, while still in a place of safety, the unit commander can give armour and weapons a quick inspection, and await further instructions.

And wait, and wait, and wait. All the while with a cold, damp wind sending distant sounds of mortal combat floating over the ramparts. Weapon hammered against weapon, and we heard hoarse shouts and the screams of horses and men, muted by distance but still vivid. After the arm-twisting involved in the relocation last night, we had ended up stationed opposite the cavalry on the via Praetoria, which is the main road which runs across the top centre of every Roman camp. However, we'd kept our old stand-to point near the Porta Decumana which is basically the camp's back door. It had taken a certain amount of pushing and shoving through the rest of the army for everyone to get into place, but when we got there it bestowed a certain advantage.

Ideally, a Roman camp should be situated in a defensible position, with the main gate facing the enemy and the rear portion being uphill if that's possible. As our camp's designers had expected the enemy to come over the river, the front gate faced the Rhone and the rest of the camp gently sloped uphill from there. Textbook stuff, except the builders had neglected the 'defensible position' bit. The slope behind the camp continued upwards. In fact, it got steeper, so a child with a slingshot could stand uphill of us and hit the commander's tent with a stone. But at least, once I had scrambled up on to the rear rampart, that slope gave a clear view north over the rain-slick tents of the camp towards the mist still swirling on the river – and to the east, where between occasional sheets of drizzle I had a confused and fragmentary view of Caepio's continuing attack on the Cimbric army.

From this less-than-perfect vantage spot, I could see that Caepio had chosen Roman army Attack Option A, which is to go straight for the enemy army like a bull at a gate. (Come to think of it, there is no Attack Option B.) Trouble was, Caepio was expected. Unsurprising really. Romans like to pride themselves on their bluff, frank honesty, but in reality our leaders have used treachery and double-cross as tactical weapons for the last century. Anyone who trusts the moral integrity of a Roman general deserves to lose.

So even as they started negotiations, the Cimbri had simultaneously girded their loins for battle. The limited view from Mallius' camp did not reveal many tents behind the Cimbric army. There was not even the expected mass of waggons at the rear. This suggested that the Cimbri had left their camp followers and baggage on the safe side of the swollen Rhone. So basically, Caepio had attacked a massive field army that was merely dozing in its ranks.

He had made significant headway too. It looked as though the steel spearhead of the Roman legions was deeply embedded in the paler mass of Germanic warriors. I flinched at the sight. Ever since Hannibal had wiped out over a hundred thousand legionaries at Cannae, there is nothing a Roman soldier fears so much as envelopment.

Head-on, the legionaries were more than a match for the warriors fighting them. They were driving their opponents back. However, the checker-board formation of the fighting maniples was losing shape as the Germanic warriors flowed around the sides of the legions, forcing the spearmen of the triarii in the rear ranks to move up and face to the side to prevent the army from being outflanked. The tip of the spearhead moved in deeper as the front-rank legionaries cut into the enemy opposing them. But the lines to the side were stretching thin. This was especially so on the north flank, that is, the river side, where men instinctively turned slightly left to get greater protection from their shield arms, forcing the men next to them to shuffle up to cover the gap. Here the line was crescent-shaped, giving in the centre, but bolstered at the base as reserves were thrown in.

A group of horsemen went galloping madly from the gates of our camp, heading directly towards where I assumed Caepio's command position would be, though this was not visible from where I stood. The feathers tied to the horsemen's spears signalled that these were couriers. Naturally Mallius would want to know what his colleague was up to, and would suggest that perhaps Caepio might like to co-ordinate whatever he was doing with the other half of Rome's army, but such messengers would have gone out a good hour ago. The air of urgency about this second group of couriers bordered on panic. It took a moment or two to work out why.

The Cimbric army was not quite a huge shapeless mass. There were clumps, where different nations such as the Teutones stood together, and the soldiers always clustered closer to their chieftains and sacred banners, so the enemy army had a kind of granular appearance. Now one clump, like a mass of mist pulled by a contrary wind, was pulling loose from the side. From a distance of two miles, the mass of warriors seemed to flow in slow motion, slowly roiling away from the main body. In fact this 'clump' was some five thousand men, moving at a dead run past the outer limits of the Roman line, around the last of the reserves and towards the unsupported base of the Roman spearhead. No-one from Caepio's army had our advantage of height, and his men had not noticed this.

Surely this would be the moment for our army to move up fast in support. I readied myself to hurry down from my vantage point the moment I saw the messengers fan out along the lanes between the tents while the red battle flag broke out out over Mallius' praetorium. But nothing happened. Those of us peering over the ramparts might have been spectators at a Greek theatre, sitting in the amphitheatre watching a tragedy played out on a distant stage.

A young cavalry officer came over to me, wincing fastidiously when a loose plank on the ramparts squelched muddy water over his sandalled toes. We stared silently at the distant battlefield until another bank of rain blocked it from our view.

'What do you think is keeping Mallius?' asked the cavalryman curiously. I pulled a face.

'He'll be sacrificing.'

There was a pause while the officer worked this one out. Then he said, 'Ah. Shit.'

'Sterculinus himself,*' I agreed. Before battle, a Roman commander sacrifices a sheep to the Gods for their divine blessing on the day's events. Then a priest, called a haruspex, inspects the victim's liver for signs that the Gods will be on our side. Neutral is okay, and a creative haruspex can generally find a silver lining in every liver to gee up the general and the men. But sometimes the omens are so downright diabolical that the only option is to sacrifice another sheep and get a second opinion. And if that fails to produce a happy omen, sacrifice another and if necessary another, and then another. By now Mallius' praetorium probably resembled a feast-day slaughter-house with the Gods still refusing to hold out any hope of a happy ending. Oh shit, indeed.

Eventually either the Gods gave way, or Mallius ran out of sheep, because messengers began moving out along the lines between the tents.

'Too late,' my companion murmured.

The rain had shifted, and we could see that Caepio was now

---

*Only the Romans would have a God of Manure.

aware of the threat to his flank. Light cavalry skirmished before the oncoming block of attackers, slowing, but not stopping them. Two sets of infantry, their formations becoming ragged in their haste, were charging across the rear of the battlefield, but it was clear they would not arrive in time.

Nothing disconcerts a soldier in a battle-line more than an enemy who hits him between the shoulder-blades, and the attack from behind was throwing the entire Roman army off balance. The triarii at the base of the Roman line had turned, and in trying to defend in opposing directions had failed to defend in either. The situation there was in chaos, with triumphant groups of Cimbric warriors breaking through completely. The Roman battle line began the first stages of a slow-motion collapse.

I once saw a section of city wall come down as our besieging army undermined and burned through the timbers holding up the foundations*. At first, nothing happens beyond a slight local sagging. Then cracks start to radiate through the whole, and large sections begin to break off and crumble, then the entire edifice - though still with substantial parts intact - majestically slides down into total ruin. My gut clenched as I watched the same process bring down Caepio's army of 40,000 men. There was no point in watching the disaster unfold, and I couldn't even if I wanted to. The horseman with my orders had almost arrived, and I plunged down the muddy rampart to meet him.

'Where is Tribune Lucius Panderius of Cohors I Safinium?'

'I'm ten feet away,' I replied testily. 'You don't have to bellow.' An almost visible fog of terror surrounded the man. It infected his horse which tried to skitter away as I stepped closer.

I muttered, 'Pull yourself together, for the God's sake. You are upsetting the men. You've just come from the commanding officer.

---

*The original foundations would have been of stone, but Roman engineers replaced these with timber set to burn through just as an attack began on the surface.

At least try to pretend to be confident.'

The messenger closed his eyes, and then passed on our orders. A jerk of my head summoned Feranius and his junior centurions. I repeated Mallius' orders to them in front of the messenger so that we were all in agreement about what the cohort was supposed to do.

'Cohors I Safinium will be the flank guard. We are to take station alongside the river and hold position alongside IV Campanestris. We are to remain in position until relieved or given further orders. We'll have a turma of Spanish cavalry in support. Everyone understand?'

There was general agreement. The messenger trotted off to spread panic among his next set of listeners, while Feranius turned to address the men.

'Listen up you lot! The proconsul's army has got into some difficulty, and it will be falling back on our camp. We're going out to screen their withdrawal. Nothing to do but hold our station. We'll be back in our tents by mid-afternoon.'

Yes, I thought, and I'm going to be selected as one of next year's Vestal Virgins. 'Some difficulty?' I grunted to Feranius as the cohort went through the general orgy of armour-tightening and scabbard checking which usually follows such announcements. 'That's like calling an elephant a large mouse with a short tail.'

'Wouldn't know, Sir', said Feranius stolidly. 'Never seen an elephant myself.'

'Okay, but you might like to quietly let your centurions know that they'll have to brace for the broken remnants of Caepio's army streaming past in about ten minutes, closely followed by lots of Cimbri. I stress the word 'lots', centurion. Lots and lots of Cimbri.'

Feranius grunted, and took himself off to his junior colleagues. The unit ahead of us swung into motion and the army started marching out.

It is a strange thing, but when you see several hundred

Samnites phlegmatically fall into marching order, and the plumes of thousands and thousands of Roman helmets bobbing ahead of them, it's hard to think that you might be in danger. The human mind just can't take in such numbers. Maybe, in the distant past before legends began, when we all lived in small tribes in the forest, thirty warriors were all that anyone needed to be safe. I think some ancestral memory clings to that fact. With so many legions going out to battle, we had to have a chance. Entire provinces have been conquered with less.

The sounds of battle were louder as we approached the gate, overcoming the crunch of hobnails on gravel, the jingle of chain mail, and the patter of rain on our armour and helmets. If we did win today, there would be a huge demand for sand-barrels to scour rust off our armour tomorrow*. The fast-approaching conflict sounded like a great wind, a confused cacophony of shouts and screams with a continual blare of trumpets, battle cries and miscellaneous howls blending into a single, sustained multi-layered impact on the senses.

Someone - one of the officers I had seen in the tent earlier - was on horseback by the gate shouting out a speech. It was not Mallius, as he was presumably by the main gate, from which the greater part of the army would be leaving. Since we were headed for the extreme flank, we left by the river gate. We saw nothing ahead but banks of mist, and rain that formed puddles amid the greasy, calf-high grass, and the Rhone itself, orange-brown and swirling sullenly as it silently carried branches and debris away to our left.

'We'll form up level with the camp wall, double maniples on the right,' I told Feranius. 'Can the men hold?'

The centurion nodded, his face grim. 'They're a stubborn lot,

---

*The best way to de-rust chain mail is to put it into a bucket of sand and roll the bucket back and forth for a minute or two. The chafing of the links scrapes off the rust.

Sir.'

'Tell the centurions, one round of pilums and don't counter-charge more than a dozen paces. We need to hold formation. And ... . Okay - that knoll there, overlooking the river. If the worst comes to the worst, we fall back on that to make a stand.'

Feranius turned to study the knoll. 'It's small,' he said, 'won't get more than a few maniples on there ... .' His face twisted and he spat, then walked off without saying another word.

There was a rolling sound of hooves, and a bunch of horsemen broke out of the mist. They wore Roman armour, but had neither shields nor spears. They paid us no heed, but angled determinedly for the hill behind the camp. Some of the horses were bloodied, and all were blown, one with great streamers of bloody foam pouring from its nostrils as the riders went past. There was a solidity to the rain now, running figures which became apparent only a few hundred paces away.

'Form up! Form up at the double!' I bellowed, and windmilled my arms as I directed our units into place. A line of hastati skidded into position beside me, and I noted that the rain-beaded face of the nearest teenager was as white as a sheet.

'Cheer up,' I told him loudly. 'I've done this dozens of times, and it's never as bad as it seems just beforehand.'

Then I noted that the second line, the veteres, had formed up overlapping the next maniple, and pushed through the ranks shouting orders at the centurions as they manhandled the men into their correct places.

A detached part of my mind was howling in primal horror, and my breakfast beef hash was pushing hard at my sphincter. But as always in those last moments before battle, organizing the men kept my thoughts distracted, and I held my own terror in check with a practised effort. Bursting through the rear ranks of our hastily-formed battle line I looked around wildly for the cavalry support. The decurion trotted forward at my gesture, and leaned down over me.

'A bad business this.' His Spanish accent was thick.

'I know, I know. Plug leaks, okay? If the line starts breaking, go in and kill anyone - Roman or German - who's facing you. I'll be along with foot soldiers as soon as I can afterwards.'

I pointed south, towards the camp. 'I'm expecting trouble there. The men are going to fall back if the legion next to them goes, and it probably will. The line will hinge on those triarii getting into place now. Make sure they hold, at all costs. Got it? Good. I've got to go. Fortuna be with you.'

I plunged through a gap in the maniples, howling at the front ranks, 'Stay steady, hold! Hold!'

The leading Cimbri arrived, not in organized ranks, but like a handful of pebbles thrown at a window, the fastest and bravest first, the rest following on afterwards. At the sight of red legionary shields, they did not pause to rally, as sensible soldiers might have done, but came on at us in a dead run, winded as they were. The legionaries in our front line methodically chopped them down as though they were two-legged timber.

Behind these fore-runners came the main body of the enemy, moving at a steady jog trot, a huge, compact mass of humanity so many men deep that the back ranks were lost in the mist and rain. They pressed close against the river bank, and from there off to the right in a ragged line stretching as far as the eye could see. Banners and standards wobbled colourfully a few ranks back, and a pilum sailed out of our ranks aiming for one of these.

The thrower would be one of the new hastati, I thought. The front ranks of our army were composed of young men with at most a few years service. They would take the edge off the barbarian attack before falling back on the veteres, the second line formed of men with over a dozen years service. Generally speaking, the veteres would see the business through without need of the triarii, our third and last line of defence, where every man was a seasoned veteran. Most of the triarii were currently resting, each on one knee, long pike held forward at an angle, the better to deflect any javelins reaching that far.

The Roman proverb, 'Things have come to the triarii,' meant that the situation had become desperate. Today, I'd not worry if things came to the triarii, but I would be eternally grateful if things stopped there too. Ominously, apart from those first cavalrymen, I had seen not a single Roman fleeing the ruin of Caepio's army.

The legions had been in very deep amid the mass of Cimbri when their line collapsed, and that was not an easy situation to get out of. If there were any survivors, they would probably be a bit nearer the centre, fleeing to our camp. Still, I hoped none of my men were paying much attention to the river. The water was starting to run red as thousands of gallons of human blood found their way into its flow. The debt to Tolosa had been paid in full.

The Cimbri had taken up a chant, something like 'Wo-tan-da'. With the sound distorted by tens of thousands of voices, and accompanying drums and trumpets, it was hard to get sense from the repeated crashing waves of noise.

'Wo-tan-da, wo-tan-da wo-tanda,' the beat became faster, almost frantic, and then suddenly climaxed in a huge roar as the huge mass of the Cimbric army threw itself in a body at the Roman line. I saw the shoulders of my legionaries flex, and the pilums flew from our ranks like a great flock of startled birds, arcing down into the lead ranks of the barbarians just as our men hit them in a short but savage counter-charge.

A quick, anxious glance from left to right showed that our ranks were solid. The formations merged shoulder to shoulder, and the clang of swords on armour hammered into the air, mingled with hoarse shouts and screams as the slaughter got up close and personal. Cursing the mud sucking at my ankles I hurtled down the rear of the line yelling at the centurions to control a section of infantry which was bulging forward. Behind

me came the thump and jingle of fifty men I was holding as a
flying reserve, and we barely hesitated for a last deep breath
before throwing ourselves into the gap opening up between the
advancing unit and their steadier colleagues.

Suddenly there was a confused mass of legionaries and
German warriors before me, and I had my sword under the ribs of
a heavily-muscled, pigtailed warrior before he even saw me. Hot
blood splattered over my face from somewhere as I ducked a
spear coming at my eyes, and I skidded on a mass of entrails
before rolling backwards between the shields of my advancing
bodyguard. Then it was back on my feet again, pushing men into
line by their shoulders, and taking my place among them with a
shield I had grabbed while down.

Just as I had done for hour after hour at drill, I slammed my
shield upward, stepped forward into the stab, blocked a counter,
took an opportunistic slash at the opponent facing the man at my
shoulder, and took out the throat of the man before me on the
back swing. Something hit me hard enough on the helmet to make
me see stars, and I automatically countered with a rising parry that
cut deep into a wrist even as I jammed my shield down to block a
stab at my groin. It was reaction fighting. One did not see a target
and hit it, one struck, and then realized why. Rational thought
stepped back and let the primal beast fight, the beast's reflexes
constrained only by years of training and discipline.

Here's a secret. Romans are never outnumbered when fighting
barbarians. We fight shoulder-to-shoulder and shield to shield,
with our swords flickering out between them, stabbing like
serpent strikes. The barbarian warrior in the front ranks has a
sword half as long as he is, and needs four feet of space to swing
the thing properly. So we get three men to their two all along the
battlefront, and the surplus enemy have to wait in line for their
turn to get at us. Replacement in the front ranks of a barbarian
army is done by stepping over the corpse of the warrior who was

fighting in front of him, while in the Roman ranks, one slips out of the front rank by turning slightly sideways as soon as there is a hint of a break in the action. The man behind takes the hint, inserts his shield into the gap, and you rotate out of your place in the line even as he steps into it. It's a dance move that takes a lot of practice, but it is one of the reasons why we so often win against the odds.

That's something else. Swinging two and a half feet of metal at maximum force takes a lot out of a man. Even with the hour or two of practice the average legionary puts in every day - even when stood down at home - it only takes a few minutes for exhaustion to set in during a battle, especially as there is a lot of other stress going on anyway. Fortunately we were fresh and our opponents had already gone one round with the Romans before jogging two miles to re-engage with the next lot. Right along our line the centurions were screaming at the men not to follow up as their tired opponents disengaged. In some places enemies stood only a few feet apart, glaring at each other as they leaned on swords or shields while desperately sobbing breath back into tired lungs.

My own lungs were heaving as I staggered back and looked south along our line, seeking out the standards of IV Campanestris. Bugger! The standards were flat against the line of my own legionaries, and my own legionaries were falling back, pivoting smoothly to form a line parallel to the river as the unit beside them collapsed. The Spanish cavalry were busy at the edge of the line, darting in, hurling javelins and wheeling away, but so far no Cimbri were loose behind us.

Damn Mallius to Hades. He had been so long a-sacrificing that it looked as though the main army had not had time to fully deploy. Instead the Cimbri had hit them halfway through the process. Squinting through the rain, I struggled to distinguish the standards between us and the camp ramparts. Some of them did not look Roman, and those that definitely were ours were a lot further back than they should be.

My shoulder had that hard, itchy ache that comes from pushing muscles too hard, and my legs were urging me to take a break. But I forced air into my lungs and trotted across to where our line bent towards the river under the press of barbarian attackers and men of the broken IV Campanestris. Without the river anchoring our flank, that broken unit could easily have been us. Probably with the same thought in mind, our legionaries opened their ranks where possible, and allowed the soldiers of the routed unit to push through. Many of these men lacked shields or swords, but they still had a standard bearer. The man came blundering through our triarii, white-knuckled hands wrapped around the standard firmly fixed to a socket belted to his waist.

'Stop!' I ordered, but the signifer was past listening. He simply dropped one shoulder and ran at me, intent on bowling aside the human obstacle in his path. Feranius - whom I had not even noticed beside me until then - suddenly stepped forward, and smashed his sword back-handed across the standard bearer's face. He turned the blade at the last moment, so that he hit with the flat rather than the edge, but there was still an ugly splat as the steel hit flesh, and the man went down as though smitten by a thunderbolt.

The centurion bent forward and tugged the standard free. He passed it to me, and bellowed furiously, 'IV Campanestris. Rally! Campanestris! Rally on the standard!'

The cavalry were working the edge of our line, turning their horses sideways to block off fugitives heading for the hill behind the camp, and beating them back with the butts of their spears. At Feranius' hoarse shout, many looked over their shoulders, and seeing a sketchy line forming at their standard, trotted back to join it. I saw a steady-looking fellow with a centurion's phalerae on his armour, and passed him the standard. 'You're standard-bearer for the unit. You take orders from whomever that man sends.' A quick jerk of the thumb indicated Feranius, who was already waving over one of our *pilus posteriori* centurions.

Meeting that centurion as I moved back to our own battle line, I gasped, 'Keep them steady. Send foraging parties forward to scavenge shields and swords for those who've lost theirs. Make sure that they don't fight until they are all armed and have their breath back. Then put them at the back. Stay near the hill and stop the gods-damned Germans from getting behind us.'

The once-cold rain now felt downright refreshing and I tipped my head back to let a shower patter on my face. Doing so brought two horsemen looming into my vision. The sodden cape of one of these riders was the red paludamentum of a Roman general. 'Caepio?'

The proconsul's piggy jowls quivered. 'Good work, man. Keep this part of the line holding as long as you can. Cover the retreat of the cavalry.'

'What? Er, seriously, what? The cavalry are meant to cover our retreat. Cavalry provide cover for retreating infantry, not the other way around. Without the cavalry we don't have a chance.'

Caepio's expression told me plainly we didn't have a chance anyway. 'I'm taking your cavalry and pulling back ... to regroup.'

A slow surge of fury began building within me.'Regroup? That's total nonsense. Regroup what? You've lost the fucking army!' My wild gesture indicated the hill behind the camp, which was alive with Cimbric warriors swarming over it like ants. There was not a Roman in sight. 'If they weren't busy plundering our camp, the Cimbri would be all over us by now. We've got to make a stand. There's nothing to regroup.'

'I have to pull back ... rally the survivors ... regroup. Hold here as long as you can. Do your duty.' There came a roar from the river bank and our fragmentary battle line shivered as the men braced against a fresh charge. Caepio wheeled his horse.

'You are abandoning the field? Running away from the mess you've made?' I was incredulous, and almost incandescent with rage. Caepio ignored me, and gestured urgently at the leader of our cavalry turma. He banged his heels into the flanks of his horse as I grabbed a spear off one of the centurion's men. 'You coward. You filthy, stinking cunnus!'

Caepio stopped at my words, pulling back on the reins. This was unfortunate as the spear which would otherwise have taken the general in the neck sailed harmlessly over his horse's head. Caepio looked incredulous, jaw literally dropping open. For a moment it looked as though he was going to say something, then he looked past me to my embattled cohort. He took a hand off the reins to make a hopeless gesture, and then he was gone. His companion paused to give me an apologetic look and a shrug, then he too galloped off. Behind him, scattered plumes of black smoke were rising over the ramparts of the camp.

Half an hour later, and our battle-line was a curved lens bending around the base of the knoll at the river-bank. The tidy maniples of hastati, veteres and triarii were now confused lines with all three jumbled together with the remnants of IV Campanestris. Centurions and optiones moved around the backs of the exhausted men, encouraging, threatening and cajoling. The top of the knoll had become a sort of first-aid station, where the severely wounded tended to the mortally wounded, and where I and Feranius - both soaked with blood, sweat and rain but otherwise intact - tried to conduct the defence.

Apart from the three hundred or so utterly weary legionaries in front of me, there seemed nothing left of the tens of thousands of Romans who had been on the battlefield that morning. Smoke drifted in mournful, tattered streamers from the camp, and the rain had settled into a steady downpour. We survived because the great crowds of Germans roaming the battlefield were intent on looting corpses and finding plunder, and those who discovered that we were ready, willing and able to fight moved on to find less pugnacious prey.

It was quite probable that other knots of resistance remained on the field; units which had through luck or discipline kept their formation. The rest of Mallius' army had been blown away by that first charge, broken before it was even fully deployed. We remained, partly hidden by the steady rain and the mist from the river, simply because there was no-where else to go. Retreat was impossible, and it was plain that the Cimbri were taking no prisoners. My last forlorn hope was that we could get through the hours remaining before nightfall, and somehow slip away in the dark.

Even that hope was quickly dashed. A Cimbric warrior on horseback, magnificently dressed in golden armour, came trotting through the river gate of our wrecked camp with a retinue of armoured men at his back. He pulled up his horse when he saw us, turned to his men and gestured in our direction.

Beside me, Feranius groaned, 'Here we go, then.'

It took a while for the barbarians to get organized, but in the end their commander put together something like a thousand of them; a mixture of bare-chested spearmen, bodies gleaming in the rain, and sword-bearing warriors, many of the latter wearing blood-stained chain mail stripped from dead legionaries. They milled about, occasionally turning to shout defiance at our men, who remained grimly silent.

'Wedge,' I muttered to Feranius, and he hurried off the knoll to brace our shield-wall. A wedge is a total pain, even for a fresh legionary line. It is a sort of human battering ram which has well-armoured warriors on the outside, and a huge mass of spearmen who push from within and give the whole thing momentum. About five hundred of the Cimbri were forming up for this, ten deep, with the heroes at the tip a mere five men. The wedge would push these men onto our swords and spears, and - alive or dead - through our ranks and out the other side. Then, with the line broken, it would be open field fighting, which we would lose.

The only chance was to stop the wedge breaking through in the first place. With shouts and gestures we pulled the fighting line back so that the slope at the base of the knoll gave us a slight advantage. The wounded were dragged further back to add extra depth to the ranks, and the Germans began that accursed 'wot-an-da!' chant which meant they were winding up for a charge.

We had pulled German and Roman corpses in front of us to form a rough, thigh-high rampart. This ex-human barrier would delay but not stop the enemy, and in the event it hardly even slowed them down. The front rank of the wedge burst our impromptu barrier apart, but it brought the men at the front of the wedge to their knees. Thereafter they did not have a chance, as the rest of the Germans simply steamed over them and hit our lines. I was in the third rank, and still felt my armour creak as my arms were pressed between cuirass and shield so tightly I thought they would break. We pushed at each other for all of a minute, with Roman and German pressed face-to-face in a crush so tight that it was hard to breathe, let alone find space to fight. Then another five hundred barbarians hit us in the flank, and it was all over.

I felt the pressure at my back ease as the men supporting me fell back, and reeled away from the press to confront a barbarian warrior in Roman mail who slammed a blue-and-white shield into my ribs. I hooked my own shield inside his, pulled the shield away from the barbarian's body, and slammed an elbow into his face. Around me, the Roman line dissolved into a mass of individual combats, with many legionaries simply being knocked over and stabbed by a scrum of opponents.

The barbarian gave a mighty shove that sent me staggering toward the top of the knoll. Even over the shouts and screams of the fight, I heard the implacable rush of the river at my back. I swung a backhanded cut at my opponent, who ducked, and then neatly filleted a Cimbric warrior who had come up to support him. The dying warrior gave a reproachful look as he fell back, blood streaming from his mouth, and I said incredulously, 'Madric?'

Madric charged me, and we met shield to shield. He grinned at me over the top of his.

'Hello boyo. I've been in the Cimbric army since about noon. A quick switch of helmets and shields was all it took.'

We did some desultory skirmishing at each other with swords, and everyone left us to it. 'The view's better from this side of the battle, really it is. There's quite a few of the Tolosans and other Gauls here.'

Madric faked a chop at my thigh and I faked a block, taking another step back. 'You've got to try the river,' said Madric clearly, and then he attempted a swing at my head, accompanied by a wild Celtic battle cry that established his bona fides with the warriors around. From the corner of my eye I saw a man rise from his knees with Feranius' head in one hand. Several other warriors already had such grisly trophies dangling from their belts, and another German with a severed head grasped in his teeth bounded in pursuit of a fleeing legionary.

'Now is good,' insisted Madric. He grunted something to another warrior who had joined the duel. The German left with a nick in his ear from my sudden lunge.

'I can't keep this one-on-one for long.'

He was right. Few other Romans remained alive on the knoll. My wet, tired fingers scrabbled with the buckles in my cuirass as Madric and I parted from our fight, both gasping for breath. The duel had acquired half a dozen curious spectators. I hurled my helmet at them, and a scramble developed for possession of the silver-and-gold embossed booty. Madric came at me again, and with a heave of my shield I pushed him back into the ranks of the Cimbri, using the brief respite to fumble free the last straps of my cuirass.

The bank of the knoll crumbled under my feet as I stepped back. The Cimbri plus Madric came at me in a pack as I lifted off the cuirass, holding it high over my head.

I howled a last message to the Gods. 'Curse you for a stupid slut, Aphrodite, and sodding well sod you, Apollo!'

Then I hurled my cuirass with full force into the startled, feral faces of the men closing in, and let the force of that throw take me backwards off the ledge and down into the tumbling brown waters of the Rhone.

Appendix

Original Ancient Texts in Translation

1. Extracts from Strabo's *Geography* ch 4.13   Vol. II of the Loeb Classical Library edition,1923

Tectosages
The people who are called Tectosages closely approach the Pyrenees, though they also reach over small parts of the northern side of the Cemmenus; and the land they occupy is rich in gold. ... Among these are also those people who have taken possession of that part of Phrygia [central Anatolia] which has a common boundary with Cappadocia and the Paphlagonians. Now as proof of this we have the people who are still, even at the present time, called Tectosages; for, since there are three tribes, one of them - the one that lives about the city of Ancyra - is called 'the tribe of the Tectosages'.

The Gold of Tolosa
They fared wretchedly after their retreat from Delphi and, because of their dissensions, were scattered, some in one direction, others in another. But, as has been said both by Poseidonius and several others, since the country was rich in gold, and also belonged to people who were god-fearing and not extravagant in their ways of living, it came to have treasures in many places in Celtica; but it was the lakes, most of all, that afforded the treasures their inviolability, into which the people let down heavy masses of silver or even of gold. At all events, the Romans, after they mastered the regions, sold the lakes for the public treasury, and many of the buyers found in them hammered mill-stones of silver. And, in Tolosa, the temple too was hallowed, since it was very much

revered by the inhabitants of the surrounding country, and on this account the treasures there were excessive, for numerous people had dedicated them and no one dared to lay hands on them.

Tolosa and Caepio

And it is further said that the Tectosages shared in the expedition to Delphi; and even the treasures that were found among them in the city of Tolosa by Caepio, a general of the Romans, were, it is said, a part of the valuables that were taken from Delphi, although the people, in trying to consecrate them and propitiate the god, added thereto out of their personal properties, and it was on account of having laid hands on them that Caepio ended his life in misfortunes - for he was cast out by his native land as a temple-robber, and he left behind as his heirs female children only, who, as it turned out, became prostitutes, as Timagenes has said, and therefore perished in disgrace.

---

2. *The history of Orosius* 5.15 -16 (Translation by the author)

After the capture of the gold

The proconsul Caepio captured a Gallic city called Tolosa, and took 100,000 pounds of gold and 110,000 pounds of silver from the Temple of Apollo. He had this treasure escorted to Massalia, a city friendly to the Romans. But according to witnesses, the men ordered to guard and transport the gold were attacked from ambush. Caepio was believed to have somehow expropriated all the treasure. Because of this action there was later a huge inquiry held at Rome.

The Battle of Arausio

In the six hundred and forty-second year from the founding of the city C. Malius and Q. Caepio, proconsul, went against the Cimbri, Teutons, Tigurini and Ambrones, tribes of Gaul and Germany. These were then closing on the Roman lands via the provinces through which flows the Rhone river. Here envy and discord caused the most damaging dispute between them, and brought great shame and danger to the name of Rome.

They were defeated ... the two sons of the consul were killed, 80,000 Romans and their allies were slaughtered, along with 40,000 camp followers, according to [the historian] Antias. So complete was the destruction of all the army that only ten men survived.

Having gained possession of both camps and of a huge amount of booty, the enemy seemed as though driven by a strange and unusual curse. They completely destroyed everything they had captured, clothing was cut to pieces and strewn about, gold and silver were thrown into the river, the breastplates of the men were hacked to pieces, the trappings of the horses were ruined, the horses themselves were drowned in the water. Men had nooses fastened around their necks and were hanged from trees.

Thus the conqueror seized no booty, while the vanquished received no mercy. In Rome, then was not only great grief, but fear that the Cimbri would immediately cross the Alps to destroy Italy.

---

3. Plutarch *Life of Sertorius* 2-3 In *The Parallel Lives* published in Vol. VIII of the Loeb Classical Library 1919 edition.

Quintus Sertorius

Quintus Sertorius belonged to a family of some prominence in Nussa, a city of the Sabines. Having lost his father, he was properly reared by a widowed mother, of whom he appears to have been excessively fond. ... As a result of his training he was sufficiently versed in judicial procedure, and acquired some influence also at

Rome from his eloquence, although a mere youth; but his brilliant successes in war turned his ambition in this direction.

To begin with, when the Cimbri and Teutones invaded Gaul he served under Caepio, and after the Romans had been defeated and put to flight, though he had lost his horse and had been wounded in the body, he made his way across the Rhone, swimming, shield and breastplate and all, against a strongly adverse current; so sturdy was his body and so inured to hardships by training.

In the next place ... Sertorius undertook to spy out the enemy. So, putting on a Celtic dress and acquiring the commonest expressions of that language for such conversation as might be necessary, he mingled with the Barbarians and after seeing or hearing what was of importance, he came back.

---

4. Plutarch *Life of Marius* 14 (Author's translation)

Finally

And now [after the battle of the Arausio], Marius enjoyed great good fortune. For the barbarians unexpectedly flowed back, so to speak, in their course for Rome, and flooded instead into Spain.

The Servant of Aphrodite
Philip Matyszak

After returning from the dead - or at least from the river Arausio - Lucius Panderius finds himself back in Rome, and an unwilling participant in the snake-pit of Roman politics. Whether dodging assassins in the back-alleys, or ducking missiles at political rallies, our hero finds that the streets of his home city can be just as dangerous as the battlefield. And on the battlefield, at least you know who your enemies are
. . .

Rome, 104 BC is a city on edge; torn by social conflict and threatened with destruction by a massive barbarian invasion. To survive the turmoil, Lucius Panderius needs to be every bit as ruthless and duplicitous as his shadowy and powerful enemies.

'The Servant of Aphrodite' is the second of the Panderius Papers, and as with its predecessor, this novel combines detailed historical research with non stop action and adventure.

ᴧᴧᴧᴩ
Monashee Mountain Publishing